Mad Carew

a&b

Mad Carew

KEN McCOY ,

First published in Great Britain in 2004 by
Allison & Busby Limited
Bon Marche Centre
241-251 Ferndale Road
Brixton, London SW9 8BJ
http://www.allisonandbusby.com

Copyright © 2004 by KEN YERS

The right of Ken YERS to be identified as
author of this work has been asserted by him in
accordance with the Copyright, Designs and
Patents Act, 1988

A catalogue record for this book is available from the British Library

ISBN 0 7490 8310 7

Printed and bound by
Creative Print + Design, Ebbw Vale

KEN McCOY was born in wartime Leeds and has lived in Yorkshire all his life. He ran his own building company for twenty-five years, during which time he worked as a freelance artist, and after-dinner entertainer. He has appeared on TV, radio and the stage. Married with five children, he is now a full-time writer and the author of six previous novels.

To my son, Tom

There's a one-eyed yellow idol to the north of Khatmandu,
There's a little marble cross below the town;
There's a broken hearted woman tends the grave of Mad Carew,
And the Yellow God forever gazes down.

J. MILTON HAYES

Prologue

Aromatherapy's supposed to be quite good, as is yoga, origami and pottery. There's a bit of a question mark over basket weaving, but what few people know is that as a therapy, bricklaying beats the rest of them into a cocked hat. It empties the mind of all the clutter of life and clears the way for fresh thinking. Winston Churchill spent many hours working out his wartime strategy whilst happily building himself a wall in his back garden at Chartwell, and if it was good enough for Winnie, it was certainly good enough for erstwhile detective sergeant and budding private investigator, Sam Carew, who got many a bright idea walling bricks. Sadly though, it is a declining skill. There's a rumour going round the building trade that if you want to find a good bricklayer nowadays, you need to take a shovel to the cemetery.

1

Sam tapped the corner stone into place with the handle of his trowel and looked down at Sean, loading the mixer fifteen feet below him. His gaze switched to a recently fitted security camera pointed at the Irishman's back and the seed of an idea formed in Sam's brain. It bore fruit as he was setting up the line for the next course of stone.

'That's it,' he murmured to himself, 'knocking shop like that. There's bound to be one.'

His work had been occupying ten per cent of his concentration, with another eighty per cent engaged in thinking up a way of avoiding a cold, boring winter afternoon observing the comings and goings at Sonia's Swedish Massage Parlour. Sam hadn't mentioned taking the afternoon off to his dad who was working industriously beside him. As yet, Sam hadn't thought up a believable excuse. This had been occupying the remaining ten per cent of his thoughts.

The closed-circuit camera had not yet been connected to a monitor, but it was still being treated with caution by Sean, Carew and Son's plasterer-cum-labourer, who was often more plastered than his walls. He had a well justified suspicion of such intrusive devices, having once starred in an incriminating video that saw him nicked for pocketing a bottle of Tia Maria in Fothergill's Famous Wine Stores. It was meant to be a peace offering to his wife, who was giving him grief over his drinking habits.

Sean was standing with his back to the camera as he covertly squirted Fairy Liquid into his mixer, in which he was mixing compo for Sam and Ernest. When the sand is gritty, a dash of washing up liquid makes the mortar easier to work, and in truth, doesn't take any of the strength out of it. Some brickies prefer Squeezy, but Sean favoured Fairy Liquid, with it being kinder on the hands. The building inspector may well have frowned upon this practice, but let's face it, building inspectors hate to see brickies making life easier for themselves.

Carew and Son Ltd were working on what for them was a major contract, converting Greerside Hall into a nursing home. They were contracted to re-build much of the frontage, rip out the rotting innards and replace them with modern materials. Ernest, Sam's dad, considered this a crime, but Sam thought the combination of old on the outside and new on the inside was the best of both worlds. Despite popular belief to the contrary, some of the old building methods were a bit suspect to say the least.

Ernest Carew looked up momentarily from his work, his mouth opened, about to ask his son what he was on about, then closed again. No point wasting his breath, it'd be something barmy. Ernest couldn't understand why a clever lad like Sam had chosen to come back on the tools. A year ago, the lad had a bright future mapped out for him. Still, he musn't grumble, his son was gradually taking over the reins and Ernest was slowly succumbing to the beckoning finger of retirement; a very persuasive finger when you're sixty-four.

Sam allowed himself a smile of quiet triumph as he tied off the line. He took a mobile phone out of his snap tin, blew off a few bread crumbs and dialled PC Owen Price of Unsworth Police.

If God gave the world an enema, he'd stick the tube in Unsworth, is one of the many cruel jibes Unsworthians have to endure. Unsworth has long been an easy target of comics, plying their trade from a safe distance beyond the town's blurred boundaries: Unsworth isn't twinned with anybody – it has a suicide pact with Grimsby; The Germans dropped an atom bomb on Unsworth and did ten million pounds worth of improvements, etcetera, etcetera. Boring after a while, but most Unsworthians rise above all this and, as soon as they can afford it, move out.

The town had always had an inherent poverty, which the natives accepted and made the very best of. But the poverty had recently been made worse by the closing down of various industries such as Unsworth Tannery and Bickersdike's Chicken Sheds. A profitable by-product of this latter business had been a fertiliser produced by the burning of chicken shit, which had had an adverse effect on the nasal ambience of the area.

The return of fresh air to that part of town was of small consolation to the newly unemployed. Beauty, they say, is in the eye of the beholder, and to behold Unsworth and see beauty, you need to be on something strong. Bootham's Yorkshire Bitter was generally regarded as being up to the task. Sam was on his second pint when Owen walked in, eating a Mars Bar.

It was the day after Sam had made his phone call to Owen Price and it had got off to a bad start. Overnight drizzle had washed away all the mortar from the previous day's work, leaving streaks of crusty khaki on the stonework. He had been heatedly discussing this with Sean, who had failed in his job of covering up the wall with polythene, when Mr Fosdyke, the building inspector, who wasn't due that day, had called in on his way to work and condemned it all. A harsh decision, because the stonework could have been cleaned off with a chemical cleanser and re-pointed, but Sam knew better than to argue. Carew and Son had a reputation to maintain and Sam's dad wouldn't thank him for damaging that reputation for the sake of a day's work.

Last night's drizzle had turned into a downpour and Sam had rained the men off and called in at the Queen's Arms, or the Clog and Shovel, to give the re-vamped pub its present, quirky title; an additional source of annoyance to Sam, the traditionalist. The name apparently reflected the pub's location, between Batty's the Clog Makers and Unsworth Light Tools. Both now defunct and re-born. One as an office block, the other as a car park. At least the idiots hadn't re-vamped the beer.

Not normally a daytime drinker, Sam decided to justify his visit by putting it down to business and arranged an impromptu meeting with PC Owen Price. He waved a hand to attract the attention of the tall, thin police constable, who was taking off his rain soaked parka to reveal his off duty sports jacket and corduroys. Owen looked furtively around, drawing attention to himself.

He spotted Sam's wave, gave a nod of acknowledgement, and made his way across the room, bumping against a chair occupied by a young woman who mouthed the words 'clumsy prat' to her male companion. As Owen apologised with his mouth full of Mars Bar, he backed away from her and knocked the arm of a man returning from the bar with a full glass in each hand, spilling both drinks liberally on the carpet.

'Sorry, boyo – didn't see you, see,' he explained, but made no offer of recompense. The man treated him to a glare which Owen diffused with a toothy smile.

He had been a police constable for twenty of his forty-two years and looked more like a chemistry teacher than a copper. But Owen had a way with him, which more than outweighed his unprepossessing features. Over the years he had scattered the seed of his fruitful loins liberally around Unsworth and district, arousing the interest of the CSA and incurring crippling Attachment of Earnings Orders. Penury beckoned, forcing him to retire from the paternity business. He now lived in respectable adultery with the local post mistress, who appeared to take her title a little too literally. Her husband was glad of Owen's assistance in satisfying the needs of his libidinous wife, as he himself could only manage it once a fortnight. The rest was down to Owen, in lieu of rent. Sam had once asked to see his Tenancy Agreement, curious as to the wording, but Owen had told him not to be so bloody smutty.

'For Christ's sake, sit down before someone calls the cops!' urged Sam.

'I *am* a cop,' protested Owen. He gave the well-appointed room one last visual sweep to ensure he didn't know anyone. There were a couple of dozen people in the place, all sitting politely and talking in muted tones as befitted their surroundings. When the evening crowd rolled up, all that would change. The resident DJ would crank his alleged music up to mind-numbing volume, obviating the need for the teenage clientèle to enter into intelligent conversation; a forgotten art.

Owen sat down and slipped Sam a large Jiffy bag beneath the table. Sam felt like a dirty old man accepting dodgy videos from a fellow member of a porn ring.

'Anything of interest on them?' he asked, as he stuffed the package into his pocket.

Owen shrugged. 'Haven't looked at them – and if anyone asks you where you got them, don't mention my name, or me and you are finished.' He looked at Sam's glass. 'Aren't you supposed to thank me by buying me a drink?'

Sam got to his feet. 'What'll you have?'

'Pint of Stella please.'

'Stella? What sort of a drink's that?'

'It's lager.'

'It's expensive.'

'I thought a change would be nice.'

'Really.'

Sam trudged off to the bar and returned with Owen's drink. 'Why can't you drink beer like normal people?' he grumbled, 'I nearly had to take out a sodding mortgage to pay for this.'

Owen eyed his glass suspiciously. 'You barmy bugger! You got me a woman's glass, isn't it?' His odd Welsh syntax sometimes threw Sam, but he could have been right. Sam's glass had a handle, Owen's was shaped like an anorexic cooling tower.

'It's what I was given – maybe they think you're my boyfriend.'

Owen looked around, startled. 'Oh heck! You've not brought me to a bloody gay bar, have you?'

Sam shrugged. 'Never used to be, but everything's changing. Look at you, drinking lager. You've been a Bootham's Bitter man as long as I've known you. Is there something you want to get out in the open, ducky?'

'Now then, boyo,' remonstrated Owen. 'Remember what you did to Bowman when he called you a poufta?'

'Point taken,' conceded Sam. He inclined his head towards a

19

young woman sitting on a barstool. 'Besides, I don't think she'd be sitting there if it was a gay bar.'

Owen looked. She had an artificial tan, low cut frock, little left to the imagination, especially in the top of fishnet stocking area. A black suspender was clearly visible, plus a tantalising strip of pale thigh, blatantly advertising the delights beyond. An attractive young woman in a brassy way, her profession was more than obvious. But not to Owen, who, for a policeman, was amazingly naïve. He treated the woman to a winning smile which failed to win her over. 'If she played her cards right,' he said, 'she could have her wicked way with me.'

Sam grinned. 'The only card she'd be interested in is a gold card.'

Owen twigged and reddened. 'Maybe she'd take Access,' he said, with a forced grin to cover his embarrassment.

'It'd be more appropriate,' remarked Sam who was sorely tempted to relate his latest gag about the Welshman and the black sheep, but with admirable self-control he denied himself that simple pleasure. Owen took a single gulp of his pint that left about an inch in the bottom of the glass.

'I want those tapes back tomorrow,' he insisted.

'Trust me.'

Owen eyed Sam with acute mistrust and finished off the last inch of expensive lager, screwing up his face in disgust. He'd no need to drink it, but he hated wasting any kind of drink. He suddenly grinned at Sam, displaying an array of gleaming white teeth; his only redeeming feature.

'Sergeant Bassey has been warning everybody about the dangers of associating with undesirables. Your name was specifically mentioned.'

'What? me – undesirable?' protested Sam. 'You can tell old Shirley that he'll be hearing from my solicitor. The cheeky sod!'

Owen got to his feet. 'And how can I tell him that, if I'm not supposed to associate with you? I'll see you tomorrow. I'm off to a proper pub.' His eyes flickered, cheekily, on the woman at the bar.

'She's all yours, boyo,' he whispered from the side of his mouth. 'In fact I'll go halves.' Taking a pound coin from his pocket, he put it on the table.

He was laughing as he left, but he was on Sam's side and that was all that mattered.

Sam surreptitiously studied the prostitute. His eyes were drawn to an unusual tattoo on her upper arm. A black cat's head with luminous green eyes. She looked as though she catered for the top end of the market. Their eyes met and Sam's quickly dropped, not wishing to give her the wrong message. Too late, she was approaching him; her Chanel No 5 arrived first. Must get some for Sally Grover, he thought. She stopped beside him, took a gold-tipped cigarette from a gold case and lit it with a gold lighter.

'Don't look at what you can't afford!' she said, a bit too haughtily for his liking, blowing a cloud of smoke Sam's way. Then she carried on past him and took the arm of a wealthy looking man in his sixties, with a vaguely familiar face, discreetly beckoning from the door. Bloody cheek! He'd never paid for it in his life – but what made her think he couldn't afford her? Sam looked at himself in one of the many mirrors and pondered his reflection. The fact that he was wearing his working clothes might have put her off, but apart from that he had a lot going for him.

Grey hairs wisping from the temples would alert most men to the advent of middle age. But to Sam, who had never been weighed down by the burdens of false modesty, they merely added an air of maturity to what he regarded as his boyish good looks. His eyes were dark brown, like his dad's. He'd no idea what colour his mother's eyes were, nor any interest. In truth, he was not unattractive, but he was no Mel Gibson either. Now in his mid thirties, and apart from an on/off betrothal to Sally Grover, he was more or less unattached. There is, of course, a certain type of woman who looks upon any unattached man as a challenge and Sam was nothing if not a challenge.

2

Sam pressed the first tape into the machine, picked up the remote, kicked off his boots, and sat back in the only decent chair his room had to offer. He examined the hole in his left sock and it crossed his mind, not for the first time, that Sally Grover was right. Three pairs for five pounds was a false economy. Most of his socks failed to survive a second wash. Next time he'd lash out and go for the two pairs for five pound range. Hang the expense. Much of his income went to his first wife. He didn't begrudge paying it. Far better to spend his money on his two boys than on high living. Although, according to Sally, decent socks didn't qualify as high living.

As the tape ran through the preliminaries he glanced, despairingly, around his flat. A mimimalist's dream. On the top of the TV stood a photo of his two sons and on one wall a cute amateur painting of his childhood pet dog, Scruff, the only female he'd ever loved, his mother and ex-wife included – especially his mother. A tiny drop-leaf dining table, two dining chairs, a dresser he'd bought at a furniture auction for seventeen pounds, and a coffee table with a dodgy leg and cigarette burns completed the total furnishings of the fourteen by twelve room.

There was a kitchen with just enough room for a sink, cooker, fridge and microwave: the latter being his main tool in warding off starvation. Background music was provided by the strange occupants of the flat below. One of whom was attempting to play *When The Saints Go Marching In*, on an out of tune sitar. Although to Sam, all sitars sounded out of tune.

He pressed "pause" on the video remote as the microwave started to ping. Then, rising from his chair, he padded into the kitchen – switching the kettle back on in passing to bring it back to the boil. He gave the cornish pasty a cursory glance through the microwave window and pushed the button to open the door.

Gravy, he thought to himself – why not wallow in luxury for a change?

Peeling open an Oxo cube, he crushed it into the bottom of a cup, poured in a couple of inches of water from the now boiling kettle and stirred it with his left hand. With his right hand he filled another cup with boiling water, into which he dropped a Tetley's tea bag, a spoonful of sugar and a splash of milk. Quietly proud of his ambidexterity, he poured the Oxo gravy onto his soft, warm pasty and cast an approving eye over the end result. A grand meal for a growing lad. Tomorrow he'd have his lunch at the Station Road café. Meat and potato pie probably. Melvin, the chef de cuisine, had promised Sticky Toffee Pudding for dessert. A balanced diet is important.

All his dirty washing was done once a week at the Skweeky Clene Launderette round the corner. In the bedroom was a double bed, which took up most of the floor space. He'd shared it regularly and vigorously with Sally until she became a little too presumptuous about where their relationship was leading. Sam had foolishly allowed himself to become engaged simply to realise his carnal ambitions, and remained so until she began pressing for a wedding date.

'No engagement, no nooky,' was her cruel ultimatum when he called it off on the grounds that he wasn't ready to commit himself to another long-term relationship. She had relented on occasions, having her own needs in that direction.

His divorce had financially flattened him, which was why, he told himself, he was doing this private eye work. But he was contributing to another husband's downfall, so who was he trying to fool? Let's face it. He was doing it because he couldn't let go of being a copper – and what's more, he'd continue to do it. But no more of this – this was seedy. No more jobs like this.

The video was monochrome and grainy, like an old Buster Keaton film. But the sign above the door was clear enough. Sam gave a despairing shake of his head at the name, no mistaking what went on in there. He sliced off a piece of cornish pasty and stuck it in his mouth, congratulating himself on the fact that it was vaguely palatable. He then prepared himself for hours of concentrated boredom. Still, it was better than sitting outside the place in a car with a long-lens camera all day long. A gulp of tea washed down his first mouthful of pasty. The CCTV idea had been a stroke of a master, as were his powers of persuasion to get Owen Price to check on the security cameras in the area, then to persuade him to use his influence as the Community Constable to get Sam the tapes from the one pointing directly at the front door of Sonia's Swedish Massage Parlour.

The comings and goings proved much less boring than Sam expected. He recognised several of the clients, including one elderly man of the cloth who turned up in mufti, but he didn't fool Sam, who tut-tutted when the parson made his furtive exit. The clients were many and varied. George Morley, the newsagent from whom Sam bought his morning paper appeared in the top of the screen, looked as though he was about to walk straight past, but did a Chaplinesque half pirouette, and disappeared like lightning through the doorway. Sam conjured up a mental picture of George's harridan wife and found himself nodding his understanding, if not his approval.

Before the prime object of Sam's interest arrived, his cornish pasty was thoroughly digested and his after dinner cigarette was down to its last inch. It was another half hour before Sam got a clear view of the man's face as he came out.

'Bingo!' he exclaimed and reached for the phone.

'Sue? it's Sam ... Oh, you know, so so. Is Tom back from school? ... Thanks.'

Sam drummed his fingers as he waited. His relationship with his ex-wife had been tenuous until she'd found herself a new man called Jonathan Kingsley. It had crossed Sam's mind that Jonathan's posh surname may have gone in his favour. She'd always hated Sue Carew. Said it made her sound like a cheap Japanese car. Now she was all sweetness and light, which in some ways was worse.

'Tom? ... I was wondering if you could pop round and help

me copy a video ... No, nothing like that, you know me. I wouldn't do anything illegal ... Great, see you in half an hour.'

Tom was thirteen and much more au fait with videos than both has father and his twin brother, Jake, the artistic one. They were fraternal twins and unalike in many ways, except that they both thought the world of Sam. To her credit, their mother didn't discourage this.

Sam thanked Tom and put the phone down before Sue had time to come on the line and bore him to death about her vastly improved quality of life now she'd got a decent man at long last. He dialled another number.

'Mrs Gladstone? ... Sam Carew. I've got the evidence you need ... No, it's better than that, I've got a CCTV video of him leaving the place. Time, date, everything, couldn't be more incriminating. I'll bring a copy round this evening ... What? Well cash is always handy.'

That's what he liked to hear. A client who was so pleased with his efforts that she couldn't wait to pay him. So long as it was in cash not in kind. He grimaced at the recent memory of a certain portly Mrs Porteous, for whom Carew and Son had built an extension. Early one morning, she'd summoned him into the house, displayed her ample charms from within a diaphanous housecoat and asked him what he would want to Artex her bedroom ceiling. Sam had scratched his chin and said ten pounds fifty a square metre, which was not what Mrs Porteous had in mind.

'Mum says the garage roof's leaking and can you fix it?' The words were delivered with monotone swiftness as Tom came through the door – as though he just wanted to rid himself of the message as soon as possible. Sam's first thought was to ask why Mum's new boyfriend couldn't fix it, but it would be unfair to burden his son with yet another message.

'Tell her I'll see what I can do.'

His son nodded absently and asked, 'Where's the tape?'

Tom and Jake had been the result of one night of intoxicated passion, legitimised by marriage, because it was the right thing to do, or so Sam had allowed himself to be persuaded. He smiled at his son and not for the first wondered if he should have worked harder at his marriage, if only to be nearer to the boys. But with Sue there would have been just too much work involved and marriage was supposed to be about happiness and love and contentment. Laughing with each other, sharing each other's sorrows, sharing each other's joys and all that stuff. Sam fingered his broken nose which had stopped one of Sue's many missiles. There hadn't been too many joys. Tom seemed to understand and Jake just accepted it, the way kids do.

Mrs Gladstone took the video tape as proof positive of her husband's infidelity. Sam wasn't entirely sure whether or not paying for sex actually counted as being unfaithful, but decided against airing such doubts to Mrs Gladstone, who was counting out his money. He was learning as he went along.

'I'll play the tape to him tonight –' she decided, handing Sam a welcome wad of notes, '– just before I boot the seedy little sod out on his ear.'

She looked much older than her errant husband, but she was a formidable woman, perfectly capable of doing what she threatened.

'I know he married me for my money,' she sighed, 'but I thought he'd make more of an effort. Ah well, back to the drawing board.'

Mrs Gladstone threw Sam a longing glance that had him backing towards the door. She let out a sudden laugh.

'My God – you look terrified!'

'No, no. It's just that I've got to meet my girlfriend in, er –' Sam looked at his watch. 'Well, later on and –'

'Girlfriend? Make sure you treat her right.' She smiled and shook his hand firmly. 'You don't look as if you need me to tell you how to treat a woman. Thanks for what you've done.'

Three of the men at the end of the bar seemed to be taking it in turns to look at Sam. Had he been aware of their attention, he'd have recognised at least one of them and might well have been on his guard. The men were mingling with a group of Unsworth Town supporters, there to drown their sorrows. Unsworth Town supporters always had a lot of sorrows to drown.

Sam was sitting at a corner table waiting for Sally and weighing up the pros and cons of inviting her back to his flat. The trouble was that Sally was talking engagement language again and would definitely see his proposition as some sort of commitment. So how could he get her into bed this time without giving the wrong impression? He was pondering this question when he noticed a man standing in front of him.

'You Carew?' It sounded like a little rhyme the way the man said it. But there was no poetry in this man's voice.

'Who wants to know?' enquired Sam, guardedly.

'I were told I'd find yer in here – and they were right weren't they?'

Sam became aware of two more men standing one either side of him, between them they hoisted him to his feet. Recognition dawned as Sam faced the man in front of him. 'Ah, Mr Gladstone, the man from the massage parlour.' He said it out loud, hoping to embarrass the man into backing off.

'There were no need for it, yer know,' said Mr Gladstone. 'I married her for her brass, she knew that. But when yer a young man like me, yer need summat else.'

'I imagine you do,' sympathised Sam, watching the man's eyes for signs of trouble. The eyes always harden slightly just before delivering the initial blow.

'She nearly bloody kicked me out.'

'Sorry,' commiserated Sam, surprised that Mrs Gladstone seemed to have let him off the hook.

'She's not happy. I can tell yer that for nowt.'

Sam already knew that, but he kept such thoughts to himself.

'I'm not happy neither,' continued Mr Gladstone. 'I just hope you're happy.'

Sam saw no cause for happiness. 'I'm packing it in,' he lied. 'Honest.' He was hoping that his honesty would be shining from his eyes. All three were six footers, marginally taller than him. His last twelve months on site had hardened his wiry frame, and whilst in the force he'd spent much of his time learning various forms of unarmed combat from an ex-SAS instructor, who knew a few moves which weren't in the text books. Still, three on one, he'd need surprise on his side.

'Bit too bloody late fer me, innit?' snapped Mr Gladstone, his eyes suddenly hardening.

Sam brought his knee up hard into Gladstone's groin, producing a howl of agony. The man's two cronies sought retribution. Fists flew at Sam from all directions. He backed off and picked up a chair, holding them off like a lion tamer. They darted towards him and he whirled it about his head, knocking one of them to the floor, but accidentally catching one of the Unsworth Town supporters a glancing blow. It was enough to bring them into the conflict. The air suddenly filled with flying bottles, glasses, fists and obscenities – a welcome release valve for the frustrated football fans. Chaos reigned as Sam's attackers fought off their new assailants, leaving the way clear for Sam to make a strategic withdrawal. He was just stepping clear of the fray when a blow to the back of his head stopped him in his tracks. He awoke an hour later on a trolley in Unsworth General Hospital.

'This one's woken up.'

A passing porter had stopped to take a look at him. There was little sympathy in his voice, nor in the voice of the nurse, who hovered over Sam for a second.

'He'll live.'

Her prognosis was delivered with a note of disappointment. Sam was looking around, wondering what was happening. He was in hospital, he figured that out fairly quickly; it was by no means his first visit to Unsworth General as a client. But surely someone should be ministering to him – he gingerly ran his fingers through his hair – not just leaving him there with a lump on the back of his head the size of a golf ball. Then he remembered the fracas in the pub and it all fell into place.

A uniformed policeman came to check him out. He laughed and called his colleague over. 'Hey Johnnie! Have yer seen who this is?'

A second uniform joined him. Sam's vision was too blurred to identify him immediately, but he recognised the voice. PC Johnnie Slattery.

'Mad Carew, as I live and breathe! It must be like the old times, you in here. How long have you been a football hooligan?'

'Get stuffed, Slattery!' Sam was in no mood for his stupid banter.

'But we're here to arrest you for being drunk and disorderly.'

'If you think I'm drunk, why don't you breathalyse me? NURSE!'

The unsympathetic nurse returned. 'These men are tormenting me, nurse,' complained Sam. 'First I'm attacked by hooligans and now I have to put up with these jokers.'

'Do you know him?' she addressed her question to the two constables who had now wiped the smiles off their faces.

'Oh yes, he's known to us alright,' said Slattery, mysteriously. 'Very well known indeed. He's known as *Mad Carew*.'

'Mad Carew?' The nurse gave Sam a scathing glance. 'So, he *is* a football hooligan then?'

A doctor paused in his step as he passed by. 'Hello Sam, haven't seen you in here for a while.' Before he walked on he explained to the nurse, 'He used to be one of our regulars.'

The nurse looked puzzled and Slattery burst out laughing. 'He used to be one of ours, love,' he said.

'So, he's not a football hooligan?'

'Football hooligan?' grumbled Sam. 'Do I look like a football hooligan? Christ, my head's killing me!'

The nurse looked down at him with a tilted head, her compassion returning. Sam treated her to the best smile he could manage. It seemed to do the trick. With his reputation partially restored, his treatment now accelerated. The trolley set off down a corridor and he lay back, as happy with his lot as he could be, under the circumstances.

3

Sean Joseph Henry cycled the three miles from his house to the site. With him not being one of nature's cyclists his bushy brows were set in concentration. Plasters and scabs on his arms and legs were evidence of his many falls. He rode upon a circa 1948 J.T. Rogers Tourer, which he'd found abandoned in the cellar of a house he'd worked on. The rain had gone now, but the threat of more was still there and Sean had come out without his cap. His hair was black and bushy. More of the same escaped through his grimy shirt collar, betraying a hairy torso. Medium height and thick set, Sean was not a handsome man. His features were not uniform. His two profiles could have been two different people. One ear cauliflower, the other almost normal. One eye lazy lidded, the other twinkling with mischief. Mouth turned up on one side due to battle scars. Broken nose, teeth like a row of bombed houses and huge, gnarled hands.

His brakeless bicycle took him at a dangerously high speed down the long slope of Athelstone Avenue. It would level out eventually – hopefully allowing him to regain control of his machine in time to turn into Athelstone Terrace. Using his huge boots as a brake, he managed to negotiate the bend and turned into a long street of once select Victorian terrace houses, now dilapidated and untended, like Sean. A tunnel of old trees lined the road; the winter sky beyond the leafless branches was dark and leaden and miserable. He didn't want to be late. Sam had seemed unusually upset at him the previous morning and there was crawling to be done if his job was to remain secure. Grey concrete lamp-posts grew beside grey tree trunks. The lamps shone amongst the branches, casting a jaundiced glow. Between the lamps was a stretch of contrasting gloom, scary to a man still half inebriated. He'd had a long session in the pub after being rained-off the day before. His wife had once again been displeased with him – made him sleep downstairs, which was handy in a way as he would have struggled to get up them. His son and daughter had regarded him with something bordering on scorn as they bustled around him, getting ready for school and work. It wasn't easy having a father who was an embarrassment. Sean was persona-non-grata in many quarters, especially at home. Still marginally drunk, he had rolled off the settee and left the house before his razor-tongued wife came down to heap further humiliation upon him.

A sharp wind disturbed the damp branches, scattering icy water onto this cycling, cursing, capless Irishman. He stood on the pedals and the squeaks from the wheels merged into one continuous grating sound as he sped through the eerie tunnel.

The noise of his arrival on site scared the hell out of two dogs, shamelessly copulating beneath the scaffold. Their retreat round the back of the building was hampered due to the male being either reluctant or unable to detach himself. This strange sight gave Sean the last smile he'd have for a long long time. He leaned the bike against a wall and started up the mixer. When Sam arrived he would already be hard at work mixing compo and loading it onto the ligger boards; perhaps such efficiency would wipe out the black mark he'd incurred the day before; perhaps Sam would forget his threat to dock his pay. He wasn't a bad boss, not as unforgiving as his dad, who still turned up to give a hand now and again. Sean stared up at the many gabled roof, now latticed by scaffolding, and wondered if he was up to carrying hods of stone and mortar up there all day long.

Agnes, the last Greerside to occupy the Hall, had died of boredom in 1998 at the age of a hundred and one. Her executors had employed a maintenance firm to prevent it falling into ruin and eventually sold it to an enterprising developer, who had seen its potential and decided to convert it into a nursing home. The top half of the Georgian stone frontage had been dismantled and was being re-built in its original style. Carew and Son were one of the few builders in the area who could be trusted to carry out the work properly. Sean knew this and took pride in being part of such a company.

Starting up the mixer, he squinted at his watch, five to eight. The mixer was a small 3:2 machine. This meant three cubic feet of loose material went in and produced two cubic feet of consolidated composition, or compo or mortar or gobbo or any number of less complimentary words to describe sand and cement mix. He threw in four generous shovels of sand then picked up a bag of cement and emptied the last quarter of it into the swishing drum. Then he lifted up a tarpaulin to bring out another bag and said, 'Shite!'

There was none left, only empty bags. He'd have to lug some more from inside the house. He was searching through his numerous pockets for the house key when a noise from inside the building made him look up. Raised voices, arguing voices. He picked up a short length of scaffolding tube and listened intently, wondering how on earth anyone could have got inside the building, which was being used as a store and kept locked up. He walked towards the door, listening as he went. The argument was becoming more heated – a man and a woman – the woman now verging on hysteria. There was a choked off scream, then silence.

'Hello?' called out Sean, tentatively, his cauliflower ear pressed against the door. An internal door creaked open, then footsteps, then nothing. He turned the key, pushed open the front door a few inches and shouted through the gap.

'Hello?'

No reply.

Clutching the scaffold tube, he cautiously entered a spacious hallway, in which the bags of cement were stored. To his right was a half finished staircase. In front of him, slightly ajar, was the door to the room from where he thought he'd heard the voices. He pushed it open and froze with shock. On the dusty floor, lying on an old sleeping bag, was a young woman. Her denim shirt was ripped open, revealing a naked breast, the rest of her clothes were in disarray and she was obviously quite dead.

Ernest Carew arrived on site at two minutes to eight, aggrieved at having to be there at all. But news of his son's predicament had reached him late the previous evening. He'd called in to visit Sam; satisfied himself that the lad would be okay, and offered him no sympathy at all. Fighting in pubs at his age. No wonder they'd kicked him off the force.

The rumble of the mixer had him nodding with approval; at least someone had started work – probably Sean. He smiled to himself. This wasn't the first time Sean had arrived early to compensate for some misdemeanour or other. He'd worked for Ernest for over ten years. On balance he was worth keeping on – just. Now he was Sam's problem. No sign of him though, probably taking a leak somewhere. He usually spent half the morning draining off last night's ale. Ernest put his glasses on and looked up at the scaffold. The ligger boards weren't loaded up with compo yet, still, you can't ask for everything. He noticed the open door and made his way towards it.

Sean, still clutching the scaffold tube, knelt beside the girl, his ear against her mouth, listening in vain for signs of life. Her eyes were partially open, empty, focused on nothing. There was livid bruising around her neck. She couldn't have been any more than seventeen. He touched her, tenderly, to see if she was still warm. She was. Then he respectfully covered up her naked breast and felt an anger rising within him. Who could do such a thing to a lovely young girl like this, the same age as his daughter, Kathleen? A disturbing thought struck him. Whoever did it was still in the building!

'What the – ?'

The shout came from behind him and had Sean instinctively springing to his feet and whirling round with the metal tube. Too late he realised it was Ernest. Too late because he'd already landed a blow which sent his old boss reeling back, tripping over a missing floor board and falling onto a pile of stone. Sean could not believe what he'd done. He looked down at Ernest, who'd struck his head with a sickening thud and looked as dead as the girl. The blood drained from the Irishman's lumpen features. He walked blindly to the outside door and watched dumbly as

Mr Fosdyke, the building inspector, got out of his van and walked towards him.

'Morning,' said Fosdyke, 'I thought I'd pop in early before you took the wall down. The boss says it's okay to clean it off wi –'

His mouth dropped open as he looked beyond Sean at the man lying behind him. He then took a nervous step past the Irishman, went into the building and did a double take of the dead girl. Too horrified to speak, he backed away as Sean stepped towards him, the scaffold tube still in his hand. Sean's mouth opened and shut and he sank to his knees in shock.

4

Despite a vehement plea of Not Guilty, it was an open and shut case. It turned out that Sean had a criminal record, albeit for small time theft. None of this was known to the jury, but they all suspected he had some kind of form. He had that look about him. Had they known more about him, they might have been swayed in his favour. Petty thieves, generally speaking, don't go round raping and murdering. Sean was found guilty on two counts of murder. His eyes met Sam's as the sentence was passed. Two life sentences, with a recommendation that he serve at least fifteen years. Sean didn't seem to be listening to the judge, he was looking at Sam and mouthing the words, *I'm sorry.*

'Serve the bugger right if you ask me,' commented Owen as he led Sam and Sally Grover through the doors of Leeds Crown Court and out into the sunlit street. *A freedom now denied Sean.* Sam shook his head. It didn't make any more sense now than it had three months ago when he first heard the awful news ...

Owen had taken it upon himself to be the bearer of the dreadful tidings. Sam had been getting dressed, ready to leave hospital when the Welshman's lugubrious face appeared round the curtains.

Sam's grin switched slowly off as Owen searched for the words. During his career he'd had to do this many times, but never to a friend. The words stuck in the Welshman's throat.

'What?' enquired Sam.

'It's your father, see.'

'Dad? What about him.'

Owen was struck dumb.

'Has he had an accident?'

Owen nodded.

'Is he okay?'

The look on the Welshman's face told him not to finish the

question. Owen was slowly shaking his head. 'He was killed this morning. We don't know the precise details, but one of your workmen has been arrested.'

Sam sank back onto the bed, his mind numbed with disbelief. The shock and pain would come soon. Questions needed to be asked, but where to start? His dad, dead. What was he going to do without his dad? His guide, his mentor, his rock – his friend.

No tears arrived that day, they came later. The following day he took himself back to his flat and got all that out of his system in one long, blubbering bout of grief. That first day was a day of numb confusion. Mixed emotions. Sadness. Annoyance at not being able to see his dad to say goodbye until after the post-mortem. Incomprehension as to why Sean had committed such a crime. The police questioning didn't seem to make sense.

Did Sean have a grudge against Sam's dad? No. He might have had a grudge against Sam after the bollocking he'd given him, but Sam was always giving him bollockings.

The police tried to paint a picture of Sean that Sam didn't recognise. Sean had asked to see him, but Sam was too confused. Too overcome with grief. He was in no position to believe or disbelieve Sean's story. He certainly wasn't in a mood to forgive the man who had killed his father.

Ernest Carew, who had fully intended living at least another twenty years, died intestate; although he'd had sufficient foresight to name Sam as beneficiary of an insurance policy, which was just about enough to pay for the funeral and a round of drinks. His mother missed the burial but turned up at the funeral reception that Sam had arranged at his dad's house. Doris Carew hadn't come to mourn. She'd come to collect.

'The trouble with your father,' she said, sipping a larger than decent vodka and tonic she'd poured herself, 'was that with him being a Catholic, he believed in the sanctity of marriage. That's why he never divorced me. Suited me down to the ground. I understand there isn't a will.' She looked round the house. 'I believe this comes to me now. Me being the bereaved spouse.'

Sam studied her carefully. He hadn't seen her since he was eight, when she had walked out of the house on the arm of a man called Giles who, she claimed, was some sort of an aristocrat. The first of many, apparently. She'd been a good looking woman, who had preferred the life of a down-market courtesan to the wife of a builder. But she hadn't aged well. Exposure to the sun had given her leathery skin, dotted with liver spots. Her ostentatiously ringed hands were bony, with incongruous red nails which obviously were no more her own than her flowing auburn wig. She wore a dark blue, size fourteen, two piece trouser suit, which was losing the battle to contain her size sixteen body. Her feet were crammed into high-heeled shoes which were too high for safety in someone her age.

'Who did you say you were?' enquired Sam, with deliberate cruelty. 'You can't be my mother, I imagined her to be so much younger than you. Round about Dad's age.'

A vaguely hurt look flickered across her face but she decided not to cross verbal swords with him. 'I could take the business as well,' she threatened, pleasantly.

'I'm a shareholder in the business and it's only worth anything if I go with it,' countered Sam.

This wasn't strictly true. Carew and Sons owned a piece of building land which was worth more than the house, plus various items of plant and machinery. But she wasn't to know that and Sam had no intention of enlightening her.

'Hmmm – that's what I figured,' she mused, lighting a cigarette and studying him. There was no hint of affection in her pale eyes.

'And I could contest the probate on the grounds that you deserted him,' added Sam, acidly. 'You haven't been technically his wife for thirty years.'

'True,' she accepted. 'And the lawyers would end up with most of the money.'

'Correct,' agreed Sam. 'So, you take the house and leave me Dad's share of the business.'

He was being more than fair and she knew it. She stubbed her cigarette out in her empty glass and held out a limp hand, which Sam ignored.

'It's a deal,' she said, withdrawing her hand.

'One more thing,' Sam said.

'Oh?'

'I'd like you to leave and come back when everything's settled. I feel I'm insulting Dad's memory having you in his house.'

Sally had been watching them from the other side of the room. When his mother left, she went across to Sam.

'Everything okay?'

'Yeah. She wants the house.'

'Surely she can't, not after all these yea – '

'She can and she has,' interrupted Sam. 'I get the business, it's worth more.' The determined poise he'd held in place all day suddenly sagged. It was probably the confrontation with his mother, having to hand his dad's house over to her without a fight. He looked at Sally. 'I'm staying here for a while, Sal. It's much more comfortable, especially the sleeping arrangements.'

She took the hint. 'I'll stay with you tonight, just to see you through all this. But don't think I'm going to make a habit of it.'

'It'll take more than one night to see me through it,' Sam said, perking up. 'Grief's a funny thing. You never know when it's going to come back and get you.'

'You're taking advantage of my sympathetic nature, Sam Carew. Marry me and you get me full time.'

'Now who's taking advantage?'

'I love you, Sam Carew.'

Sam smiled and kissed her on her forehead, eliciting a tear. He saw it coming and retreated to the kitchen where Owen was generously dispensing Sam's drinks. Perhaps it was good that she insisted on marriage as a pre-condition of living together. It was becoming an old-fashioned concept, but for the moment it ensured Sam his independence. As far as women were concerned, his mother and ex-wife had left him a legacy of mistrust which Sally would be hard-pressed to overcome.

Sally wiped away the tear and switched on a smile as Sam's

Auntie Maureen introduced herself. Her eyes were mostly on Sam as she offered her condolences to Ernest's younger sister. Maybe it was unfair of her to press him at a time like this. But she wouldn't wait forever.

The evidence against Sean was circumstantial but weighty. He'd been found by the building inspector with a lump of scaffold tube in his hand, standing over the body of Ernest Carew, with the body of a young girl lying behind him. There was no possible exit from the house other than the front door, through which Ernest Carew and subsequently, the building inspector, had entered. The time of death of both victims was put at 8 am.

Sean's own version of events did his case no good. He'd heard someone, presumably the girl, shout out. No one had passed him as he went in. The building inspector had seen no one leave. All the windows were locked on the inside and the only other exit was the back door, which had been locked and bolted from the inside. He admitted hitting Ernest, but his reason for doing so seemed so far-fetched as to have the press smiling in disbelief at such a weak effort. Fabricated stories usually had a certain amount of artistic merit, but Sean's effort had little to commend it.

The prosecution had drawn up a scenario which fitted events. The girl had left her home the previous evening after a row with her parents, who assumed she'd stayed overnight with a friend. But the friend in question knew nothing about it. It wasn't uncommon for the victim to do this, she'd stayed out the previous night and turned up safe and sound. Somehow she had managed to let herself into Greerside Hall – it wasn't explained how – and Sean's barrister failed to raise the question. Sean had gone into the building, seen the girl and in his drunken state had killed her in an attempted rape. The fact that he'd also killed Ernest simply emphasised how deranged he was at the time. Okay, she'd had sex with someone other than Sean a few hours before her death. They put this down to a lover from the previous evening, who was too scared or embarrassed to come forward. There was no evidence that Sean had actually raped her, but it didn't mean to say he hadn't tried. The main thrust of the prosecution's case was that no one else could possibly have committed the crime. The trial was over in less than a week. Sean's barrister shrugged, philosophically, when the verdict was announced. He'd done his job sufficiently well enough to justify his Legal Aid fee, but they didn't pay him to work miracles.

Sam was sitting with Owen and Sally in the bar of the Victoria behind Leeds Town Hall, enjoying Tetley's beer as it should be served, when a priest walked through the door.

'Wasn't he in court?' asked Sally, nodding in the direction of the black-suited cleric.

'Didn't notice,' said Sam, who had noticed very little that morning.

'I saw him,' confirmed Owen. 'He was sitting at the back. I heard him sigh when the judge passed sentence.'

The presence of a dog collar threw cold water over the filthy stories being exchanged by a group of guffawing young suits standing at the bar. The priest caught the trio's eyes and made his way over to them. The stories resumed behind him as he held out a hand of greeting.

'Michael Donnelly,' he said, leaving off his obvious title. He was a small, round man with a face like a map of Ireland.

Sam, whose Catholicism had lapsed around the time his mother had run off and left him and his dad to fend for themselves, shook the priest's hand.

'Hello, Father. I'm Sam Carew, but I suspect you know that.'

'I do indeed. Would ye mind if I join ye?' There was a gentle West of Ireland lilt to his voice.

'Not at all,' said Sam, pulling out a chair. 'Can we get you anything to drink?'

The priest eyed the three tempting looking pints on the table. 'I wouldn't mind a half pint of what you're drinking.'

Sam looked at Owen, 'Could you get Father Donnelly a half of bitter, Owen?'

Owen, being a lapsed Methodist, didn't agree with men of the cloth drinking in public houses and went off to the bar with bad grace.

The priest watched Owen depart then placed the elbows of his shiny suit on the table and brought his hands together as if in prayer, interlocking his fingers and resting his chewed thumbnails against his teeth.

'I'm Sean's parish priest,' he began.

Sam and Sally nodded, wondering what was to follow.

'And I know Sean well. He's a good Catholic.'

Sally was tempted to say, "So was Mussolini," but she didn't.

'He'd like you to visit him.' The priest held Sam in a steady gaze, as if daring him to turn the request down.

'He's asked before,' answered Sally, on Sam's behalf. 'But Sam was advised not to.'

'It was sub-judice then, it's not now.'

Sam nodded his understanding before posing the question, 'Why would I want to visit the man who murdered my dad?'

The priest took his time to answer. Experience had taught him that a considered reply carries more weight. 'Because ye don't believe Sean murdered your father, any more than I do!'

The reply took Sam aback. The priest seemed to know more about what he was thinking than he himself did.

'I was watching you in court,' added the priest, to reinforce his theory. 'I could tell by the look on yer face, by the way ye kept shaking your head. The whole idea's too preposterous.'

'I don't know what to believe, Father,' Sam admitted.

'Then I'll tell ye what *I* believe, shall I?' said the priest. 'I believe that someone else killed the girl and that Sean found her. Yer dad came up behind him, and Sean's first reaction was to hit out. He thought whoever was behind him was the killer. It was a tragic accident. Sean just wants to tell ye how sorry he is.'

Owen arrived with the priest's half pint. Father Donnelly thanked him, drank it off in one go and stood up to leave. As he turned to go he said, casually, 'Ye know, I heard the lad's confession last week.'

Owen looked shocked. 'Aren't you betraying the secrets of the confessional?'

'And have I breathed a word of his confession to a living soul?' protested the priest. 'I'm entitled to me opinion the same as anyone. And me opinion is that Sean Henry is as innocent as you are, my friend.' He handed Owen his empty glass and left.

'If it's true,' commented Owen, 'and I'm not saying for one minute that it is, look you – but if it's true it's a hell of a miscarriage of justice!'

Sam looked first at Sally and then at Owen. His thoughts weren't difficult to read. Lapsed Catholic though he was, he knew that lying in confession was totally pointless.

5

As jails go, Armley has little to recommend it. Fortress-like from the outside and gloomy and oppressive within. He'd visited before on a couple of occasions, to interview prisoners during his time in the police. Sam left the jail with what seemed like a lump of lead in his stomach. He was now totally certain of Sean's innocence, but hadn't a clue what to do about it. Sean's faith in him had been touching.

'You bein' an ex-copper ought ter foind out the truth, no problem. Then, when I get out I'll be able ter pay yer fee wid me compensation.'

Sam's part time private-eye business seemed to have died a death, along with his dad and Nicola Fulbright, the murdered girl. When the police kicked him out he found he missed the thrill of the chase so he'd started up the Carew Investigation Bureau. But there wasn't much thrill in catching errant husbands, especially those who took exception to being caught. He absent-mindedly fingered the tender spot at the back of his head. This was different though. Although Sean was the instrument of his dad's death, he wasn't the original cause of it; Sam was certain of that. He'd been a good, albeit, erratic detective. During an unusually prolonged bout of sanity, he'd even made sergeant, with the potential to to go further. Detective Inspector Bowman had put paid to all that. The bastard! One day he'd get his comeuppance.

He shook Bowman from his thoughts and turned his attention to the job in hand. Somehow the real killer had escaped unseen, there was no doubt about that, no doubt at all. Thoughts of hollow walls and secret passages and tunnels ran through his mind. Before he joined the police Sam had served an apprenticeship as a brickie and spent three years at night school. He also knew architects, engineers and surveyors. If there was a secret exit from Greerside Hall, he was the man to find it.

6

He'd been waiting on site for twenty minutes when the men arrived at 8.15. He knew he'd been letting things slip. A quarter of an hour would soon turn into half an hour and so on. Sam looked at his watch.

'Right lads. The day after tomorrow's Wednesday. That's half a week gone and nothing done!'

They smiled sheepishly because they knew he was letting them off lightly. Some muttered lame excuses, to which Sam replied he'd heard it all before, just get your bloody fingers out.

In a month the Greerside Hall contract would be into penalties. He could argue unforeseen circumstances as a reason for running over time and his argument would carry some weight, but he didn't want to. He just wanted to get away from the place. He'd spent too little time there over the past three months, delegating the supervision to Alec Brownlow. A good man at his job, but the men knew he wasn't their real boss and took advantage.

Sam stood behind Alec as the short, middle-aged joiner mildly berated his teenage mate.

'How many times have I told yer? Yer hang a door ter blind the room. It's been standard practice since Adam were a lad.'

The lad looked baffled but Sam knew what he meant. When a doorway is positioned near or at the end of a wall, the hinge should be on the side nearest the middle of the room, so that when the door opens inwards, the room is afforded privacy until the last moment. This is doubly important in toilets, bathrooms and bedrooms, where that extra second of time can save the occupant unnecessary embarrassment.

Alec turned to Sam. 'It's like talking to a bloody wall. He's a good lad from the neck down.'

The lad protested sullenly. 'I can't do it on me own. There's nobody to hold it while I'm hanging it.'

Alec nodded, sympathetically. 'Tell yer what, Tim lad,' he

suggested. 'Nip across to Harry and see if he can fix yer up wi' a long stand.'

Sam grinned. The men had played that one on him when he'd been apprenticed to his dad. Being the boss's son had earned him no respite from the practical jokers. He'd been sent to the builders merchants for a long stand and waited two hours before being told he'd stood long enough. The following week they sent him for a set of sky hooks, but he'd wised up by then and spent an hour reading the paper in a transport café before returning to sniggers from the men who had had an arduous hour off-loading a wagon.

He'd fallen for the portable benchmark though, and had struggled to carry a one hundred pound block of concrete, engraved with an arrow, almost a quarter of a mile, only to have it explained by his grinning dad that a benchmark was a fixed point engraved into something permanent, such as a wall, from which surveyors took their levels. Nothing in the world was less portable than a benchmark.

It all seemed a long time ago. He'd spent sixteen years in the police force since then, not to mention a failed marriage. Sam watched the youth make his way over to where Harry the plumber was working, then he turned to Alec.

'I'd like you check all the walls downstairs, especially the ones in room six.'

Alec recognised the room number as the one where the killings had taken place. He threw Sam a glance. Sam shrugged.

'Okay, I'm looking for secret passages. Some means of getting out of the house that we don't know about – it's just a daft idea I've got into my head.'

'Yer don't think Sean did it, do yer?'

Sam shook his head. 'Not for one minute.'

'No,' said Alec. 'Neither do I, nor any of the lads neither. He were a brainless pillock were Sean, but he'd never do nowt like that.'

It struck Sam that Alec was referring to Sean in the past tense. As though he was history.

'Whoever did it,' said Sam, 'managed to get out of that room without Sean seeing him. He either went through the wall, through the floor, through the ceiling – or vanished up his own arsehole. I'd like to find out which.'

He looked at the stone flagged floor and envisaged the entrance to an underground passage, maybe an old, disused culvert, not shown on any survey maps.

'I think we'll have this floor up,' he said suddenly, and walked outside to enlist the help of a pair of groundworkers, who were busy laying the drains.

Carew and Son lost a day and a half, not to mention a lot of the patience of the owners who were now threatening to invoke the penalty clause as soon as the contract period had expired. He'd had a JCB digging trial holes, looking for passages, culverts, drains, wells, anything. He'd checked and double checked the wall thicknesses, the ceilings, the door and window locks. Houdini himself couldn't have got out of Greerside Hall without being seen.

There were only two possible conclusions. Either Sean did indeed commit the murder, or the murderer was still inside the room when Sean discovered the girl's body. But there was nothing in the room to hide behind. No cupboards, no walk-in fireplace, nothing.

Hang a door to blind the room. That was it! The killer had been hiding behind the door as Sean opened it, then, when Sean entered the room, he'd sneaked out and made his getaway. Hang a door to blind a murderer more like. Why hadn't anyone else thought of that? It was so simple. A chat with Fosdyke, the building inspector who was first on the scene might reinforce his theory. Sean had been convicted because it was impossible for anyone else to have done it, so all Sam had to do was cast doubt on this theory and Sean would be set free.

It was a start if nothing else.

Sam had spread the ground floor layout of Greerside Hall on the front counter of the Unsworth Building Services Department.

When the building inspector appeared, he was studying it intently. Fosdyke disturbed Sam's concentration by announcing:

'I'll need twenty-four hours notice before I can test the drains.'

He was tall, dark, and slim, with shallow, grey eyes divided by a larger than desirable nose. An unfussy woman might find him attractive.

Sam looked up into Fosdyke's slightly harrassed face and said, 'Pardon?'

'We've an inspector off sick,' explained Fosdyke. 'And I'm having to cover for him, but if you fill them up with water overnight I'll test them first thing in the morning.'

'I'm not with you,' said Sam, puzzled.

'I said I can't test the drains today,' repeated Fosdyke, impatiently. 'I've got too much on.'

'Oh right – no, I haven't come about the drains, I'd like you to look at this and tell me something.'

'Oh!' Fosdyke went round to Sam's side of the counter to get a better look at the drawing. 'What am I looking for?'

'Well,' began Sam. 'It's to do with the two murders. I can't believe Sean killed the girl ...'

Fosdyke swiftly returned to his own side of the counter as though wanting a defensive barrier between him and Sam.

'You used to be a policeman, didn't you?'

Sam nodded, his eyes still on the drawing.

'But you're not anymore.'

'No. You see, I was wondering if the killer could have been hiding behind this door and made his esca–'

'Mr Carew,' cut in Fosdyke, sharply, 'I'm a building inspector, not a police inspector. I've spent several hours talking to the police, not to mention two days in court. I was hoping the matter was closed.'

Sam looked up slowly, holding Fosdyke in his gaze until the young man lowered his eyes. 'The matter isn't closed for Sean Henry. He's in prison.'

'I should have thought that's the best place for him. After all, he did kill your father.'

'Look, Mr Fosdyke, I'm not here to give you grief, I just want you to give me your opinion on something.'

Fosdyke looked at his watch. 'I can spare two minutes,' he said officiously.

Sam took a pencil from his pocket and drew a short line on the plan to represent an open door. 'When Sean opened this door,' he began, 'he wouldn't be able to see anyone hiding behind it, would he?'

'Not if he didn't turn round, no.'

'But he wouldn't turn round, would he? He'd walk into the room and bend over the girl, looking at her. A bit distracted, wouldn't you say?'

'So, you're saying the killer sneaked out while Sean Henry was distracted. Wouldn't your father have seen him?'

'Doubt it. According to Sean, Dad was only a minute behind him. My guess is that the killer heard Dad coming in and hid behind these stairs,' Sam made a cross on the hall stairs with his pencil. 'Then made his getaway as Dad walked into the room.'

'That wasn't the only thing he walked int – Sorry, that was in bad taste.'

'Yes, it was,' agreed Sam.

Fosdyke tried to steer the conversation away from his faux-pas. 'I'd have seen him if he'd run out of the building after your father went in.'

'Ah – now that's what I'm here for,' said Sam. 'Did you see my dad go in the building?'

'No.'

'So the killer could have run out the front door and dashed round the back of the building just before you arrived.' Sam ran his pencil across the plan, drawing the killer's possible escape route.

'It's unlikely. I'm fairly certain it had all just happened when I arrived,' said Fosdyke.

'It'd take the killer just a few seconds to make himself scarce,' challenged Sam. 'You can't be certain, can you?'

'No, I can't be certain,' conceded Fosdyke, grudgingly.

'And you'd have to say that in court, wouldn't you.'

Fosdyke scowled. 'Are you saying I've got to go through all that again?'

Sam grinned. 'You're a Local Government Officer – it's your duty!'

'Marvellous!' replied Fosdyke. 'Bloody sodding marvellous! Is there anything else?'

'Now you come to mention it, we would like the drains testing tomorrow morning. I'll make sure they're filled up by the time you get there.'

'If they fail the test it'll be another three days before I can test them again,' replied Fosdyke, testily.

'No problem. They'll pass.'

Sam looked down the trench at the two ground workers, Mick and Curly. 'I've arranged for the building inspector to test the pipes in the morning.'

'Jeez! We're not ready,' grumbled Mick. 'We just put a test on ourselves and there' s a bit of a leak somewhere. Tell yer man ter come in the afternoon.'

'He won't. He reckons he's got too much on, and if they fail it'll be three days before he comes back.'

Mick opened his mouth to grumble again, but Sam had gone.

Drainage pipes are water tested by putting a stopper in the lower end and filling the line of pipes with water. The drain will run between two manholes, where the pipe becomes an open channel. The inspector will check that the level of water in the higher manhole channel stays at a constant level for several minutes, thus proving that there are no leaks in the pipeline.

A wise inspector will then go to the lower manhole and see the stopper released and watch the water flow out. It's not beyond the scruples of certain drainage men to insert a second stopper at the top end, just a few feet down from the manhole, then fill that few feet up with water, ensuring a successful test. Fosdyke had been told to watch out for this.

He nodded his approval of the stationary water after standing almost half an hour over the manhole, then strode quickly down the line of pipes to where Curly was unscrewing the stopper.

'Hold it!' he shouted. 'I want to see the water released.'

'Would ye like ter unscrew the stopper yerself?' teased Curly. 'Oim up ter me neck in shite down here.'

'Just let it go,' said Fosdyke, testily.

Curly unscrewed the cap and jumped clear as a stream of water shot out. Fosdyke strode briskly back to the top of the line. That manhole was now clear of water, no trickery here, the test was good. He walked across to Sam, who was watching proceedings with some trepidation. If the pipes had failed he'd be into penalties for sure.

'They seem okay, Mr Carew. You can do the concrete surround now.'

'Thanks Mr Fosdyke. By the way, I told Sean's solicitor what you said. It'll go in his favour at the appeal.'

'Right,' said Fosdyke with a marked lack of enthusiasm. 'Don't backfill the trench before I check the concrete surround.'

'We can be trusted to do things right, you know,' said Sam, sharply. 'I thought you had a lot of work on.'

Fosdyke spun on his heels. 'I'll be here in the morning,' he called out, over a departing shoulder.

'I thought you couldn't come back for three days,' muttered Sam, to Fosdyke's departing back. He strolled over to where Mick and Curly were lighting up cigarettes. 'Thanks for getting the pipes sorted, lads. I'd have been in trouble if they'd failed.'

The two Irishmen looked guiltily at each other. 'We couldn't actually find the leak,' admitted Mick. 'But there's nothin' much wrong wid the pipes.'

Curly nodded his agreement. 'It'll be an awful dark night when the shite won't find its way down dem pipes.'

Sam closed his eyes. 'Jesus! You used a balloon, didn't you?'

Mick nodded, causing Sam to explode.

'Hellfire, Mick! He'd have closed the site down if he'd found out – re-checked everything we've done – it wasn't worth it. I've a good mind to sack you both!'

He stormed away before he did just that. Sacking them wouldn't be clever. They were good lads, and they'd been clever enough to get away with it. Getting away with things always impressed Sam, who got away with very little. The balloon trick was the oldest in the book. Too old for young Mr Fosdyke, obviously. He turned and shouted back.

'Find that bloody leak and fix it!'

Mick and Curly looked at each other, slightly put out that their efforts on Sam's behalf hadn't received proper recognition.

Instead of using an illegal second stopper they'd inflated a balloon and pushed it down the top end of the pipe. It had enough strength to hold back the few inches of water in the top manhole. Then, when the water in the bottom end of the pipe was released it created a vacuum which burst the balloon and released the water from the top manhole. Simple physics. An illusion. Just like the illusion that was keeping Sean in jail. The law was like a building inspector, a sucker for a good illusion. But who was the illusionist?

7

Sam's divorce from Sue had been acrimonious and had, indirectly, been the cause of his dismissal from the police force. Never being one to respond to unwanted advice, he'd rejected the many friendly warnings about him moving in with Darren Feast. Darren was an old friend of Sam's, going right back to his schooldays. Darren had helped Sam with his English and French homework and Sam had acted as Darren's protector.

He had been more curious than repulsed by Darren's revelation that he was probably homosexual. The word 'gay' had not entered into common usage in those days.

'You mean you don't fancy girls?' asked a sixteen year old Sam, as they made their way home from school behind a group of fifth formers from Unsworth Girls High. 'Not even her?'

He pointed to the swaying hips of Fiona Clarkson who was well aware she was being followed by at least one lad she fancied and was putting on an exaggerated display. This was having the desired effect on Sam, who was unaware that it was Darren Feast she was aiming her hips at. Darren was tall and soft-faced and pretty. He was also polite and charming, which set him apart from his contemporaries. Polite and charming were qualities much admired by the girls of Unsworth High.

'No, I don't know what you see in her,' admitted Darren.

'Come on, Darren! I mean, look at that bum. It's like two grapefruits in a hanky.'

'I'd prefer the grapefruits.'

It took Sam a while before he accepted it. Darren was a queer, a woolly woofter, a shirtlifter, but first and foremost he was his pal. Darren knew better than to make any amorous advances on Sam, but Sam often used Darren's charm and beauty to entrap girls, who turned in frustration to Sam when they realised Darren wasn't available. Sam was always very accommodating in this respect.

Darren became an English teacher and found it wiser to keep his sexual proclivities under wraps, seeing no advantage at all in 'coming out of the closet'. So how the police found out about him was a bit of a mystery, but the police have an aptitude for finding out about most things. Sam's marriage had finally collapsed and Darren had put him up in his flat on a temporary basis, until he found somewhere of his own. He'd been living there for over a year when Detective Inspector Bowman began his cheek-pinching campaign.

'Finally gone over to the other side, Sammy darling?' he sniggered, pinching Sam's cheek in the station canteen. 'No wonder your wife kicked you out.'

Sam hadn't a clue what he was talking about and turned to Owen Price, who was standing behind him in the queue.

'Is that it then? Has he finally flipped?' Sam had no love or respect for Bowman.

Owen looked around the canteen in that conspicuously secretive way of his. 'I think it's to do with you living with Darren, isn't it?'

'Me living with Darren?' The penny dropped. 'Oh right.' Then in a louder voice, he added, 'I thought everyone on the force was grown up. I didn't realise we had a big daft baby among us.'

The whole room heard it and knew what was going on. Bowman had no answer, other than a mental resolution not to let the matter drop.

The cheek pinching went on for weeks, whenever Bowman got near him, once during a briefing, to the amusement of Bowman's lackeys – all two of them. Sam's unorthodox policing had always got up Bowman's nose. He resented Sam's popularity with officers of the lower ranks. Sam resented Bowman's childish teasing, and spent much time dreaming up a suitable retaliation.

Darren himself came up with a suggestion, which he later bitterly regretted. 'Do you remember mucking about with the Van De Graaf generator at school?'

Sam laughed. How could he forget? His science experiments had cost him a three-day suspension.

'There's one in our science lab,' said Darren.

'Really?' Sam considered the implications of what Darren was suggesting and grinned. 'Could you bring it home sometime?'

'I reckon I could sneak it out for the weekend,' said Darren. 'The head of science has been lusting after me for quite a while now. Can't stand him of course. Bad breath. The man could strip pine from ten paces.'

'You're too fussy, you know that, don't you?'

'I have my standards. That's why I don't fancy you.'

'Oh Darren! You can be so cutting.'

The Van De Graaf generator, as every schoolkid knows, is a method of charging up a metal sphere with static electricity. This can be transferred by touch to the human body without any ill-effects, providing the body is insulated from the ground. The charge can then be passed on to to anyone coming in contact with the aforementioned body.

Such as Inspector Bowman.

As an instrument of revenge, Sam thought it was the very thing. He also thought it would add to the fun if he let everyone in the CID room in on his little joke. There was a hush of happy anticipation as Bowman's heavy shoes clattered down the corridor, Sam was standing just inside the door, with his hands on the sphere, charging himself up. As Bowman entered the room, Sam stepped forward, hair standing on end. The detective inspector saw him and grinned.

'Having a bad hair day, Sammy darling?' he sniggered, reaching for Sam's cheek. 'How's your boyfri – !'

The size of the flash took everyone by surprise, including Sam, who was bracing himself for little more than a jolt. He hadn't bargained on a mini thunderbolt-jolt. Of course nobody was more surprised than Detective Inspector Bowman, who was lifted off his feet and sent flying across the CID room, catching his arm on the edge of a filing cabinet and smashing his elbow. The acute pain was mercifully anaesthetised when he hit his head on a table, knocking him unconscious. There was a shocked silence, broken by DS Janet Seager. She knew more about physics than

Sam, who was lying on his back, holding his cheek, burnt by the flash.

'I told you not to put too much charge into yourself, you mad sod!'

'I thought if I wore thick rubber soles I'd be okay!' grumbled Sam, who had a history of overdoing things.

Sam counted the houses down Water Lane until he came to number seventy-six, the Fulbright's house – Frank and Jean. He'd got their details from Owen who had once again sworn him to secrecy as to his source of information. Sam had sworn on his mother's life.

His departure from the force had been low key. Faced with a disciplinary hearing and the strong possibility of at least being reduced to constable, he told the chief superintendent that he could stick his job where the sun didn't shine. Perhaps if he hadn't, his dad would be still alive. Left to his own devices, Ernest wouldn't have taken on anything as big as the Greerside Hall job. He only took it for Sam's benefit, to give him something to get his teeth into.

Sam didn't really blame himself, not after the first few days anyway. He'd heard enough *If Only* stories during his time on the force to know that it was possible to trace almost any tragedy back to one's own movements. Something to do with the chaos theory. It would help lay his dad's ghost if he found the real killer though. The old man would want him to get Sean out of jail, despite him being a troublesome old reprobate. An obvious starting point seemed to be the parents of Nicola Fulbright, the murdered girl. It had always seemed odd to him that they hadn't been to court to see any of the trial. In his experience this just wasn't normal.

The house was a substantial semi in what for Unsworth was a select area. The garden was large and untended and the front door could have done with a lick of paint, as could the rest of the house. A window above him creaked open in response to his knock. Sam took a step back and stared up into the face of one of the ugliest men he'd ever seen.

'She's out,' said the man, just before he disappeared from view.

Sam knocked again. The man re-appeared, this time with a mouthful of gleaming teeth which Sam hadn't noticed before. They helped to enhance his appearance, but not much.

'Mr Fulbright?' enquired Sam.

'I told yer, she's out.'

'Are you Mr Fulbright?'

There was a moment's hesitation before he said, 'Aye, lad.'

'It's you I've come to see.' Sam tried to sound cheerful.

'Me? What do yer want? There's no money in the house, she's took it with her. She'll have ter pay yer when she gets back.'

'I'm not after money,' Sam reassured him. 'In fact, if you're a bit short I can let you have some.'

He'd no idea why he said it, but it seemed to work. The man gave him the most frightening smile he'd seen in a long time and disappeared again. A minute later he was holding the door fractionally open.

'How much can I have?'

Sam took out a twenty pound note and held it between two fingers, just out of Mr Fulbright's reach.

'Do you mind if I come in?' he asked.

The door opened wide enough for Sam to enter the house.

'Thanks, Mr Fulbright.' He handed over the note.

Fulbright stuck it into his back pocket, and asked, uncertainly, 'What do I have ter do?'

'Well, first of all I'd like to say how sorry I am about your daughter.' Sam realised as he was saying it that this man might not actually be the father, he looked easily old enough to be her granddad. The man's face contorted into the most mournful expression Sam had ever seen outside a cartoon.

'Aye – she were a good lass were our Nicky.'

Sam allowed the man a moment's silence before he introduced himself.

'My name's Sam Carew. My father was killed as well.'

He followed Mr Fulbright into a large living room which, unlike the house's exterior, was kept neat and tidy. He sat down on a worn leather Chesterfield, Fulbright sat on the edge of a chair opposite; his eyes full of uncertainty. Had he done the right thing in allowing Sam in? Would his wife have something to say when she got back?

'The reason I'm here,' began Sam. 'Is that I think they've locked up the wrong man.'

Fulbright's head nodded and shook simultaneously as if keeping his options open.

'She's dead yer know,' he blurted. Tears appeared in his eyes.

Sam nodded, the futility of his visit was becoming apparent. A door opened behind him and a rough-tongued woman enquired, 'Who the hell are you?'

Mrs Fulbright came into the room, many years her husband's junior. Sam stood up and held out his hand.

'Mrs Fulbright?'

'Yes – who are you?'

'Sam Carew. It was my father who was killed by –'

'That bleedin' paddy!' She finished his words for him.

Sam nodded. 'Something like that. Which is why I'm here.'

'Why's that then?'

'I told him she's dead,' interrupted Fulbright.

'I think he knows, Frank,' she said, then, in a low voice to Sam, added. 'He's not full shillin' any more. Yer know – a bit doolally.'

'Right,' said Sam, who'd worked this out for himself.

'It's been comin' on for a couple o' years. He'll have ter go in an 'ome before much longer. I'm Jean, by the way.'

'Pleased to meet you, Jean.' He held out a hand.

'Likewise.'

She shook Sam's hand and smiled down at her husband, who returned it with one of his own. 'He's an ugly owd bugger, as yer might have spotted,' she said, kindly. 'Face like a bulldog pissing on a nettle. But he's been good ter me. Married me when no bugger else would. He were a good father ter my Nicky an' all. He's not her real dad, yer know.'

Sam had worked that one out as well. Nicky had been a pretty girl. Her mother was no oil painting, so the father must have had something going for him in the looks department.

'Why did yer say yer've come?' she asked, taking off her coat and walking back into the hall to hang it up. Sam followed her.

'I don't think Sean Henry killed your daughter,' he said, bluntly.

Her back was to him as he said it. She froze momentarily at his words, then continued to hang up her coat. 'What about your dad?' she asked.

'He killed Dad alright, but I don't think he killed your daughter.'

She walked past him into the living room. 'Frank,' she asked, gently. 'Be a love, mek us all a cuppa tea.'

Frank rose from his chair, happy to be useful. Staring hard at Sam, he asked 'Do yer tek milk an' sugar?'

'Milk and one sugar, thanks.'

'Just pour it out, love,' said his wife. 'I'll see ter the milk and sugar.'

Frank shuffled into the kitchen.

'He'll be gone a while,' she said. 'He'll make a pot o' tea, he hasn't got Alzheimer's or nowt. Not yet anyroad.'

'I imagine your daughter's death hit you hard.'

She paused before answering, as if examining her true feelings on the subject. 'It were a right sickener, I haven't got over it yet.'

'I'm sorry.'

'Ter tell the truth – Sam, did yer say?' Sam nodded. 'Ter tell the truth, Sam, she'd been a pain in the arse for a couple o' years. Couldn't do nowt with her. I hate ter speak ill o' the dead - 'specially when it's one of yer own, but she were an absolute pain in the arse. Did what she liked, when she liked. She were cheeky ...' There was anger and sorrow on her face as she shook her head at the memory of her daughter. 'Mind you, what kids aren't, nowadays?'

She inclined her head in the direction of the kitchen, where her husband was clattering about, singing an unintelligible, tuneless song. 'An' she talked to him like he were a piece o' dogshit.'

Sam didn't know what to say. Mrs Fulbright seemed to see his dilemma. 'She'd have grown out of it I suppose,' she conceded. 'They all do.'

'I'm sure she would,' agreed Sam.

'She were me only one. When he's gone, that'll be it – on me own.'

Tears weren't far away. Sam sat there, awkward. To his relief, the sound of breaking crockery broke the moment. Mrs Fulbright laughed and shook her head. Her husband stuck his head round the door and said, 'I think I broke a cup or summat.'

'I bloody know yer've broke a cup. We'll have no bloody cups left at this rate, yer clumsy owd twat!'

Sam winced at her language. Frank grinned and disappeared. His wife returned her attention to Sam. 'Me mother told me not ter marry a good looking man. I think I've taken her advice a bit too far. I should've taken the middle road – married someone like you.'

'Gee, thanks,' said Sam, insulted.

'Frank were a brilliant dad to her. Treated her like his own. She never appreciated him. Pity that.'

She took out a packet of Benson and Hedges and offered one to Sam, who accepted it gratefully.

'Thanks. I didn't know whether you smoked or not so I didn't like to –'

She interrupted him. 'It's the one vice I've got left. I never did drink much – and as for the other.' She inclined her head in the direction of the kitchen. 'Frank were never – yer know – much cop between the sheets.' A grin flickered across her mouth as she thought of something. 'I've been thinking of putting him on Viagra – I reckon if nowt else it should stop him pissin' on his slippers.'

Sam grinned. He liked a sense of humour in a woman – a handy thing to have when you're married to Frank, it seemed. As they lit their cigarettes, Jean remembered why he'd come.

'So, yer reckon it weren't that paddy what killed my Nicky?'

'I'm pretty sure it wasn't.'

'Who d'yer reckon it was then?'

'No idea,' admitted Sam. 'That's why I came to see you. I know Sean. Killing your daughter's about the last thing he'd do.'

'He killed yer dad.'

'I know he did – but I reckon that was an accident.' Sam held her in his gaze and asked, 'Did Nicky have many boyfriends?'

Jean laughed humourlessly. 'I'm afraid ter say that our Nicky were a right little tart. She had a different lad every week. Every night sometimes.'

'Do you have any names?'

She rubbed her chin, thinking. 'Michael Elvington – he lives on the Robertstown estate, in the Elmtrees. She went out with him last year for a couple of months. Nice lad, pity she didn't stick with him.'

'What about recently?'

Jean was hesitant on this one. 'Well, I don't know his name, but I had a feeling she were seeing this married feller. Nowt serious as far as I know. Nowt were ever serious wi' our Nicky.'

'What about her dad? By that I mean her real – sorry – biological father.'

Even more hesitation here. She drew hard on her cigarette, tilted her head and blew a cloud of smoke towards the ceiling. 'Yer gonna be diggin' deep on this, aren't yer? You're the one what used ter be a copper.'

'Used to be – not any more.' More hesitation, so he tried a different tack. 'How did you meet her father?'

She smiled thinly. 'Well, it were sort of through work, yer might say.'

'Really?' he tried to sound interested. 'What sort of job did you do?'

She laughed as she stubbed her cigarette out in a heavy glass ashtray with *King's Arms* written on it. Looking him in the eye, she said, 'I were on the game if yer must know. I haven't a bloody clue who Nicky's dad were.'

'Oh, sorry. I didn't mean to pry.'

'Didn't mean to pry? You've done nowt but bloody pry ever since yer walked through that door.'

'Yes, you're right – what I meant was, I didn't mean to pry into your private life. It's none of my business.'

She took another cigarette from the packet. Sam's hand went to his pocket from where he pulled his own cigarettes. 'Please, have one of mine,' he insisted.

'No thanks love, I stick to me own brand.' Her hands were shaking as she lit up. 'I packed it in for a bit when I fell on wi' Nicky. Wish I'd stuck to it, costs me a fortune.'

'I'm the same,' sympathised Sam. 'I've stopped three times this year.'

Jean smiled and unconsciously blew a smoke ring that Sam watched enviously. Mastering the smoke ring was one of his many unfulfilled ambitions.

'After she were born, Frank took us both in,' continued Jean. 'He's a good bloke is Frank, no matter what folk say. He had a bit o' brass an' this house had been left to him. He only worked on t' railways, but he were comfortable off. I suppose that's why I married him.'

The tears had arrived at last. Sam was always uncomfortable with tears of any kind.

'I've never talked ter no one about all this, yer know,' she confessed. 'Frank doesn't really understand and I've no family ter speak of – or to speak *to*, for that matter.'

Sam desperately didn't want to be the one she confided in.

'There *are* people you can talk to,' he suggested, getting to his feet. 'They're really good – I can recommend it.'

'Did you go to anybody?'

He nodded, untruthfully. 'I'll ring you with a name if you like. It's good to get things off your chest.'

'I'd like that.'

Frank appeared at the kitchen door with two cups of tea in his hands.

'I'm going now,' said Sam, 'thanks for your help.' He looked at Frank and smiled. 'See you, Frank.'

Frank winked at him and tapped his back pocket containing the twenty pound note. 'Aye – see yer lad,' he grinned.

9

'Michael Elvington lives with his mother at 49 Elmtree Close and he's got no form to speak of – and you owe me yet another bloody favour, boyo.' Owen had driven his police Astra onto the Greerside Hall site.

'Thanks Owen,' said Sam. 'There was no need to come round. A phone call would have done.'

'Don't flatter yourself. I'm in the area on police business.'

'What sort of business?'

'Burglary business. Burglary number six to be precise. Same MO for each one. No sign of forced entry. At first we thought the house owner was working an insurance fiddle, but there's been too many since then. The burglar must have keys to let himself in and out. Shirley's pulling his hair out.'

'Shirley hasn't got any hair.'

'I was speaking metaphorically, you illiterate bugger!'

Sam couldn't help himself, crime still fascinated him. He leaned in Owen's car window. 'Have you worked out what sort of people would have keys to someone else's house?'

'In most of the cases,' retorted Owen, 'nobody. We've already checked the builder angle. None of them have had any recent building work done.'

'Do you mind if I come with you to this latest one?' asked Sam. He was becoming surplus to requirements on site. All the stonework was complete and Alec Brownlow was handling most of the supervision. On top of which he'd been giving Sam grief about which job they were going on to next. Ernest had always provided continuity of work, but it had been all Sam could do to finish off the Greerside Hall job. He'd promised to sit down and chat about this to Alec, but he decided that Owen's problem was more pressing – and more interesting.

'If Shirley finds out, he'll have my guts for garters,' grumbled Owen, as Sam got in the passenger seat. 'And my guts have been playing up as it is, without you upsetting me even more.' He stuck a couple of Tums in his mouth to prove his point.

'It's all those Mars Bars you eat.'

'Helps me work, rest and play.'

'I suppose you'll need the energy to pay your board and lodging. How is the post mistress, by the way? She hasn't put the rent up has she, you're looking a bit haggard?'

'My rental arrangement is none of your business.'

'Don't be such an old misery. I may have information which will lead you to the burglar.'

Owen brightened. 'What information?'

'How the hell do I know? I haven't examined the crime scene yet.'

'I don't believe I'm doing this!' moaned Owen as he drove off the site.

'Owen,' mused Sam, his mind wandering as they drove. 'Would you say I'm good looking or middle-of-the road?'

'What?'

'Oh, nothing. I was just thinking. You wouldn't be much of a judge anyway. I think she was so used to Frank's ugly mug she wouldn't know handsome when it stared her in the face.'

'Sam, have you ever thought of booking yourself into a lunatic asylum? I reckon they could straighten you out in a couple of years.'

The old woman shouted through the partially opened door to Owen. 'It's about bleedin' time!' she grumbled, before opening it fully to let him in. Sam, as instructed, stayed in the car.

He waited until Owen was in the door before getting out and walking round the back of the house. When Owen returned Sam was back in the passenger seat.

'I tell you,' said Owen. 'It's got me baffled. She had enough bolts on the door to keep out an army and locks on all the windows.'

'Have CID got themselves involved yet?'

'Sort of. They're leaving it up to uniform to do the legwork,' replied Owen. 'You know Bowman. Too scared of getting egg on his face. He'll only step in if we give him a decent lead.'

Sam lit a cigarette, much to the annoyance of Owen, who was trying to give them up. He unwrapped a Werther's Original instead.

'Could you take me on a quick tour of all the other houses that were burgled?' asked Sam.

'Only if you tell me you know how it was done,' insisted Owen.

Sam looked at him, despairingly. 'Owen, even Sherlock Holmes needed to see the full picture before making his dazzling deductions.'

An hour later, Owen and Sam had driven past four of the other five houses.

'Call back to the site before we look at the last house,' requested Sam. 'I'd like Alec to come along.'

'It's not a bloody sight-seeing tour, look you,' grumbled Owen. 'Why does he have to come?'

'To help me show you how it's done. It's a two man job is this. The only thing I can't figure out is how they covered up their tracks.'

The final house was an end terrace, or Town House as the estate agents preferred to call it. Built in the 1970s, when builders could get away with eighteen houses to an acre.

'I've brought a couple of builders with me to try and throw some light on how the burglars got in,' explained Owen to the young man who opened the door. 'It was your wife I spoke to last time, my name's PC Price of Unsworth Police.'

'Oh, right. The wife's at wor ... at the shops.' His correction was made with the guilty look of a man on the dole who wasn't declaring his wife's income. Sam spotted it, but Owen didn't. Not that he'd have done anything about it.

'May we come in?' asked Owen.

'We'll just have a look round outside,' chipped in Sam. 'Could you lock us out – all the doors and windows? I want to show you something.'

He took Alec round the back of the house. The young man locked the door and led Owen into the miniscule living room. Ten feet square with a dining area off, into which was crammed a table and six chairs. The living room was furnished with an illuminated bar and a four-seater settee facing an old television set which stood on a coffee table.

The young man went into the kitchen to lock the door, excusing the state of the television as he did. 'It's me old telly,' he called out, as if having an old TV created some kind of social stigma. 'The thievin' bastards took me Bang and Olufsen, and me video and stacking system, and the microwave and a Rolex me wife bought me for me birthday.'

Owen wondered if the young man was confusing Rolex with Rotary, but decided to leave that one to the insurers.

'I were watching *This Morning*,' he said. Owen nodded, he liked Fern but he wasn't so struck on Phillip Schofield. Too pretty for his own good.

'I'm waiting for that doctor comin' on. He's gonna talk about arthritic hips. That's what I've got yer see. I'm on the sick.'

He emphasised his ailment with a pronounced limp which Owen hadn't noticed on the way in. Sitting down on a worn settee, the young man invited Owen to do the same.

'It's a crap picture innit?' he said, apologetically. 'Yer ought to have seen me Bang and Olufsen widescreen. It were like being at the bleeding Odeon.'

Owen thought the picture looked okay, easily as good as the 19" Baird in his room. It crossed his mind to ask his landlord for a better telly. Perhaps not, the landlord's wife might put his rent up and she was wearing him out as it was. He sat beside the young man, watching the TV doctor advising on many types of relief for ailments ranging from arthritic hip to irritable bowel syndrome. Owen became deeply interested.

'Oh, I'm a martyr to my bowels, see,' he said, cramming a handful of Tums into his mouth. 'Play me up something awful they do.'

He was happy to have found a soulmate. Stories and sympathies were exchanged about their ailments. A common empathy was struck when the conversation reached haemorrhoids. Interrupted by a cough from behind, they both turned to face a grinning Sam. Owen introduced him.

'This is Sam Carew. He appears to have solved the mystery.'

'A mystery to a bobby,' corrected Sam. 'But no mystery to a builder. Follow me.'

The two of them trooped obediently behind Sam into the kitchen. Alec was standing outside with a screwdriver in his hand and an expression on his face which said: "I don't want to be here."

'Out and back in ten minutes flat,' said Sam. 'And we haven't been practising.'

'What's he talking about?' enquired the young man. Owen shrugged.

'I'm talking about your plastic windows,' explained Sam. 'The ones with the beading on the outside. Dead easy for whipping out the glass and putting it back so no one's the wiser.'

Owen leaned over the sink and tapped the window for reasons best known to himself. 'I suppose the other houses all have plastic windows?' he queried.

'Same type, same age. Could have been put in by the same firm. The window firms have wised up since then and put the beading on the inside, but there's still a lot of the old type about.'

'At least six round here,' commented Owen.

'And the rest,' said Sam. 'I'm surprised the insurance companies didn't twig.'

'What do I do now?' asked the bemused young man.

'Well, if you don't want the same thing happening again, you should get some new windows,' advised Sam. 'To a burglar, these are like walking through an open door.'

'I can't afford new winders. I'm on t' sick.'

'Maybe your wife'll pay for them out of her wages,' suggested Sam. 'Or failing that, you can always get a big dog. That usually does the trick. You could maybe get one from the Social.' He said it with a straight face.

'Good idea, thanks.'

Sam's humour had fallen on deaf ears. The young man might even capitalise on the idea.

As they left the house, Sam turned to Owen. 'Do me a favour, find out who they're all insured with. I can do a spot of business here.'

'I suppose it's the least I can do,' sighed Owen. He hated being indebted to Sam, who always seemed to call in his debts straight away. 'I'm going to have to hand it over to CID though.'

'What? To bloody Bowman! Have you gone raving mad? I've handed you the case on a plate and you're about to give it to that pillock.'

'It's not exactly on a plate,' pointed out Owen. 'The general idea is to find out who did it, or have you forgotten that bit?'

'Owen, now we know how it's done, it's all downhill from here.'

'I hope you're talking about the case and not my career.'

'You can't see it, can you?' said an exasperated Sam. 'Whoever did it took great pains to cover up their method – and their tracks. They must have walked on duck boards or something, so's not to leave footprints. And why did they bother putting the windows back? They're obviously worried about the glaring clue that'll make life difficult for them once you lot find out how it's done.'

'What glaring clue would that be?'

Sam sighed. 'Good God Owen! You could chop chips on your head at times. So far we know that the only houses they're breaking into are ones with plastic windows beaded on the outside. Once word of that gets out – into the papers say – all the people with that type of window are going to be on their guard. And the last thing a burglar wants is someone who's on their guard.'

Owen was offended, but weakening, so Sam tried another angle. 'On top of which our villain seems to know exactly which houses have got this type of beading.'

'Inside knowledge, you mean?'

'Probably worked on these houses himself at one time,' said

Sam. 'Owen lad, it's your career I'm thinking of. How long have you been trying to make sergeant? Ten years? Fifteen? This could do it for you.'

'Look boyo, you done me a good turn, but I can't handle a thing like this on my own. Once I tell Sergeant Bassey, he'll just pass it on to Bowman.'

'I know all this – thinking's never been Shirley's strong point,' said Sam, 'but it'll be a hell of a feather in your cap if you solve the whole thing on your own.'

'It'll certainly do Bowman no good if a mere plod solves one of his unsolvable cases – make him look a right plonker,' conceded Owen. Pointing the ignition key at the car, he clicked open the locks and turned to Sam. 'You'd like that wouldn't you, you crafty bugger?' He was still suspicious of Sam's motives.

'The thought never crossed my mind,' lied Sam. 'Anyway, down to business. I reckon those houses were all built by the same builder back in the seventies.'

Owen was wondering how he could tell. Sam read his thoughts. 'Little things. Similar design, same bricks – London Tudors; same roof tiles, stuff like that. First thing we need to do is find out who the builder was and take it from there. He shouldn't be to hard to track down. If the owners don't know, you can go down to the council offices and speak to a building inspector called Fosdyke. He'll check back through the records and tell you all you want to know about who built what and when.'

'Fosdyke,' Owen was writing down the name. 'Didn't he have something to do with your dad's ... you know?'

'Well, he was there, but I wouldn't go round accusing him of anything sinister, he might take it the wrong way. It might be as well if you don't mention my name.'

'I'd no intention of mentioning your name, boyo. Mentioning your name has never done me any good as long as I can bloody remember.'

Alec had been standing patiently by the car door throughout

the conversation. 'Have we finished playing cops and robbers now?' There was a distinct edge to his voice.

'What's the problem Alec?' asked Sam, getting into the passenger seat as Alec got in the back.

'The problem is that I don't want ter be out of a job this time next month, nor do any of the lads.'

'You have my deepest sympathy,' said Owen, starting up the car.

'Thanks,' said Alec. 'But yer can't put sympathy on the table. What jobs have yer got lined up fer us?'

Sam had switched his mind from the burglaries to the address Owen had given him earlier in the day. Nicola Fulbright's boyfriend's address. He'd be paying Michael Elvington a visit that evening. No, it'd have to be tomorrow, he'd promised to take Sally to the Grand Theatre in Leeds that evening. Opera North were doing *Othello*. She was determined to inject a bit of culture into him. He'd wanted to see Ken Dodd at the City Varieties but Sally had hinted that opera was a bit of an aphrodisiac as far as she was concerned and Ken Dodd was no match for a sexually aroused Sally Grover.

'Sam! I asked you a question,' said Alec, impatiently.

'Sorry Alec. What was that?'

'The lads are worried about their jobs. They think yer've got nowt lined up for them after Greerside Hall's finished. What shall I tell 'em?'

Sam considered Alec's problem. It had been locked away in a reluctant recess of his mind. He knew he needed to do something, but simply hadn't got round to it. He was a bricklayer and fairly new to the game at that. 'Alec,' he admitted at last, 'I'm a detective and a brickie, but that's all. I know nothing about pricing up jobs.'

'I know a man who does.'

'Who?'

'Me.'

Alec paused before explaining himself. 'I had me own business up to six years ago, then I went bust.'

71

'Alec, there seems to be something lacking in your job application technique,' commented Owen, drily.

'Shurrup Owen!' said Sam, brusquely. 'Just keep your eyes on the road. 'Go on, Alec.'

'I was sub-contracting, to Brighouse Estates,' continued Alec, 'when they went down.'

'Taking you with them,' concluded Sam. 'Could have happened to anyone.'

'Sorry Alec,' apologised Owen.

'Anyway,' went on Alec. 'I could do all your pricing for you. I offered to help your dad out, but he'd have none of it.'

'He was a stubborn old so and so, was my dad,' agreed Sam. Owen drove on in silence as Sam thought about what Alec had told him. His dad had held the joiner in high regard, which was testimonial enough for Sam.

'Look,' he said at length, turning in his seat to face Alec. 'Suppose I put you in charge of the company. You get all the work and do all the pricing. I'll do the bricklaying and sort out the money side. How does that sound?'

'Sounds like you're making me a partner,' said Alec.

Owen nodded his agreement to this. 'That's what it sounds like to me, boyo.'

'Owen!' complained Sam. 'Just keep this out will you?' He tapped the side of his nose. 'I'm conducting business negotiations with my new partner.' Turned back to Alec, he held out his hand. 'Fifty-fifty on everything we make from now on. I'll get the assets valued and you can buy your half as you go along.'

Alec was taken aback at the generosity of Sam's offer, which seemed to have been made on the spur of the moment. 'Are you sure about this?' he asked.

'I'm not sure about anything right now.'

'Makes a change,' said Owen. 'I've never come across a man so bloody sure of himself when he has no right to be.'

Sam ignored him and added, 'But I've never gone back on a handshake in my life.'

'That's true,' conceded Owen.

Alec shook Sam's hand. It was more than he ever expected. From Sam's point of view it was the most astute business move he'd ever make.

10

The news that Sean Henry had been granted leave to appeal against his conviction came as an intense irritation to Fosdyke. It should have been obvious to an idiot that the man was guilty – who else could have done it for God's sake? Now he'd have to stand in that blasted witness box again, and be asked stupid questions by some stupid barrister. Such thoughts were milling around in his head as he arrived to do a final inspection on Greerside Hall.

He climbed out of his council van and stretched his long legs. That was another thing. Why couldn't they give him something decent instead of a crappy old Maestro van? He'd got an HND in municipal engineering, which was a damn sight more than any of the other inspectors had. Most of them were jumped up tradesmen. His boss, Chalky White left school with two O Levels and a spirit level. Someone was going to suffer this morning and the hot favourite was Carew and Son. He'd already made them excavate back down to a sewer to confirm it had been surrounded with concrete. The JCB had just finished digging when Fosdyke arrived. He took a notebook from his pocket and was examining it carefully when Sam walked across and stood beside him.

'Damp course trays over the windows,' read Fosdyke.

'What about them?' queried Sam.

Fosdyke looked up from the notebook. 'Are there any?'

'Of course there are.'

'I didn't see any,' commented Fosdyke, returning his attention to his book. It was within his power to ask Sam to provide proof, which would have been impossible without breaking out yards of stonework. Sam breathed deeply. It wasn't a good idea to upset the building inspector, but everyone had their breaking point.

'Wall plates, what size are they?'

'Four by three, as specified,' replied Sam, patiently.

'The specification's metric, you shouldn't be talking in inches.'

'A hundred by seventy-five,' said Sam. He was beginning to crack. 'How come you're having to ask me? Shouldn't you have checked this stuff already?'

'I can't be everywhere.'

Fosdyke walked to the edge of the newly dug trench and looked down. The excavation clearly revealed that the pipes had been concreted.

'How do I know it's a hundred and fifty millimetres thick?' he enquired.

Sam wanted to hit him, but he settled for sarcasm.

'It isn't.'

'How thick is it?'

'My lads aren't metricated yet. They settled for six inches.'

Fosdyke was trying to work out which was the greater. Sam helped him out.

'That's a hundred and fifty-three mil to the layman. We threw in the extra three mil for good measure and hang the expense.'

Fosdyke wasn't happy at being called a layman. 'Give me one good reason why I should take your word for it.'

'If you'd bothered to turn up when we were concreting, you could have seen for yourself,' snapped Sam. 'Then we wouldn't have to waste time and money digging it out again!'

Fosdyke could see he was getting to Sam and he was enjoying it. 'It's like I just said,' he retorted. 'I can't be everywhere at once. You shouldn't have back-filled the trench until I'd checked the concrete.'

The re-excavation of the trench had left the ground unstable. Sam could see the edge of the trench, where the building inspector stood, was beginning to slip. He took a quick step back. Fosdyke realised too late what was happening and, still clutching his notebook, he slid slowly and comically downwards. A miniature landslide buried him up to his chest. Alec, Mick and Curly came over to join Sam. They all looked down, not quite knowing how to help. Fosdyke looked to be in pain.

'Are you okay?' enquired Sam, with genuine concern.

'Okay? Do I look fucking okay? Ow! Jesus! I think I've broken my ankle. Ooh, shit and corruption!'

'Oh,' said Sam, wincing in sympathy. 'Sorry about that.'

'Never mind fucking sorry. Do something, you idiots!'

'That's very strong language for a buildin' inspector,' muttered Mick to Curly. Curly nodded his agreement. People in authority should set an example, especially in trying circumstances such as these.

It was an hour before Fosdyke was finally loaded on to an ambulance. Mick and Curly had dug him out as gently as they could, which wasn't very. The building inspector had cursed and promised all manner of recriminations on Sam for contravening site safety regulations and not having the trench properly shored up.

Sam had patiently explained that you can't shore a trench up while you're digging it out and that they'd only finished digging a few minutes before Fosdyke had arrived. Besides, it was just four feet deep and they'd only dug it out to look down, not to work in – and it shouldn't have been necessary anyway.

'Never mind, I'll explain it all to your boss,' Sam said, as they put Fosdyke into the ambulance. 'He's a decent bloke, I'm sure he'll understand.'

Fosdyke began to warn Sam about not talking to his boss, but the ambulance doors cut off his words.

'Serves the pillock right,' said Chalky White, Fosdyke's boss, later that day. 'Causes more trouble than he's worth. Never came up through the trade like the rest of us, yer see, straight outa college. It's like having a football referee who's never played himself. Thinks he knows it all and he knows nowt.'

He was preaching to the converted. 'Find out what ward he's in and we'll send him a get well slowly card,' said Sam, through Mr White's van window. The job had passed final inspection without problem.

'Hey! He'll appreciate that,' laughed White. 'Yer'll get the

Certificate of Habitation in a couple o' days.' He slammed the van into reverse, then leaned out of the window. 'For what it's worth, I reckon yer've not done a bad job.'

Such double negatives are high praise indeed. Sam blew the gnarled old inspector a kiss. Kind words are rare birds in the building trade.

'I been in to see your Mr Fosdyke but he's in hospital see,' said Owen on Sam's answering machine. *'And his boss was out and no one else seemed to be able to help so I may as well hand the whole thing over to Shirl ... Sergeant Bassey. I thought I'd ring and let you know as it's only common courtesy, being as how it was you who found out how it was done.'*

Sam rang Owen at his home as soon as he picked up the message, but the post mistress said he was indisposed. Whatever that meant.

Detective Inspector Bowman was conducting the briefing. There'd been a seventh burglary and the press, as his superintendent put it, were beginning to take the piss. He'd taken Bowman to task that morning. Bowman had tried to shift the accusation of incompetence onto uniform, but as it was officially a CID case, this didn't wash with his boss.

Before Owen had the chance to pass his information on to Sergeant Bassey, the two of them had been summoned to a CID briefing concerning the burglaries, ostensibly to add what little knowledge they'd gleaned so far. In truth, Bowman was determined not to shoulder any more blame than he had to. He opened proceedings with a question to the sergeant.

'You've had a lot to do with the case, Sergeant Bassey, how much progress have you made? For example, do we know how the burglar gets in and out?'

Bassey wasn't going to take this. 'We know about as much as the experts in CID – and by the way, it's been your case all along. We've just been helping out of the goodness of our hearts.'

'I think I know how it was done, sir,' called out Owen.

Bassey glared at the constable, wishing he'd keep his mouth shut.

'They get in through a window, see,' explained Owen. 'They don't smash it, they just take out the whole pane.'

They was a silence as the room digested Owen's revelation.

Bowman took the idea a stage further to illustrate its stupidity. 'I see,' he said, rubbing his chin, theatrically. 'How cunning. And they put it back after they've left, exactly how they found it, with no trace of it ever having been taken out. No footprints, finger-prints, nothing.'

'Yes, sir,' said Owen, uncertainly.

'Maybe they wash the dishes and do a bit of hoovering while they're at it.' His remark generated a few smirks.

'It's the only possible way they can get in sir,' persisted Owen. He wished he'd asked Sam to be a bit more technical in his expla-nation. 'It's plastic windows, see. They're easier to break into.'

Owen had reached the boundaries of his knowledge on the subject. The significance of internal as opposed to external bead-ing had escaped him. If Sam didn't exasperate him so much, he'd have taken the time to glean a bit more information on the subject. Grins were appearing on the faces of the CID officers.

'I've got plastic windows at home,' said Bowman. 'Being bur-glar-proof's supposed to be one of the big selling points.'

Owen took a step back to indicate the end of his contribution, but Bowman wasn't going to let him off the hook.

'It's very good of the burglars to put the windows back after they finished. We must remember to thank them when we catch them.'

The amusement became audible. Bowman had few fans at the station and it pleased him to find so many men on his side.

'Why do you think they go to all this trouble, constable?' he enquired. 'Putting the windows back and leaving no trace.'

'To throw us off the scent.' The answer seemed obvious to Owen. 'So we don't twig that the only houses they're breaking into are the ones with plastic windows. It narrows everything down, see.'

'So, now that we've solved that mystery, the burglars should be easy to find, should they?' said Bowman, sarcastically.

Bassey jabbed an elbow into Owen's ribs, hinting at the Welshman to shut up. Owen obliged, he saw no reason to help the grinning detective inspector.

'Right,' said Bowman. 'So much for uniform's contribution. For the time being we'll take a risk and ignore Constable Price's idea about the windows and explore some more practical suggestions, such as the burglars having access to the house keys ...'

He was still talking when Sergeant Bassey ushered Owen from the room. He confronted the flustered constable in the corridor. 'What the hell was all that about, Owen?' he snapped. 'You made uniform look right bloody plonkers in there!'

'Sorry Sarge,' protested Owen. 'It was just an idea that's all. Sam Carew thought – !'

That was as far as he got.

'Sam Carew?' exploded Bassey. 'Why are you listening to that mad bugger? What have I told you? Never mind Carew. In future, run your ideas past me!'

He was gone before Owen had a chance to run his ideas past him. Unkind thoughts, centred on Sam, occupied the Welshman's mind. Doubts about the worth of Sam's conclusions. His weird ideas. Sam was always so convinced that he was right, even after he'd been proved wrong. Although, admittedly, many a villain had ended up behind bars courtesy of Sam's weird ideas.

Owen wasn't the only one having unkind thoughts about Sam. Jean Fulbright was sitting outside his flat in her Cavalier when Sam pulled up behind her in his Range Rover, a legacy from his dad and much less embarrassing than his old Cortina, which he claimed was a classic car but in truth was a heap of junk and all he could afford. She'd obviously been crying as she got out of her car to confront him.

'Yer know Frank was arrested this afternoon!' She said it in a way which had Sam feeling guilty.

'No, I didn't know.'

Her face displayed a mixture of anger and distress. The anger was clearly directed at him. 'He's not supposed ter drink, yer know. I never keep a drop in the house, but that wouldn't stop him going ter the pub if he had any money ter go with. That's why I never left any money in the house when I went out.'

'Oh,' said Sam, inadequately.

'He never was a big drinker,' she went on. 'But he used to enjoy a pint with his mates at the Pear Tree. That's where he was when they arrested him. Some silly git gave him twenty quid.'

She obviously knew who the silly git was, but she wanted Sam to stew in his own discomfort.

'He had three pints and had a piss at the bar. He never does that at home. Mind you, he's never drunk at home.' There were tears in her eyes. 'He ... he took it out and pissed all over the carpet. Women watching and everything.'

Sam felt wretched. 'I ... I suppose you know it was me who gave him the money. I don't know what to say. I didn't realise, I'm sorry.'

Her brow furrowed as she looked up at him. 'Why, though?' she asked. 'Why did yer give him money?'

Sam did many things which didn't make sense to anyone but him, and this was just one of them. 'I did it because ... look, I'm sorry. I suppose the correct answer is I did it because I'm stupid. It comes from having been a copper. When someone seems a bit, well, reluctant, money often smooths the path.'

'It'll take more than money ter smooth Frank's path. They've locked him up. He'll be scared.'

'I'll see what I can do.'

'I think you'd better.'

Sam took out his mobile and rang the police station. What he didn't realise was that they were in the process of letting Frank go. Jean had been in an hour ago and explained what had happened, placing the blame squarely on Sam's shoulders. When her story reached Bassey's ears, Sam's involvement was enough to convince him. The irate sergeant came on the phone and gave Sam an ear bashing. As Sam listened he nodded and smiled at

Jean. Then, when the sergeant came to the bit about Frank being released, Sam said: 'Oh, by the way, you have a chap in there called Frank Fulbright, you'd be doing me a favour if you let him go without charge. He's a good bloke who's had a few problems recently ... You will? Thanks Sarge.' This provoked further fury in Bassey who thought this idiot was really taking the piss. Sam clamped the phone to his ear so the noise of Bassey's rage wouldn't escape and be overheard by Frank's now relieved wife. He concluded the call by saying, 'I owe you one, Sarge.'

Sam clicked off the phone and smiled at Jean. 'Right,' he said. 'I've sorted it. You can collect him now. He's been released without charge.'

She got back in her car and drove away without a word of thanks. Sam watched her disappear into the traffic. It had been a mixed day, one minor triumph and one mini-disaster. Perhaps the scales would swing in his favour when he visited Nicola Fulbright's boyfriend, Michael Elvington, that evening.

Elmtree Close was a cul-de-sac on a council estate. A game of football was in progress, probably a reaction to the recent FA Cup Final, despite it being won by Arsenal. Before the war, Unsworth Town had reached the fifth round and would surely have their glory days once again. According to the football strips on view there appeared to be several teams playing. Unsworth Town, Leeds United, Manchester United [needless to say] and for some obscure reason, Tranmere Rovers.

Sam found it reassuring, despite the ball bouncing off the roof of his Range Rover. It made a change from seeing kids sniffing glue or just sitting gawping at a television. He got out of his car just as the ball came flying his way and nodded a neat header into the path of a small, brown-skinned boy in a Manchester United top. The boy struck it on the volley straight through the window of number 49. The street cleared of footballers in a matter of seconds, leaving Sam to cope with a barrage of abuse from the irate Mrs Elvington, who had apparently seen enough through the now broken window to know that Sam had played his part.

'What sort of idiot are you, playing football wi' kids? I just hope you're gonna pay for this winder, cos I bloody aren't, I can tell yer that for nowt!'

Sam went on the attack, the only way in such situations. 'Mrs Elvington – it's bad enough being hit on the head by a ball without copping a mouthful from you into the bargain!' His tone was enough for her to to back off. He also knew her name, this was worrying. What had her Michael been doing now?

'And who are you when yer at home?' Her belligerence was mingled with a hint of caution, which Sam spotted.

'My name's Sam Carew, I'm a private detective investigating the murder of Nicola Fulbright.'

'Nicky Fulbright? Oh aye. What's that got ter do wi' me?'

'I was actually wanting to speak to your son.'

'Private detective? So yer not a proper copper then?'

'No, but my dad was killed at the same time. I need to get to the bottom of it and I was wondering if Michael could tell me anything about her.'

She stood her ground, considering her position. He wasn't a proper copper so he probably had no rights. A large dog emerged from within her house, mainly Alsatian, but no Crufts contender.

'Heel, Sabre,' she commanded, optimistically.

Sabre sauntered past her and took a nonchalant pee against the gateless gatepost.

'Perhaps he's a bit deaf?' ventured Sam.

'Nah – one word from me and he does as he likes,' she admitted. 'Mind you, he barks like buggery when a stranger comes in t' house, so he's good that way, yer know, burglars an' stuff.'

'Scares off intruders,' said Sam.

'Them an' all,' she agreed, trying to weigh him up. Should she tell him to clear off or what? He looked a nice enough bloke.

'I'm willing to pay for your window,' he offered. 'In fact I can get it made safe for you right now, and have it fixed first thing in the morning, if you like.'

This swung it, her face softened. 'Awright, yer'd best come in.'

She absently ran her fingers through her bleached blonde hair as though tidying it for her visitor. Sam thought her hardly old enough to have a grown up son. The fact that there seemed to be no husband around maybe had a lot to do with it. Teenage pregnancies were not a new phenomena, not around Unsworth anyway. She had never been a pretty woman, now probably in her mid-thirties, although much older around the eyes. Slim, but shapeless, bare-legged and high-heeled. Not Sam's type.

He was already ringing an emergency glazing firm as he followed her through her door. Being a builder with so much help on tap was a godsend. He closed the door, shutting out a panting, drooling, Sabre. Loud, thumping music was coming from upstairs.

Mrs Elvington poured him half a tumbler of whisky which would have had him reeling had he drunk it. She kept it especially for hospitality purposes. Sam smiled and held up his hands.

'That's very kind of you Mrs Elvington, but not at the moment.'

'Fair enough, waste not want not.' Putting the glass to her lips, she tipped half of it into her mouth. A good double. She drew in a sharp breath to ventilate her burning throat. 'Drop o' good stuff that.'

'I understand your son used to be friendly with Nicky,' Sam began 'and I was hoping he might be able to throw a bit of light on who her boyfriends were. Nicky's mother only knew about Michael, but I suspect there might have been others.'

'Yer suspect right, mister. I don't like ter speak ill o' the dead but she'd had more pricks in her than t' Unsworth Labour Club dartboard.' She tipped the rest of the whisky down her throat, took another sharp breath and eyed him steadily. 'She were a prostitute, were young Nicky.'

The thought had been at the back of Sam's mind, so it came as no great shock. He nodded. Mrs Elvington went into the hallway and shouted up the stairs.

'Michael!'

No answer.

She returned momentarily, 'I'll pop up and gerrim. He can't hear nowt when he's got that racket blastin' in his ear'oles.'

Sam looked through the broken window at the cautiously returning footballers. The ball lay on the carpet amid shards of glass. He threw it back out through the broken pane and proceeded to pick up some of the larger pieces, placing them on one of the many old newsapers scattered around the room. Mrs Elvington had catholic taste, from the *Mirror* to the *Guardian*. Tidiness was not one of her virtues. Sam could relate to that. A half eaten Chinese meal lay on the coffee table in its foil container, chicken fried rice with a portion of sweet and sour sauce. The music upstairs stopped and a few seconds later a youth walked into the room. Medium height, overweight, shaven headed and suspicious of Sam.

'Me mam says yer want ter talk ter me about Nicky Fulbright.' Simple words, but articulately spoken. The lad was nowhere near as thick as his haircut and teenage acne made him look. Mrs Elvington followed him back in.

'I've told him she were a prostitute,' mentioned his mother.

'That's right, she was,' confirmed Michael. 'But she wasn't a slapper!' he said in Nicky's defence.

Sam tried to equate being a prostitute with not being a slapper.

'She used ter be a right laugh did Nicky,' went on Michael. 'I went out with her for nearly a year. Then she started using E – that's Ecstasy,' he explained, for Sam's benefit.

'I think he'll know what E is,' interrupted Mrs Elvington. 'He's a detective.'

'Oh,' said the youth. 'We used to go to the clubs in Leeds,' he continued. 'It's brilliant there – and that's where she started using it.' His eyes grew sad at the memory. 'Other stuff as well.'

'He thought a lot about her, didn't yer, lad?' said his mother. She put an arm round her son and gave him a hug.

Michael shrugged, mildly embarrassed. It was all in the past. 'She started going out with a crowd o' right idiots. Packed me in.'

'If she'd stuck wi' our Michael, she'd be still alive,' said Mrs Elvington. 'He's a bright lad is our Michael. He dunt look it but he is.'

'Anyroad,' continued Michael, frowning at his mother's unintentioned insult. 'She ended up meeting this black feller called Chisel Joo.'

'Did you ever hear of such a stupid bloody name?' commented his mother.

Sam had heard of Chisel Joo. He was very bad news indeed – a pimp, drug dealer, and very violent. Nicky's murder was taking on a new, unwanted, dimension.

'It's his street name,' explained Michael. 'They all have street names. Somebody once told me his real name was Cedric.'

Sam knew this. Cedric Jewison, not a name to strike much fear into anyone. But Chisel Joo was a very different proposition indeed – a proposition Sam didn't know how to tackle without police resources. And it was unlikely the police would take much notice of Sam Carew.

'I know a bit about Chisel Joo,' he said. 'So he was Nicky's pimp, was he?'

'She couldn't help it.' Michael was still springing to Nicky's defence. 'He supplied her wi' drugs and she couldn't pay, so he made her go on the game.'

'He wants bloody locking up!' said Mrs Elvington, heatedly. 'How come they haven't locked the bugger up?'

'Because everyone's scared to give evidence against him,' explained Sam, who had often wondered why Chisel Joo seemed so bullet proof. 'The police have been after him for years.' It crossed his mind to pass his suspicions on to the drugs squad, who had Chisel Joo constantly in their sights. Sam chose his final question carefully.

'Michael,' he asked. 'An Irishman called Sean Henry has been locked up for her murder. Do you think he did it?'

Michael shook his head. 'Nobody round here thinks he did it. Nicky were trying ter give the game up. Reckoned she'd got a regular boyfriend, some married bloke. Chisel wouldn't have been too pleased about that. It were just too much of a coincidence.'

'So, you reckon Chisel had something to do with it?'

'I never said that. You'll have to fathom it out for yerself.'

'Thanks Michael,' he turned to go. 'And thanks Mrs Elvington. Sorry about the window, but there should be someone around shortly to make it secure.'

Michael looked at the broken window, noticing it for the first time. His loud music had drowned out the crash.

'Your mam'll explain,' said Sam as he left.

A small girl stood by his car, hand outstretched. A marginally older boy stood beside her, nudging her to speak.

'We looked after yer car, mister,' she announced.

'Ah,' nodded Sam, appreciatively. 'Security guards, eh?' He walked slowly round the vehicle, examining it, much to the amusement of the children who looked at each other with supressed giggles, holding their hands over their mouths to stop any incriminating laughter falling out. Sam gave them fifty pence each, which apparently was an acceptable amount.

The small, brown-skinned boy, now disguised in a Leeds United shirt, flashed Sam a row of smiling white teeth and passed the ball to him as he was about to step into the Range Rover. Sam trapped it neatly beneath his foot and wagged his finger at the boy.

'You've got me into enough trouble for one day, thanks very much.'

He flicked the ball in the air and watched in amazement as the boy kept it up with head, feet and knees, far longer than Sam had ever been able to. And Sam had turned out for Unsworth Boys in his heyday.

'Keep that up, young 'un, and you'll be playing for Unsworth Town in a few years,' he called out.

The boy gave him disparaging look.'Don't talk daft, mister. It's bad enough bein' black!'

Sam got into the car, reflecting on what Michael had told him. It had been a fruitful interview, but the end result wasn't what he'd been hoping for.

11

The word 'frog' has several different meanings. To a builder it's an indentation in the top of a brick, the purpose of which is to hold additional mortar and form a stronger bond. Sometimes nowadays replaced by holes through the brick, which cuts out the practice of lazy brickies walling bricks upside down to save on mortar. Ernest had sacked brickies for doing this and Sam was wondering whether to do the same. The facing bricks they were using to build the boundary wall around the Fletchers Field site had a deep frog and by turning the brick upside down, it made walling them a good deal easier – and faster. This suited Arthur, who was on piecework. He'd boasted about being a twelve hundred bricks a day man and Sam was beginning to see why. It was approaching Monday dinnertime and Arthur, who had only been set on that morning, had laid at least five hundred.

'Did you ever go to night school, Arthur?' asked Sam, having put down his own trowel and strolled over to the sub-contract brickie's section of the wall.

'Three years, City and Guilds,' boasted Arthur, slapping mortar on the sides and top of a brick, this time the right way up. 'Got the Silver Trowel in me final year.'

This was an award made to the best student. Bobbie, Arthur's labourer, grinned. He was picking up extra money to labour for Sam as well, but still managed to find time to follow on behind Arthur and do the pointing. They were a good team, their brickwork was neat and would continue to look neat for a few years, until the cracks appeared.

'Really? I missed out on the Silver Trowel,' admitted Sam, who had been expelled from night school for walling up the school entrance as a prank. His teacher had complimented him on his workmanship, but the principal, a humourless man, had insisted on him leaving. He watched Arthur walling for a few minutes. He was good and fast and had no need to cut corners.

'The building inspector'll be round this afternoon,' he said. 'When we're walling with frogged bricks, he's got this annoying habit of taking a random brick out of the wall and checking it's been laid the right way up. If he found one the wrong way up he'd make us take the whole lot down and start again. It's never actually happened to us because we never do that sort o' thing – and what with you being a Silver Trowel man, you'd never wall them upside down – would you?'

In truth Sam, had never known a building inspector do such a thing, but these men were a law unto themselves and were capable of anything. Arthur looked worried.

'Well, I've never heard o' nowt like that. Are yer sure?'

'Positive,' lied Sam.

Arthur studied his boots carefully, then looked at Bobbie. 'We might o' let one or two slip through,' he admitted.

'Oh no!' exclaimed Sam. 'That one or two could knacker up the whole job for us. Just make sure you've sorted it by the time he turns up.'

He didn't really want to lose Arthur. Good brickies were hard to come by. Sam walked away and picked up his own trowel. From the corner of his eye he could see a discussion taking place. They could either cut their losses and walk off the job – a course of action many brickies would take – or they could take their punishment and start again. Arthur came walking over and stood behind an industrious Sam.

'Look, Sam, er, ter tell the truth.' Sam recognised this as a prelude to a lie. 'We're not so sure where we've walled 'em upside down, so ter be on t' safe side we'll take 'em all down and clean 'em off. We'll soon catch up.'

Sam continued walling. 'Fair enough,' he said, happy with the way he'd dealt with the problem. Arthur hesitated for a second, wondering if Sam had anything to add, then walked back to where his labourer was waiting for the signal to start taking the wall down.

* * *

A month had gone by since Sam had found out about Chisel Joo. A month of indecision, not having a clue how to handle that side of things. Owen had advised him to let it lie.

'Owen, an innocent man's in jail,' Sam had argued. 'A friend of mine. How the hell can I let it lie?'

'How the hell can you tackle this Chisel Joo character on your own is more to the point,' was Owen's answer. He didn't like the situation any more than Sam, but he was marginally more practical. He was also disappointed that the trail had dried up on the plastic window installers. He'd found out the name of the builder only to find they no longer existed. There had been no more burglaries and it was destined to remain on file as an unresolved case.

Sam had taken out an advert in the Yellow Pages for the Carew Investigation Bureau. This had produced a string of enquiries, all of which were for jobs he didn't want. Mostly domestic: divorce, following people, keeping overnight watch, serving writs. He'd turned them all down on the grounds of overwork and told the Yellow Pages he wouldn't be renewing his ad. Once he'd got Sean out of jail he'd think again.

Alec had taken to the job of managing director like a duck to water. He'd picked up a nice contract from Manston Holdings, a property development company, to do all the groundworks and superstructure on the Fletchers Field site, a twenty house development on the edge of town. This meant building the houses, banging the roof on, then leaving most of the first, and all of the second fixings to someone else. First fixing being the flooring, glazing, staircase, stud walling, door casings, electrical wiring, plumber's piping and plaster boarding. The plasterer would follow, then back would come the joiner, plumber, electrician to do their second fixings. Not to mention various other trades: painter, floor tiler, wall tiler etc. All tricky, time consuming work. Carew and Son Ltd had got all the meaty stuff. Sam was well pleased with his new MD.

To help Mick and Curly with the groundworks, Alec had brought in a new man, a large, Afro-Caribbean called Jacob Marsden, who'd once been a maintenance man on Greerside Hall, before Carew and Son had moved in. Jacob would lead Sam to Chisel Joo.

It was a warm Wednesday in July and Jacob was at the bottom of a deep manhole finishing off the benching, under the watchful eye of the building inspector. Sam arrived on site with Mick and Curly in his car.

'Alec sent a new bloke this morning to help you out,' he informed them as he pulled up. 'He looks handy enough – apparently he's pretty good on the drainage side of things.'

A turbaned head emerged from the manhole as the Irishmen climbed from the car. The man in the turban bent down and held out a helping hand to Jacob, who climbed out behind him.

Curly strode across to confront them. The ginger curls which had given him his nickname had gradually eroded to a small island of salt and pepper locks marooned on top of his head in a sea of freckled skin, around the perimeter of which grew more unruly hair, covering his ears as far as his grimy collar. He folded his arms, accusingly, across his chest and called out to the two brown men emerging from the manhole ...

'Aha! So that's how yer gettin' into the country, is it?'

There was an awkward silence as Jacob and Mr Singh turned to confront the smiling Irishman.

'It was a joke,' explained Curly. 'Me bein' one of yer ethnics, I'm allowed ter make ethnic jokes.' He inclined his head towards Sam. 'Now if yer man was ter crack a joke like that, it'd be racist.'

Mick was walking away, distancing himself from his pal.

'Shut up, Curly!' ordered Sam. 'This is Mr Singh, the new building inspector. If you offend him, you offend me!' He turned to Mr Singh. 'Has he offended you, Mr Singh?'

Singh smiled, displaying a row of gleaming teeth. Curly

returned his smile, his own teeth a bit hit and miss, like a NAAFI piano.

'No offence taken,' said Mr Singh. 'We ethnics have to join in with the great British tradition of taking the piss out of each other.'

'He's not speaking for me,' growled Jacob, scowling down at Curly.

Curly held out a hand of friendship. 'Curly Kilbane,' he said. 'You'll be the new feller. I never knew you was a black feller.'

'I was hoping ter keep that a secret,' said Jacob, taking Curly's hand and crushing it.

'You're all Yorkshiremen now,' said Sam. 'And we Yorkshiremen take as we find.'

Three assorted heads looked at him. Wondering what the hell he was talking about.

'The lads have been talkin' about Chisel Joo,' said Jacob. 'Word is that yer looking for him.'

It was the following day and Sam had stopped to chat with his new groundworker.

'I wouldn't exactly say looking for him. If I was looking for him, I'd have probably found him. It's just that I think he might have had something to do with Nicola Fulbright's murder.'

'That's what I heard. And I didn't hear it on site either. You should keep your thoughts ter yourself, Mr Carew, if you don' mind me sayin'.'

'Where did you hear it?'

'In a club. Chisel Joo isn't pleased with you accusing him of murdering the girl.'

'I didn't accuse him,' said Sam.

'Chinese whispers says you did.'

'Irish whispers more like,' said Sam. Mick and Curly frequented the blues clubs, where rumours were quick to circulate.

'You want ter tell them ter keep their mouths shut,' warned Jacob. 'Chisel's a very unpleasant man.'

'It's difficult for an Irishman to keep his mouth shut, or hadn't you noticed?' pointed out Sam. 'It was probably my fault for telling them. Anyway, thanks for the warning.'

'Any time. Chisel Joo's got it comin' to him. If you need any help ...'

'Really?' said Sam.

Jacob nodded. 'He's not my favourite person.'

'I'll bear it in mind.'

12

There was a time when Ragley Road was a better part of Unsworth, before the war that is. The main road and adjacent streets had once housed many of Unsworth's professionals and businessmen. There were mostly large, three storey residences with servant bells and high ceilings, ornate cornices, dado rails and heavy oak doors; details your modern-day builder would dismiss as being non-functional and therefore a waste of money. Then in the fifties there had been a steady exodus to the leafier, out of town suburbs. The large houses left behind had been converted into flats and bedsits for the incoming population, many of them immigrants. The inevitable ghetto appeared; not the immigrants' fault, just the way things were. Unscrupulous people take advantage. Well-meaning people in authority tolerate too much, let things slide. There's a Ragley Road in most industrial towns. Run down, unswept streets. Cheap, obvious prostitutes on every corner, and a general air of degradation, despair and dogshit.

Blues clubs are private drinking clubs. Mostly illegal and unlicensed and usually in converted cellars, which often extend beneath several houses. They are meeting places for villains of all descriptions and because of this they were tolerated by the police, who worked on the premise that it's all very well to know your enemy, but it's a bonus to know *where* he is.

There were many blues clubs in the Ragley Road area, but the best one was owned by Chisel Joo and incongruously called the Starlight Club. Despite being one of the few licensed clubs, licensing hours weren't strictly adhered to – totally ignored, in fact. It was well past Friday midnight when Sam, hoping Chisel Joo didn't know what he looked like, nervously followed Jacob down the steps and through the door into a small lobby. Beyond the lobby was a closed door and behind the door, the thump of loud Reggae music.

A smiling Rastafarian collected £5 entrance money. Beside him stood a large, tattooed bouncer, who would refuse both admittance and refund if he didn't like the look of you. Sam thought it would be fairer for the bouncer to vet the customers *before* they paid their money. But this was their way of doing things and he wasn't in a position to argue.

'This is Sid. He works with me, man,' said Jacob.

'Is he Irish?' enquired the bouncer.

'Yorkshire born and Yorkshire bred,' said Sam.

'Strong in the arm and weak in the 'ead,' added Jacob. The bouncer didn't smile, but he stood to one side and allowed them through.

Jacob opened the door and the sound hit them. The tape recorder Sam had hidden in his pocket with a tiny mike poking from his shirt would struggle in this noise.

The club comprised several small to medium rooms and ran under at least two houses. Each room had its own booming speaker. Somewhere was a DJ. His West Indian patois was a foreign language to Sam. Whirring fans distributed the mixture of smells – sweat, drink and cannabis – but did little to cool the air, which was conditioned by open windows. Sam felt the perspiration rising. Any warmer and it would be suffocating in here. Or was it just good old-fashioned fear?

Jacob led him to the bar which sold beer in cans and spirits in miniatures. No one drank from glasses. There seemed a good atmosphere about the place; lots of talking and laughing above the music; lots of candles and low wattage bulbs. The clientèle was an even mix of white and otherwise. Some coloured men were wearing fancy hats and long flowing robes and moving to the music with a rhythm which the white men couldn't match. Sam tried to relax but it wasn't easy. He took a can of Budweiser from Jacob. Seven pounds for two cans. There was a lot of tax-free profit being made down here. Sam wondered if the vatman ever knocked on the door. He made a mental note to mention it the next time they kicked up a fuss about some twopence ha'penny invoice he'd mislaid.

A young man was spraying graffiti on a wall. Very artistic grafitti where the letters were three dimensional and over-lapped one another. Sam was trying to make out what he was writing, but had to walk away as the paint fumes hit him. The whole place was an unbelievable fire hazard. How they'd got planning permission was anybody's guess. Exposed joists in the ceiling, which should have been plaster boarded over to give at least an hour's fire protection. No visible fire exits. There were many reasons to close this place down. A phone call to the fire service wouldn't go amiss. But that wasn't why he was here. The music softened as Finlay Quaye was replaced by Diana Ross.

'Thank God for that,' he said to Jacob. 'I thought my eardrums were going to burst.'

Jacob grinned. 'Keep your eyes on the dancers, man. It's worth bein' ripped off just ter watch.'

As Diana Ross gave way to Dina Carrol, the dancing couples began to entwine themselves. Sam watched in amazement at the shameless groping going on before his eyes. One couple – a black man, and an extremely pretty brown-skinned girl – having decided to be the floor show, competely undressed each other within a circle of admiring onlookers, receiving a round of applause as they both danced naked around the room.

'Chisel's the one over there,' whispered Jacob. 'Long feller. Plenty of bling, stripey shirt, white pants.'

He didn't look in Chisel's direction as he said this. His descrip-tion was enough to identify the man. Chisel Joo was well over six feet tall with a shaved head and much gold ornamentation, including one gleaming tooth. After watching the impromptu floor show for a while, Chisel pushed the dancing man aside and took his place, his hands moving over the girl's body, visit-ing intimate places. She seemed in a world of her own, putting up no objection. Her body was nothing to be ashamed of. Just as well, as she certainly wasn't showing any shame. The seemingly cuckolded man stood and smiled as he dressed himself and walked towards the bar.

'Hey! Mooky boy,' shouted someone. 'What you doin' lettin' Chisel mess with your woman?'

'She ain't my woman, man,' replied Mooky with a shrug. 'Just axed her for a dance that's all. She's a very forward lady if you axe me.'

'She's a very doped up lady,' murmured Sam.

Jacob nodded. 'Rohypnol ... Chisel does that ter girls jus' fer fun.'

'Date rape drug,' mused Sam, wondering if he was in a position to do anything to help the girl. He caught a look on Jacob's face. A look of pure hatred. 'He's done something hasn't he? – something to really piss you off.'

Jacob didn't answer straight away. He took a cigarette from his pocket that looked fatter than your average John Player. Lighting it, he offered it to Sam, who took a drag, purely for authenticity. He felt Chisel's eyes might be on him.

'That's good shit man,' he commented, passing the joint back to Jacob.

'Don't overdo the play acting,' cautioned Jacob in a low voice. 'Chisel's seen you smoking the stuff.'

'Right,' said Sam. 'What did he do to upset you?'

'Upset me? You sure have a way of understating things.' He took a long drag and offered the joint to Sam, who refused this time. 'He turned my baby sister into a hooker, that's what he did.' Jacob's eyes were on Sam as he said this. Narrow and dark and angry. Sam didn't press him for details, but he knew there was more.

The naked woman had slumped, semi-conscious onto Chisel's chest. He thrust her, roughly, into the welcoming arms of one of the male onlookers and walked into another room.

'He'll be back,' said Jacob. 'I reckon he's gone ter check up on you. See if anyone knows you. Let's just hope no one does.'

Sam's thoughts were temporarily elsewhere. 'I should do something to help the girl,' he muttered. 'She's drugged up to the eyeballs.'

'Don't worry too much about her,' Jacob advised. 'She's a very enthusiastic hooker.'

'Doesn't make it right,' argued Sam. 'By the way, I've a tape recorder in my pocket. If I can get Chisel to talk, I'll be recording everything he says. Tell him you've heard the rumours about Sam Carew looking for him. Let's see where it takes us.'

Jacob frowned. 'Tape recorder? I thought you couldn't use that sort of thing in evidence.'

'Not as such,' agreed Sam. 'But if I can get him to admit to killing her on tape, with a witness to back me up – that's you – it'll be enough for the police to arrest him. And it's amazing what comes out of the woodwork when someone's been arrested for murder. By the way, my name's Sid Charlesworth. I'm a sub-contract brickie working on the same site as you. But we're not working for Sam Carew.'

Mariah Carey began to sing *Without You* and Sam looked at his watch. One thirty-five. The behaviour of the dancing couples deteriorated – having been set such a bad example. It made an interesting and titillating spectacle. Sam moved toward a fan to cool himself down. It was warm in here, in more ways than one.

Mick and Curly tentatively descended the steps into the Starlight Club, conducting a heated, whispered argument as to whether they should be Welsh or Scottish. They each silently handed five pounds to the Rastafarian.

The bouncer blocked the door to the club. 'You Irish?' he enquired, belligerently.

'No,' said Curly.

'Scotch?'

The way he asked made the Scots sound just as unwelcome. Mick opened his mouth to say 'Yes', but Curly beat him to it.

'Welsh,' he said.

The bouncer stared at them for a few seconds then stood to one side. 'Next time, bring yer own women with yer!' he rasped.

The pair walked silently through, neither wishing to put their Welsh accents to the test.

'See,' gloated Curly. 'I told ye the Scotch were as unpopular as de Irish. English fellers tink dem Scotch fellers are like piles.'

'Piles?'

'Haemorrhoids,' expounded Curly. 'Der ones that come down an' go back up aren't too bad. But the ones what come down an' stay down, are a pain in de arse!'

Laughing at his own joke he made his way to the bar, but stopped when he saw Sam and Jacob.

'Jesus! Would yer look at who's through there,' he said to Mick.

'And who *is* through there?' enquired Chisel Joo, politely.

Curly turned to face the tall black man, who was holding out his hand.

'Good evening gentlemen, how's it going?'

'Do we know you?' asked Curly, curiously.

Chisel smiled. 'Just being friendly. It's a friendly club.'

'That's right,' agreed Curly. 'We been ter most o' dem other clubs but dey're crap compared ter dis.' The two of them shook hands with him in turn. 'I'm Mick and he's Curly,' said Mick.

'Mick and Curly,' repeated Chisel, omitting to introduce himself. He spoke well, no trace of an accent. 'That sounds Irish. How did you get past the doorman?'

Curly was hurriedly dreaming up an explanation, but Chisel smiled. 'Just joking, may I buy you both a drink?'

He turned and snapped his fingers at the man behind the bar. A minute later Mick and Curly each had a miniature of whisky in one hand and a beer in the other. They liked this tall black feller, whoever he was. The night had got off to a good start.

'Who was it you saw through there?' asked Chisel, casually.

'Ah, nobody yer'd know,' replied Mick, unsuspecting.

'Just our boss,' said Curly.

'Boss, eh? What sort of work do you do?'

'Civil engineers,' said Mick. It sounded infinitely better than shit-kicker. Same job, different title.

'And what's your boss's name? smiled Chisel. 'Maybe I can buy him a drink.'

'Sam,' said Curly. 'Sam Carew.'

The smile hardened, imperceptibly, on Chisel's face. 'Really? I must buy Sam Carew a drink.' He went off in Sam's direction, his hand checking on a knife concealed inside his shirt.

'He's coming,' warned Jacob.

Sam felt Chisel's presence behind him. He put his hand in his pocket and clicked on the tape recorder.

'Good evening gentlemen, can I buy you a drink?'

Sam turned to look at Chisel, forcing a smile to his face. 'Well, we never turn down a free drink, do we, Jake?'

'Never,' agreed Jacob. 'Very bad manners turning down free drinks.'

Chisel looked at the cans in their hands and called to the barman. 'Two more Buds, Leroy.' He held out his hand. 'I'm Chisel Joo, I own the place.'

Jacob took his hand and shook it. 'Jacob,' he said. 'And this is Sid, Sid Charlesworth. We work together.'

'Pleased to meet you, Sid Charlesworth,' smiled Chisel, the smile not quite reaching his eyes. Sam noticed this and was justifiably worried.

Mick and Curly watched proceedings for a while, slightly envious of the fact that Chisel was now buying drinks for their boss, who could well afford to buy his own. Voices from behind alerted them to the danger they'd put him in.

'Is Chisel Joo around?'

'Yeah man. He's at the bar talking to the white guy and the long black feller.'

Curly's can fell to the floor from a frozen hand. 'Holy shite! That was Chisel bloody Joo!'

Jacob had already told them about word getting back to Chisel Joo about Sam's suspicions and how dangerous they'd made things for Sam.

'Sam's gonna tink it was us what told Chisel about him,' said Curly.

'Well I didn't tell that Chisel Joo nuthin' – I never even seen Chisel Joo before now,' complained Mick.

'Neither have I,' said Curly, hoping this might absolve him of all blame.

'It was you what opened your big gob in that other club last week. That's where he got it from.'

'We're bloody sacked fer sure,' moaned Curly.

'That's if he's still alive ter sack us! That Chisel's a very bad man.'

Either way their jobs seemed in jeopardy, which was a shame as they enjoyed working for Carew and Son. Sam was a lot more tolerant than most bosses.

Other men were gathering around Sam and Jacob. A menacing buzz went through the room. Mutterings of, 'Keep out of the way, there's some shit gonna happen.' People moved away from the bar, some hurried out of the club. Mick and Curly were aware of all this, but Sam and Jacob weren't. Chisel was being very conversational and Sam was hoping to swing the topic round to Nicola Fulbright, but he didn't quite know how. Chisel did it for him:

'You and I have something in common,' he said to Sam.

'Oh?' Sam couldn't think of one thing he had in common with Chisel Joo.

'That's right – our names.'

Sam was at a total loss.

'We've both got two,' explained Chisel. 'I've got my own name and my street name – and you've got Sid Charlesworth and Sam Carew!'

The surrounding men crowded in to shield Sam and Jacob from watching eyes. Chisel's knife was at Sam's throat, drawing blood.

'There's only one thing worse than being accused of something you've done, man,' hissed Chisel. 'And that's being accused of something you ain't done. What's this thing you've been sayin' about me killin' Nicky, man?' His accent was slipping. So was the knife, down Sam's neck, opening up a shallow wound.

Had Sam been in a position to think about such things, he'd

have been hard pressed to remember being in a worse situation than this. He was deep in enemy territory, surrounded by hostile and evil men. The knife at his throat, in all probability, would soon put an end to his existence. A normal reaction to this situation would be fear. Sam was very normal in this respect. Subsequent reactions would vary from cowering submission, to desperate pleading for mercy, to offers of great wealth in exchange for life – to loss of bowel control.

No one was holding Sam's arms. Chisel's men had confidence in the terror their boss injected into his victims. No one ever fought back against Chisel. It was never worth it.

Sam brought the heel of his hand up hard under Chisel's chin, snapping it back. The knife dropped to the floor. Sam tried to kick it away but a black hand picked it up. He hit Chisel in the throat, sending him choking to his knees. Someone grabbed Sam from behind, other fists pounding into his face and body. Sam was kicking out at his frontal attacker who suddenly went down with a blow to the head, delivered by a chair held by Curly. Mick was with him, a small, stocky man with a fierce punch. The fight raged through to the next room and the next. Four against more. Sam and Jacob fought with the anger and desperation of recently reprieved men. Curly and Mick fought with Gaelic abandon, self preservation not a priority. They were having fun. The opposition was dwindling.

The bouncer came in, walked straight into a swinging stool and took no further part. Sam was seeing the advantage of no bottles or glasses in the place. The usual pub weapons weren't available, just fists, feet and furniture. Chisel apparently allowed no weapons of any kind in his club. People were leaving in droves until just the combatants and the graffiti artist, who kept pushing people away from his work, were left in the bar areas. A candle was knocked over and set fire to the paint-soaked newspapers protecting the floor from the paint splashes, producing acrid smoke. Sam threw once last punch at an attacker and backed away, coughing. Loud bangs as the spray cans exploded. Mick and Curly were on the other side of the fire, as were the rest of Chisel's men. The smoke forced them through the door and outside, where the Irishmen decided upon discretion being the better part of valour and took to their heels.

Jacob had fought with one eye on the fallen, choking Chisel. Eventually the pimp pushed himself painfully to his knees, still coughing and spitting. Jacob reached down to his belt and drew out Chisel's knife. He held it to the pimp's throat.

'Say your prayers if you know any, you pile of shit!'

Chisel spat violently at the ground then sneered at his aggressor, the gold tooth flashed in the light of a candle on the bar.

'Go on – stick me man!' He spat out a mouthful of blood, causing Jacob to jump out of range. 'You ain't got the guts!'

'I have, actually,' said Jacob, coldly. He stepped forward and forced Chisel's head back with the point of the knife. His tone wiped the sneer from Chisel's face. 'You see, you killed my sister. That's what makes it easy. What's difficult is *not* killing you.'

'Sister? I don't even know your sister.' Chisel's sneer had given way to uncertainty. Jacob obviously meant business.

'Her name was Simone. You knew her well enough, you had her working for you, you repulsive bastard.' He jabbed the knife into Chisel's neck, drawing blood and forcing him to stumble backwards. For the first time there was fear in the pimp's eyes.

'Simone was your sister? How the hell was I to know? Anyway, man, it it wasn't me who killed Simone. She OD'd man.'

'I know very well how she died,' snarled Jacob. 'And who started her on drugs and put her on the game.'

Fierce fighting was still going on in the next room. Screaming from further away, where women were desperately trying to get out of the place. Jacob and Chisel were oblivious to it all, for their own reasons.

'And mebbe you had somethin' ter do with Nicky Fulbright's death.' Jacob was emphasising each word with a jab of the knife.

There was loathing on Jacob's face. Chisel needed to keep him talking. 'Nicky? Look, I'm sorry she's dead, man. But you must know it was nothin' to do with me.'

Loud bangs distracted Jacob, making him turn. Chisel went for him, knocking the knife from Jacob's hand. The two of them made a grab for it, Chisel's hand getting there first, but Jacob's hand encasing his. They rolled across the floor struggling desperately. Each knowing what was at stake. Life. They were coughing now as smoke poured into the room, Chisel was the worst, his throat not having recovered from Sam's blow.

Sam staggered into the room away from the fire and saw the struggling pair on the floor. He tried to help, but too late. Chisel rose to his knees and looked up at him with surprise on his face. The gold tooth flashed, then he sank to the floor. The knife was embedded deep in his chest. Sam stared down at him for a second, then automatically reached for the pulse in Chisel's neck. He held the vein down for a few seconds as Jacob looked on.

'Dead,' pronounced Sam, looking across at Jacob, the fumes making his eyes run.

'Oohh shit! It was an accident, man.'

Sam accepted this with a nod. Both of them were now almost lying on the floor as smoke billowed above them, forming a cloud base two feet above their heads and sinking. Through the smoke Sam could see flames licking across the ceiling, a good time to leave. He looked around at a small open window behind him, through which smoke was escaping. There was the clang of an approaching fire engine in the distance.

'Best be on our way,' he decided.

As Sam got to his feet, Jacob felt a bar towel on the floor, beneath his hand. He picked it up, rubbed the handle of the knife and followed Sam to the window. Another bang sent flames searing into the room behind him. Sam stumbled across something soft and instinctively put his hand out to detect what it was. Naked flesh, unmistakably a woman. Jacob had passed him and was halfway through the window as Sam gave what was a coughing shout.

'There's someone here!'

The naked girl stirred as he pulled her to her feet. She placed her arms around him and nuzzled his neck, seductively.

'Bloody hell, woman! There's a time and a place!'

He hoisted the girl onto his shoulder, staggered through the smoke and pushed her head out of the window. Jacob, now outside, grabbed her and pulled her through. More explosions behind Sam sent heat searing into his back, setting his clothes on fire. The smoke and fumes were too much for him. He grabbed wildly for for Jacob's hand, but Jacob had gone.

Smoke billowing into the backstreet told firefighter Pete Thornycroft which house he was heading for, which was just as well – from the back they all looked the same. He'd left the mayhem in the front street on his boss's less than detailed instruction. 'Check round the back – NOW!'

What he was supposed to be checking for, he'd no idea. He was the new boy on the watch and eager to make a good impression, so he hadn't stopped to ask any questions that might make him appear thick. Panicking voices made him quicken his pace. He kicked open the backyard gate and saw the smoke was billowing from a ground-level window. A man was coughing and spluttering, enshrouded in the smoke, trying to pull someone out. As soon as the man became aware of Pete's presence he turned and ran, leaving a naked woman lying on the ground. The fireman dragged her well clear of the smoke and bent over to look for signs of life, taking off his helmet to get closer. As he did so, he noticed a hand waving from the window. He cursed.

'Oh shit!'

All the breathing apparatus was in the next street. He took a deep breath and plunged back into the smoke, grabbed the waving hand and yanked Sam through the window in a series of desperate heaves. Then he banged out the flames on Sam's back.

The two of them lay on the ground, coughing and spluttering – Sam by far the worst.

Beside them, the naked woman got to her knees and vomited

noisily. A second firefighter arrived, female. She assessed the problem at a glance and radioed for help. The house was becoming an inferno. She pulled and cajoled the three of them into the street, clear of burning debris. Sam lapsed into unconsciousness and woke up in Unsworth General Hospital. In his usual bed.

13

'I don't wish to appear over critical, but would you mind telling me what you were doing pushing a naked prostitute through the window of a burning blues club in Ragley Road at two o'clock this morning, when you told me you needed an early night?' enquired Sally, with a testiness, Sam thought, unbecoming in a hospital visitor.

'Sal, I've already answered that question.'

'Ah! But that was to the police. I was looking for something nearer the truth.'

Sally's annoyance with Sam had been fuelled by the anguish he'd put her through during the past few hours. The first call, from Owen, had Sam on his last legs, rushed to Unsworth General with severe burns. Throughout the night he'd graduated to minor burns to the back, smoke inhalation and minor lacerations to his neck. The latter was assumed to have been caused by broken glass – as opposed to the business end of Chisel Joo's knife. Bowman and a detective constable had been to see him. Sam had been non-committal. He owed them nothing.

'I was having a quiet drink, a fight broke out, that's all I know. A fire started, everybody panicked. I couldn't get to a door and I saw this bloke climbing through a window. I went to follow him and stumbled over this woman.'

'This woman, this *naked* woman,' said Bowman, 'was Mandy Jackson, she's a prostitute.'

'Was she really?' said Sam. 'And here's me thinking she was from the Salvation Army.'

'Cut the comedy,' snapped Bowman. 'Why was she naked?'

'I reckon she was the one who was fooling around earlier,' Sam explained. 'She and a feller did this strip-tease, then Chisel Joo started dancing with her.'

'Ah, Chisel Joo. Tell me what you know about about him,' pressed Bowman.

Sam shrugged. 'I reckon he had something to do with the fight. Didn't see much of him after it started. It's him you want to be talking to, not me.'

'We'd love to, unfortunately he's dead!' said the inspector, searching Sam's face for his reaction.

'Bloody hell!' Sam feigned shock. He was good at that. Bowman wasn't entirely convinced, but thought the shock might have been genuine. 'Were any others dead?' Sam asked, anticipating the guilt he might feel if the answer was yes, having been the root cause of the mayhem.

'No.'

'Thank God.' His relief was genuine, even the police could see that.

'There was no one else left in the club, apart from Chisel Joo,' continued Bowman. 'We assume you'll be able to help us with a few names.'

'Sorry, I'm afraid you assume wrong, Inspector. I didn't know anyone. Perhaps you should try Mandy Jackson.'

Bowman's mouth tightened in annoyance. 'So,' he said. 'To sum up. You were having a quiet drink in a blues club where you didn't know anyone – a club frequented by villains, drug dealers and prostitutes.' He shook his head. 'It's not like popping into the local for a swift half. What were you really doing there?'

'I sometimes need to fraternise with undesirables as part of my work as a private investigator,' Sam explained, off the top of his head. 'If they see me around often enough, I get to be accepted as one of them. You should try it.'

'That's a load of bollocks and you know it,' snapped Bowman.'

Sam shrugged and looked beyond the two detectives to where his coat was hanging over a chair. He could see the bulge of his tape recorder. He was a victim. They'd no right to search him, but that wouldn't stop Bowman. He feigned dizziness and closed his eyes. A nurse hovering behind the policemen stepped forward.

'I think he's had enough for now,' she decided, in that final way that nurses have. 'Could you leave now, please?'

Bowman left, reluctantly, promising to call back later.

Sally's tone was bordering on caustic. It was an hour after the police had left. The nurse had announced her arrival and Sam had confirmed he was up to seeing her.

'If it's any consolation, Mandy the prostitute is ever so grateful. She reckons you saved her life.' There wasn't a hint of hero worship in Sally's voice. 'She's calling in to see you later.'

'That's nice,' said Sam, without thinking.

'Over my dead body!' she exploded. 'I'm not having naked prostitutes visiting my fiancé.'

Sam went quiet, pondering what she'd just said. 'Sally, love,' he said cautiously. He didn't want to add fuel to her fire, but it needed to be said. 'I'm not your fiancé.'

'Well – you know what I mean.'

He didn't, but felt it best to let the matter drop. She leaned over his bed, her dark hair falling forward, shadowing her face. It was a pretty enough face, with no wrinkles appearing yet, despite her being a year older than him. She could maybe do with losing a few pounds, but this didn't bother Sam, who didn't go much on skinny women. Better to have something to hold on to. He smiled up at her. He had a useful range of smiles. This was his helpless, little boy smile. Always a winner.

'Sal, I wonder if you'd do me a really big favour.'

'What's that, love?' her eyes softened as he knew they would.

'In my coat pocket there's a small tape recorder. I'd like you to get it and put it in your bag.'

She had the tape recorder out almost before he'd finished talking. The wire to the microphone was still inside his coat sleeve. She pulled it out and wound it around the machine.

'Whatever you do, don't tell anyone about it,' he added.

She shrugged, as though it was a matter of little importance.

'Promise?' insisted Sam.

'Okay – what's the big deal?'

'And don't play the tape.'

'Okay,' she promised, mentally deciding to play the tape at the first opportunity. She also decided to make a few conditions of her own. 'And I want *you* to promise not to have anything to do with this naked prostitute. She's apparently very grateful and no doubt wants to repay you for services rendered. If I find out she's been rendering any of her own services to you I'll ...' She saw Sam's face drop and realised he was looking at someone behind her. Bowman and the constable had re-appeared.

'Hello Sam,' said Bowman, with forced cordiality. 'And this is ...?'

'Sally Grover,' said Sam. 'A friend of mine.'

'Right then,' said Sally, kissing Sam on his cheek. 'I'll be off.'

The constable stepped into her path. 'Just one moment, miss, before you go. I wonder if we could have a look in your bag?'

Sam's heart stopped. If they found the tape they'd know he was the one who started the fight with Chisel Joo – and all its implications. Sally had no option but to oblige. She put up a protest though, as any woman would. If she hadn't, it would have appeared suspicious.

'Do you mind if I ask what you're looking for?' she demanded, clutching her bag to her. 'A woman's bag is a very private place.'

Bowman looked squarely at Sally. 'No harm in telling you,' he said. 'You see, the remains of a large quantity of drugs was found at Chisel Joo's club. We're just trying to establish the real reason for Mr Carew's visit.'

Sally leaned over Sam and spoke to him as though he was the stooge in a music hall comedy act. 'The nice inspector thinks you're on drugs,' she explained.

Sam nodded his vague understanding. 'Nothing gets past the nice inspector,' he replied. 'I bet me being in hospital gave me away. It's a fair cop, Mr Bowman. I'm drugged up to the eyeballs with paracetamol.'

Sally emptied the contents of her bag on the bed. Bowman

looked disappointed at the obvious absence of drugs. He picked up the tape recorder. Sam's heart raced.

'What's this?'

Sally took it from him. 'What does it look like, Inspector? It's a dictaphone.'

'You a typist or something?' enquired Bowman.

'Secretary,' corrected Sally. 'I sometimes have to take work home. I hope you don't want to search the rest of me. You see, I haven't any pockets for you to look through, and my knickers are out of bounds, even for you, Inspector.'

To Sam's satisfaction, Bowman blushed. 'That won't be necessary,' he said. 'We'll just search Mr Carew's pockets, if that's alright with him.' He looked questioningly down at Sam, who smiled up at him.

'Be my guest, Inspector. Oh! There should be a packet of fags in there. I expect them to be still there after you've gone. I know what you police types are like.'

Bowman's face creased with annoyance as he watched the constable go through Sam's pockets. 'Nothing here, sir,' he announced.

'I'm such a disappointment to you, aren't I,' said Sam, apologetically. 'Will that be all?'

Bowman stared at him, long and hard. 'I know you had something to do with Chisel Joo's death. When I find out what it is, I'll nail your arse to the wall.'

Sam felt more resentment than fear. 'Look, Inspector. I know the world's lost a wonderful human being in Chisel Joo, but don't take it out on me.'

A most unlikely thought struck him, a stab in the dark, but it was worth an airing.

'Perhaps Chisel Joo was a friend of yours, inspector. If so, I'm sorry.'

The sudden guilt on Bowman's face disapeared as quickly as it came, but it didn't go unnoticed. 'You're an idiot, Carew,' he snarled, angrily. 'Idiots get found out, it's nature's way.'

'Goodbye, Inspector,' said Sam, marginally unnerved at the

truth in Bowman's parting words – especially in his case. But he was also wondering if Bowman and Chisel Joo *were* connected. Now that would be a turn up for the books.

14

Jacob was waiting for him when Sam arrived on site at ten past eight the following Monday morning. Sam had been discharged from hospital the previous afternoon and, although he was by no means fit enough for work he had certain things to sort out.

Alec was already in the cabin sorting out the programme for the day. He'd no doubt be giving Sam strict instructions to go home, despite Sam still being his employer. The true fifty-fifty nature of the partnership wouldn't kick in until Alec had enough in the kitty to buy his fifty percent. At this rate it wouldn't be long.

Jacob's face was a mask of concern. He hadn't known what to do. To run, to give himself up, or to play it cool. He'd attempted the latter, but was making hard work of it. The tall, black man looked anything but cool.

He diverted his boss from his intended destination – the site cabin. Sam still didn't know why Jacob hadn't been there when he so desperately needed him. He felt it hard to keep the anger from his voice.

'Where the hell were you when I needed you? If that fireman hadn't spotted my hand at the last minute I'd have been a goner!'

Jacob looked sheepish. 'I'm sorry, Sam. I thought the man knew you were there. I panicked.'

'Panicked? You don't know the meaning of the word. I bloody panicked. Christ! I thought I'd bloody had it!'

'I know, I know – and I'm sorry,' apologised Jacob. 'But I'd just killed someone. My mind wasn't right. I nearly didn't stop ter pull the girl out. All I wanted was ter get the hell away from the place. When the guy came ter help, I just left him to it.'

Sam could understand his predicament. He'd once killed someone in the course of duty. It affects people in different ways. Sam had nearly packed the job in, it just didn't seem worth it.

Being responsible for the end of a life is a weighty burden. No matter how worthless that life was.

'Okay,' he said, putting an arm around Jacob's shaking shoulder. 'I suppose I understand how you felt. It happened to me once. You were in shock, probably still are.' He looked Jacob squarely in the face. 'Have you said anything to anyone?'

Jacob gave a bitter laugh. 'Man, I haven't even *seen* anyone. If you hadn't turned up just now, I'd have gone home. I wasn't going ter talk to no one until I saw you.'

'What about Mick and Curly?'

'I don't think they turned in yesterday, but they're here this morning.'

'Good, I want a word with them. The police know *I* was there, but they don't know about you three. You'll be well advised to keep your traps shut. Not easy when you're Curly. I'll have to put the frighteners on him.'

He looked questioningly at Jacob. 'You said it was an accident.'

'It was,' said Jacob. 'I was trying ter get the knife off him. The next thing I knew it was sticking in him.'

Sam nodded. 'It happens. Who's hand was the knife in when it stuck in Chisel's stomach?

Jacob sounded uncertain. 'I honestly don't know. Anyway it doesn't matter.'

'It'll matter if the police find your fingerprints on the knife.'

'They won't.'

Sam threw him a quizzical glance.

'I rubbed the knife clean – just in case,' explained Jacob.

'Did you now?' said Sam. 'There's not many people would have remembered to do that in the heat of the moment.'

'There was a bar towel on the floor – the thought just came ter me. Did I do the right thing?'

'I don't suppose you did yourself any harm.' Sam was curious. 'Have the police got your prints then?'

Jacob gave a guilty nod. 'Probably, from years ago. I got into a bit of trouble. Nothing heavy, just kids' stuff.'

Sam didn't press him on this, Jacob was having a hard time.

'Do you think I'm in the clear?' he asked.

Sam shrugged. 'Look, Jacob, this is real life,' he said. 'You're only in the clear if you want to be.'

Jacob frowned, he didn't understand.

'You see, you're a decent bloke,' Sam explained, 'and that can be a problem. In my experience there may come a time when your secret gets too much for you and you feel the need to come clean, despite the fact that owning up to killing Chisel won't do anyone any good, least of all you. So I just want to make my position clear. As far as I'm concerned I was an innocent victim of violence, who saw nothing and heard nothing. Chisel Joo was killed by person or persons unknown. If I knew who killed him and didn't tell the police, I'd be guilty of with holding evidence, which is a serious offence. So it's a good job I don't know. If at some stage you foolishly own up to killing him, there'll be no one more surprised than me.' He paused to let his meaning sink in, before adding, 'Do we fully understand each other?'

'We do.'

'If you ever feel the urge to give yourself up, just remember what he did to your sister,' advised Sam.

'I'll do that,' said Jacob.

'Any idea who killed Chisel?' enquired Sam.

Mick and Curly shook their heads. Sam thought as much, but he needed to be sure.

'Neither do I,' he said. 'By the way, thanks for helping me out.' He took a small wad of notes from his pocket and divided it equally between the two of them. Little enough to pay for what could have been his life.

'Yer a gentleman,' said Mick.

The two Irishmen were sitting on a pile of breeze blocks, eating sandwiches designed more for the mouth of a hippo than a human being. Sam sat down beside them. 'The police are looking for two paddies,' he lied. 'They reckon they had something to do with starting the fire. I told them I didn't see any Irishmen who I knew – so don't you two make me into a liar.'

Among the many vague descriptions the bouncer had given to the police were two Welshmen and a Yorkshireman called Sid.

'We was never there, was we Curly?'

'We definitely never was,' confirmed Curly. 'I never go anywhere, and when I do, it's not there.'

'That might be as well, for a while anyway,' advised Sam. 'Arson's a serious crime. Ten years minimum.'

'Jesus! I never started no fire,' grumbled Curly, as Sam walked away.

'It won't matter if dey catch us,' said Mick. 'We're guilty o' bein' Irish. That'll be enough to lock us up. Best forget all about it. Say nothin' ter nobody.'

'Well, it wasn't exactly a night I care ter bloody remember,' said Curly.

Sam took his cup of coffee from Sally and stared up at his bedroom ceiling.

'Thanks, love. No one makes coffee like you.'

'Oh yes, and who else has been bringing you coffee in bed?' It was meant to sound like a joke, but she didn't quite bring it off. She didn't know whether to trust Sam.

He ignored her remark, which she found irritating. A bit of reassurance never goes amiss. 'What did you make of the tape?' he asked, suddenly.

She hesitated, then said, 'I didn't listen to the t—'

'Don't give me that,' he interrupted, cheerfully, sitting up and swinging his legs onto the floor. 'Wild horses couldn't have stopped you from listening. Don't worry, I'm not mad. You got me out of a spot when you put it in your bag.'

'I'll say. You'd have been locked up by now if they'd listened to it.'

'Aha! So you *did* listen to it!' he exclaimed, triumphantly.

'Only bits of it. I heard the bit where Chisel Joo denied having anything to do with Nicola's death.'

'And did you believe him?' he enquired, his eyes fixed on hers.

She thought for a while, then nodded, slowly. 'Probably. Under the prevailing circumstances he'd no reason to deny it.'

'The prevailing circumstances,' said Sam, 'were that he had a knife to my neck.' He fingered his bandaged throat, remembering the moment with a shudder.

'Oh, love!' She went to him and kissed him gently. 'Why do you have to get involved in all this? You're out of the police force now. I don't want to lose you.'

Sam had long since known the answer to such questions. The questions asked by people who wanted to change him. To change his lifestyle, to manipulate him. Sue had been like that. He certainly wasn't going to take it from Sally. Attitudes like this should be nipped in the bud before they start to flourish.

'Sal,' he said, firmly, placing his coffee on the bedside table and pulling her into bed with him. 'I am what I am. You get what you see. Just hope I never change, because if I do it'll be for the worse. The most I can promise is that I'll do my best to remain the same loveable creature I am today.'

It was the answer she expected. Slipping off her nightie she asked, 'Why don't you marry me? You slimy little ratbag!'

'Because I don't want to spoil anything. Why do you want to change things all the time?'

'Sam, I'm no longer in the first flush of youth, or hadn't you noticed? I need to have someone I can rely on. Preferably a husband. Preferably you.'

He kissed her, gently, on her forehead, then on her lips. 'Why do we have to go through all that nonsense again?' he said. 'We've both had our fingers burnt by marriage. Why can't we just live over t' brush, like normal people?'

She sat on top of him, straddling his legs, hoping it might give her an unfair advantage in the discussion. It didn't do any harm. Looking up at her like this always pleased Sam.

'Sally Grover, you naughty lady! You'd give a stiffy to a snowman.'

'Less of your crude building site talk, Carew!'

She was secretly pleased with the compliment, no matter how crude. There was visual evidence of him becoming aroused. Time to press home her advantage. Make him commit to something while his mind was elsewhere. He hated breaking promises.

'I can't live over the brush,' she said. 'Not with you or anybody.'

'Oh. Why not?'

'It's something of a family taboo.'

Sam's curiosity almost matched his passion. 'Taboo? What sort of taboo?'

'Well,' she explained. 'My grandparents came from Barnoldswick – or Barlick as they called it. Up on the Lancashire border. In their time, the place was famous for having an unusually large number of people living *over t' brush*.'

'Really?' Sam feigned shock. 'Well that's disgraceful. You hillbillies have a very racy lifestyle. What about your grandparents? Did they live ...?' he finished the sentence with a suggestive nod.

'Yes, as a matter of fact they did, much to my mother's eternal shame. The people who were properly married used to stick their marriage licence in the front window, so's not to be tarred with the same brush.'

Sam found this amusing, Sally admonished him with a mild slap to his arm.

'Ouch!'

'You deserve it. It wasn't meant to be funny. My mum and her brothers had to live with the shame, right up to leaving home. Each of them vowed never to inflict such shame on their own children.' She looked down. 'So, if you want to do anything useful with that thing, mister, you'd better come up with a proposal.'

'That's blackmail of the worst kind! I've known people get ten years for less.'

She began to ease herself away from him.

'Okay! Okay! The engagement's back on.'

'Promise?' she pressed.

He had his hands around her, with both sets of fingers crossed.

'I promise,' he lied.

15

'I'm selling the building land,' said Sam.

'Fair enough, it's yours to sell,' replied Alec.

'I'm telling you, because I'm making you a director, with forty nine percent of the shares.'

'Thanks, I appreciate that,' said Alec. 'But I thought I was only sharing the profits at the moment, not the assets.'

'After I've sold the land,' continued Sam, 'I'm splitting the rest down the middle with you. It's getting too complicated apportioning your share of the profits to buy out fifty per cent of the assets.'

'You mean you're giving me fifty per cent of everything?'

'Forty nine per cent, actually.'

'That's very generous, thanks, Sam.'

'It's very practical. You're a better builder than me. I'm also tying you up in a contract that prevents you leaving with any of the assets. You leave me without my agreement and all the assets revert to me. That includes future assets. But if at any time I decide to sell up, you get forty-nine per cent of everything.'

'I'd be a fool ever to leave you.'

'That's the idea.'

'Right,' said Alec. 'If that's all you've come to tell me, you'd better get that trowel of yours moving. I want my forty-nine percent to be worth something.'

'Yes boss,' grinned Sam as he walked from the site hut to where Arthur was busy walling footings.

'Morning Arthur. Where's Bobbie?'

'Sacked. I cleared him off last night. Silly bugger were chucking plums in t' concrete. Buildin' inspector sees yer doin' that, yer in big trouble.'

Plums are old bricks, stones, lumps of old hardened concrete that can be thrown into foundations to make the concrete go further. Once they disappear beneath the wet concrete, no one's any the wiser. Until the foundations start to crack.

'Silly sod,' said Sam. 'It's not his money he's saving. What's he want to do that for?'

'He were mixing t' concrete hisself. He thought it'd be faster. Yer know what he were like,' explained Arthur.

'I'll pull Jacob off the sewer connections until we get someone else,' decided Sam.

'I'd prefer ter do t' labouring meself,' said Arthur. 'He's a rum bugger is yon.'

'I'm paying you to lay bricks,' insisted Sam. 'You don't keep a dog and bark yourself.'

'I wouldn't call him a dog if I were you. He'd bite yer bloody head off!'

Sam looked across at Jacob wielding a pick in the distance and wondered if there was a side to him he hadn't noticed. Or was it just a reaction to his recent trauma? Probably. Killing a man can have a strange effect on some people. Sam felt an element of guilt himself. Had he not gone to Chisel's club that night, none of this would have happened. He was beginning to question his own capabilities. Up to now he seemed to have thrown up more mysteries than he'd solved, which wouldn't be difficult. A chat with his Welsh pal wouldn't do any harm.

Owen was already in the Clog and Shovel when Sam arrived. 'Why do we always have to meet in here?' he enquired.

'Because no one knows us,' replied Sam. 'I'm only doing it for your benefit.' He picked up the pint of Bootham's Owen had already bought him, noting with approval that his friend was drinking the same.

'What's the story on Chisel Joo?' asked Sam, wiping the froth off his top lip with a forefinger.

'Bowman thinks you're more involved than you say you are.'

'Does he really?'

Owen looked at him for a second, expecting him to expand on his answer, but Sam wasn't going to enlighten him. What Owen didn't know couldn't hurt him.

'He's got a real bee in his bonnet about you, boyo,' Owen continued. 'He reckons he's going to nail you. Whoever stabbed Chisel Joo had the foresight to wipe their fingerprints off the knife. That's a cool-headed thing to do, under the circumstances, isn't it?'

'Isn't it just?' agreed Sam, thinking of Jacob.

Owen was studying him, closely. 'Cool-headed, as in experienced policeman.'

'What?' queried Sam. Realisation struck him. 'Oh, come off it, Owen. You don't think I did it, do you?'

The Welshman looked almost embarrassed at being put on the spot. 'Not if you tell me you didn't.'

'I didn't,' said Sam. 'And I didn't see who did kill him.'

One probing question from Owen and he'd be into telling lies. Thankfully, no more questions came. Owen knew when to stop. He took another mammoth gulp from his pint. Sam had never seen anyone take such gulps. A pint of beer never went to Owen's lips more then three or four times before it was gone. He placed the empty glass on the table. Sam was only a quarter of the way down his, so he ignored the hint.

'Bowman thinks you went for Chisel because you think he killed Nicola,' said Owen, realising his second pint wasn't immediately forthcoming.

'I knew Nicola was working for him,' conceded Sam. 'I'm amazed the police didn't latch on to that line of enquiry.'

'Why should they?' said Owen. 'They had Sean Henry bang to rights. Police resources are stretched enough without going on wild goose chases – besides, word has it that Chisel had handed her over to someone else. Bowman seems totally convinced that Chisel had nothing to do with her death.'

'He's that sure, is he?' said Sam, curiously.

'Seems to be,' nodded Owen. 'He has information about Chisel that mere plods like me aren't privy to.'

'Maybe he has information about Chisel Joo that only *he's* privy to.'

'Anything's possible, boyo,' agreed Owen, eyeing his empty pint. 'Even you buying a round!'

Sam wasn't listening. His mind was wrestling with various permutations of events.

'If Chisel *did* kill Nicola, then Sean's locked up for good. Unless he *had* her killed, which is the more likely of the two. Then the killer's still at large, without Chisel's protection. Which should make it easier for us to sniff him out.'

'We? What's all this *we*?'

Sam looked at him, as if surprised at such a question. 'Owen, I thought you wanted to make sergeant.'

'I do. Solving the burglaries was supposed to do that. Up to now it's made me look an idiot.'

'Did you check out the builder, like I told you?' enquired Sam, reluctantly going along with Owen on the change of subject.

'I did,' said Owen. 'They were all built by a firm called Castle Homes, which no longer exists.'

'Fred Castle still exists,' said Sam. 'Tell you what, I'll do my best to track him down on your behalf.' He made it sound a difficult task.

Owen's face lit up with misplaced gratitude. 'Thanks, boyo, I'd appreciate that.'

'In the meantime,' added Sam, between finishing his own pint. 'I'd appreciate it if you could find out if Bowman had more to do with Chisel Joo than he's letting on.'

It seemed a fair exchange of tasks to Owen. Sam took both empty glasses and went to the bar, ordering refills as he took his mobile phone from his pocket. He tapped up the memory then dialled a number.

'Fred Castle? ... Sam Carew ... Oh, not so bad, thanks. Look Fred, when you were doing spec building in the seventies, can you remember who your plastic window contractor was? ... Cheers, give me a ring when you do ... thanks Fred.'

He took the drinks back to the table and indicated to the

mobile phone stuck in his top pocket. 'Just been putting out a few feelers for Fred Castle,' he said.

'Cheers,' said Owen, picking up his glass and pouring a third of it down his throat. 'You know there's something about the Nicola Fulbright case you keep dismissing.'

Sam's pint froze on his lips. 'Oh, what's that?'

'Could be that they've got the right man.'

Sam cogitated on this as he sunk his pint. Sean's guilt was still one of many possibilities. He'd dismissed it from his mind once. Now he needed to reinforce his convictions.

Sean Henry lay on his bed in Wakefield Jail, staring up at the ceiling and allowing the tears to dry on his face. Bridie had gone back to County Mayo and taken their son with her. Their daughter, Kathleen, was staying in England, but was moving down to Birmingham with her job. The stigma of being the family of a murderer was too much for them to live with. Maybe he understood, but Sean couldn't forgive them. They must have known he wasn't capable of such a crime. Life was scarcely worth living.

The three things stopping him from topping himself were the lack of tools with which to do the job; the fact that it was a mortal sin and would condemn him to eternal damnation – a strong deterrent for a devout Catholic – and Sam Carew, who'd written to him to arrange a visit. He allowed himself a rare smile. 'Good old Sam Carew. Yer man'll get me out – no danger o' dat.'

'Yer what?' asked the armed robber in the bunk below.

'Nuthin',' said Sean, who didn't realise he was thinking out loud.

'Just my luck, bein' banged up with a thick fuckin' paddy what talks to hisself!'

Sean made no reply. The man in the bunk below was in for a rude awakening if he thought Sean was going to take much more crap from him. The worst that could happen was loss of privileges. And the privileges this place offered were a fair exchange for the satisfaction of hammering his huge fist into that

124

sneering weasel face. He'd wait until Sam had been. No point risking being refused a visit.

Sam was already seated at a table when Sean entered the visitors room. In prison clothes, with a short haircut, Sean looked more respectable then he had done on the outside. It wasn't a hard transformation, but Sam was pleasantly surprised at how well he looked. From a distance anyway. Sam watched him look round, searching for him. A prison pallor was perhaps beginning to tone down his colouring, but it wasn't detrimental to his overall appearance. A look of recognition and Sean set off in Sam's direction, then Sam noticed the Irishman's eyes. These Irish eyes weren't smiling. They were grey and sad and bewildered. Despite his appearance, which probably suited his surroundings more than most, this was an alien environment to Sean. He wasn't one of life's villains. A bit of a rogue at worst, but not jail material. His criminal record wasn't squeaky clean, but whose is? A fine and a ticking off by a magistrate for his failed theft in Fothergill's wine stores and a Bound Over To Keep The Peace because of a fight outside the Dog and Gun, which Sean had only joined in for the hell of it. That was all. It hardly classified him as a murderer.

'You're looking well, Sean, considering.'

'Well, I'm not drinkin' as much. The hooch they make in here tastes like shite.'

Sam smiled and asked, 'How are you bearing up?'

'Not so good. The wife went back to Ireland and took me boy wid her.'

It didn't surprise Sam. Prisoners wives needed support. If not from friends, from family. Her family was in Ireland. For all she knew, Sean might not come out for fifteen years at the earliest.

'Sorry to hear that.'

'So was I. She done right though, I never treated her fair.'

Sam didn't know what to say – so he said nothing.

'She was no oil paintin' – as ye know yeself,' went on Sean. 'But inside she wasn't ugly. And I never treated her fair. That's why she's not standin' by me.'

'What about your daughter?' enquired Sam.

'She's moving outa town. Something to do wid her job.'

'They've got to get on with their lives, Sean. It's not their fault you're banged up in here.'

'I know that, but it's not my fault neither.'

Sam looked up at a prison officer and waved an opened packet of cigarettes in the air, the guard nodded his consent. Taking two out, Sam gave one to Sean, then pushed the rest of the packet across the table. Before Sean could pick it up, the officer appeared behind him and leaned over his shoulder, taking the cigarettes almost out of Sean's hand. He looked inside, then put it back down – open cigarette packets always merited attention, sealed packets were okay. Sam grinned at the officer. 'The gun's in my sock,' he joked. 'It wouldn't fit in there.'

It fell on humourless ears. A metal detector had already sensed that Sam carried no weapons.

'It's a laugh a minute in here,' said Sean, miserably. 'Dem screws are about as funny as a cracked pisspot.'

'It's the job,' explained Sam, unnecessarily.

The room was buzzing with different voices; hostile, friendly, sweet, harsh, guarded, stentorian. At the next table, news of a refused parole was provoking tears, then words of censure from a woman visitor who seemed to think it was her man's fault. As though he was staying on for an extra year because he was enjoying himself. Behind them, someone told a joke, provoking a chorus of loud, dirty, laughs.

'That's Bradley,' said Sean. 'I told him that joke about the lesbian and the Irishman.'

Sam smiled. He knew the joke. 'I imagine you're keeping everyone amused.'

'Not everyone,' said Sean. 'The feller in my cell's a bit of a gobshite. I'm goin' ter have ter straighten him out.'

'Be careful, Sean,' warned Sam. 'Don't do anything stupid. They can make life really tough for you in here.'

Sean said nothing, just drew on his cigarette and tapped his sausage fingers on the table, drawing Sam's attention to them.

Sean had the biggest hands he'd ever seen on a man. Gripped round the throat of a young girl they'd be deadly. A thought struck him.

'Sean, before you went into the house that morning, had you put a mixing in?'

Sean's expression lightened a little at the memory of normality. Talk of the job, his real life, where he belonged, which wasn't in this place.

'A bit o' one,' he said. 'But there was only a shovel of cement in the bag. That's why I went in the house. If I'd loaded up wid cement the night before, I wouldn't be here now.'

Sam ignored this self criticism, despite the truth of it. Sean should have made sure enough materials were on hand in order to start mixing the minute he got on site. In a cruel way he was a victim of his own laziness.

'Did you shovel the cement in, or did you pick the bag up like you normally do, and tip it in?'

Sean didn't have to think much about this, although he was puzzled at Sam's question. 'I picked up the bag. I tink it's easier that way.'

'So, there'll have been cement on your hands when you went in the house?' enquired Sam.

'There was always cement on me hands,' admitted Sean.

'Did you touch the girl?'

Sean's eyes hardened, hurt. Sam realised what he'd said. 'No – I'm not asking if you killed her. I'm asking if you touched her at all?'

Sean was relieved. If Sam lost faith in him, what hope did he have? He scratched his head, trying to remember the events of that awful morning.

'When I went in the room she was just lying on some sort o' blanket ting.'

'Blanket? There was no mention of a blanket.'

'One o' dem sleepin' bag tings.'

'You never mentioned a sleeping bag in court.'

Sean thought for a while, then said. 'I didn't, did I?'

'It's probably neither here nor there,' said Sam. 'No doubt the police checked it thoroughly. What did you do then?'

'I tink I touched her ter see if she was alive.'

'Where did you touch her?'

'I did dis.' Sean placed his hand on his forehead. 'Touched her like dis.'

'You didn't touch her neck?'

Sean shook his head. 'It wasn't me what done that, boss.'

'I know it wasn't, Sean. And if people had been doing their jobs right, you wouldn't be in here.'

'If I'd been doin' me job right I wouldn't be here,' added Sean, bitterly.

Sam faced the solicitor across the cluttered desk and enquired, 'How long before his appeal's heard?'

'The way the courts are jammed up it could be another two years.'

'But if we got some really concrete evidence to support his case, would that bring it forward?'

On Sam's advice, Sean was being represented by a different legal firm. The term "a new broom sweeps clean" had great significance in legal representation. Any cock-ups made by the previous firm would be gleefully brought to light by the new boys, whereas the previous firm would be inhibited by any such mistakes.

Roger Constant LL.B. looked up from his cursory examination of Sean's file, shrugged and scrutinised his well chewed fingernails, the price he was paying for giving up smoking. 'I can but try,' he said. 'If it's conclusive I can get him out on bail. What have you got?'

'I haven't got anything as yet,' said Sam. 'But I suspect the forensic people have – and if I'm right, I think someone should give them a bollocking.' He paused to collect his thoughts before going on. 'Sean's a labourer. We know he loaded the mixer before he went into the house that morning – it was still going when the police arrived – the thick buggers didn't know how to turn it off.

He'll have had cement dust on his hands. When the lab boys examined the girl, it should have shown up in the marks around her neck. I never heard anyone mention cement dust.'

The solicitor shook his head. 'It's not conclusive. Who's to say he wasn't wearing industrial gloves when he loaded the mixer?'

'Sean's never worn industrial gloves in his life,' argued Sam. 'In any case,' his eyes held a glint of triumph, 'Sean says he touched the girl on her forehead to see if she was alive. If the lab boys did their job properly, and let's hope they did, then traces of cement dust should have shown up on her forehead. Cement dust that could only have been put there by Sean, proving that he did indeed have cement on his hands and he wasn't wearing gloves. So, if there was cement dust on her forehead and none around her neck, it couldn't have been Sean who killed her.'

The solicitor ran Sam's reasoning through his head for a few seconds as Sam got his cigarettes out. He offered one to Constant, who pointed to a sign on the wall saying "Thank You For Not Smoking".

'Sorry about that,' he said. 'I'm not unsociable, just weak-willed, trying to give up.' His eyes dwelt longingly on Sam's cigarettes, but Sam tactfully put them away. 'Anyway,' Constant went on. 'I think you might have something. Forensic evidence played little part in his conviction – or in his defence for that matter.'

'His defence council only turned up to collect his Legal Aid fee,' said Sam, sourly.

'You could well be right,' said Constant. 'But I'm confident the pathologist and forensic people won't have missed anything.'

'Pity they didn't mention it – if they thought it relevant.'

'It's not up to them how their findings are used,' pointed out Constant. 'They simply provide information and establish the cause and time of death. How this is used is up to the prosecution and defence lawyers.'

'I always think they have a moral responsibility,' said Sam.

'You've been watching those old re-runs of *Quincy*.'

Sam smiled, there was an element of truth here. 'By the way,' he said. 'Sean mentioned that the girl was lying on a sleeping bag when he first saw her. Did you know about that?'

'I don't remember seeing anything in the file about it. He could be mistaken, you know.'

Sam nodded, Sean had been mistaken about many things in his life. He remembered something else, the thing that had triggered this idea in the first place.

'And there's one other thing,' he said. 'They should have photographic records of the bruising, so they should be able to have an accurate stab at the size of the killer's hands. I'd be amazed if the bruises match Sean's great mitts.'

The solicitor was impressed. 'The two together could be conclusive, or ...'

Sam knew what was coming.

'It could go the other way and prove he was guilty.'

Sam shrugged. 'Either way it'll be a weight off my mind. I'm sure he didn't do it though. In a way it'd make my life a lot easier if he had.'

Generally speaking, Sean was an amiable man. His circumstances were beginning to brutalise him though. In his life he'd won and lost his share of fights in equal numbers, most of them whilst under the influence of drink. When he got back to his cell after Sam's visit, he made up his mind to stop his cellmate in his tracks if he started mouthing off again.

The armed robber wasted no time. He was sitting on Sean's top bunk, smoking Sean's cigarettes and reading the letter from Bridie.

'I see your missis has gone back ter the bog, then,' he smirked. 'What's she like? She must have had a face like a pig's arse if she had ter marry an ugly bastard like you.'

Sean pulled him effortlessly off the bed, wrapped his hands around the man's neck, headbutted him into oblivion, placed him in the bottom bunk, then went off to the gym to ride the exercise bike.

Blood on the cell floor and moaning noises alerted one of the officers. The armed robber was taken to the medical block and Sean was sent for.

'Do you know anything about this?'

'Anything about what, sir?'

'About the attack on your cellmate.'

'Who d'yer tink did it, sir?'

'I think you did it.'

'No sir, it can't have been me. I was ridin' on the bicycle. The best feller ter ask is himself.'

'We'll do that, and if it turns out to be you, your feet won't touch the ground.'

Sean looked down at his firmly anchored size thirteens, as though pointing out the improbability of such a statement. The officer got the inference and wasn't amused.

'We'll be speaking to you later.'

'Tank you very much, sir.'

A week later, Sam was up on the first lift of scaffold, walling facing bricks, when his mobile rang.

'If it's my wife, tell her I'll ring her back when I've finished shagging my secretary,' called out Arthur.

'An' if it's Mick's wife tell her he'll ring back when he's finished shagging Arthur,' called up Curly from the floor below.

'How did you know I been shaggin' Arthur?' enquired Mick.

'Hello?' said Sam, ignoring the banter which went on all day and every day. 'Mr Constant ... yes ... yes. Great ... that's great Mr Constant. So when it goes to appeal he's got a good chance? ... Really? ... Thanks Mr Constant, keep in touch.'

He could scarcely keep the grin off his face.

'Good news?' guessed Arthur.

'I hope so,' said Sam. 'We've turned up some new evidence that says it wasn't Sean who killed Nicola Fulbright.'

'I could've told 'em that,' said Curly.

'The evidence that convicted him was purely circumstantial,' said Sam. 'The new evidence is factual.'

'I been convicted on circumstantial evidence,' said Curly. 'The circumstances bein' that I was found wid half a ton of lead in me bedroom.'

'The circumstances were that yer bedroom floor collapsed,' chipped in Mick. 'An' the lead finished up in yer kitchen.'

'Heavy stuff, that lead,' said Curly. 'I figured the polis would never tink ter look upstairs fer a load o' lead. I blame it on the council. Them council houses aren't built properly.'

Leaving the conversation behind, Sam walked over to the site office. He needed to see Owen. If Sean wasn't guilty, the quicker the police knew about it the better.

'I need to take a couple of hours off,' he informed Alec.

'And if I said you can't?' queried Alec.

Sam thought for a moment. He didn't want to usurp Alec's authority. 'Then it'd have to wait,' he said. 'You're the boss on this site.'

'Two hours, no more,' grinned Alec.

'I'll make it up when I get back,' promised Sam.

Sean was on the exercise bike. Others wanted to go on it but such was the reputation he'd earned when putting his cellmate in hospital that the other inmates left him to it. No point upsetting the mad Mick.

There was a meter on it that told him his speed and distance. He travelled ten miles a day now. His imagination had taken him well beyond the walls of the prison. He was back home in County Mayo, riding the green lanes around his father's farm. Sean, being one of the younger sons, had been obliged to make his living elsewhere, otherwise he'd never have left. McCloud Construction had taken him on at the age of sixteen. He'd arrived on his own, taken digs in Unsworth and worked for two years on the Unsworth Ring Road.

Sweat ran down his face as he pedalled on. There was something comforting about sweat. Something familiar. The armed robber had come out of the medical block that morning and been taken to another cell. No accusation had been made against Sean.

Only implication. Seven and a half miles. Today he felt good, he'd try for fifteen.

Maybe he'd have a ride into Ballycarra and a pint of stout in McFee's. He'd been too young to drink when he left and he could only conjure up a hazy mental image of the interior of the pub. His parents were strict about such things and although his dad drank himself insensible twice a week, he forbade young Sean to go near the place.

He pictured an interior not unlike the Dog and Gun in Unsworth. Except that a band was playing in the corner. Sean liked a good band. Drums, fiddles, penny whistle and mandolin. "Rattling Boy From Dublin Town". He began to hum it as he pedalled, then he stopped because he couldn't hold a tune in a bucket. Everybody told him that.

Sam Carew had instilled hope in him. He wasn't quite sure what Sam had been on about when he talked about cement and touching the girl, but he had seemed happy with Sean's answers and that could only be good news.

Someone had told him that if he won his appeal he could sue for a million pounds. That'd do for him. Bridie would come back like a shot to a feller with a million quid in his arse pocket – no danger of that. He was twenty one when he married her in St. Theresa's Church. She'd been a year younger and pregnant with Kathleen. It wasn't a marriage made in heaven but they'd made their bed and decided to lie on it. Nine miles. Maybe he'd try for twenty. He was oblivious to the four men who entered the gym. The other occupants stopped what they were doing and left. The men drew nearer as Sean pedalled happily on, lost in his own world. The landlord was placing a pint of Guinness on the bar in front of him. Sean licked his thin lips, he could picture it vividly, almost taste it. Black as coal with a thick white collar, standing there like a parish priest.

Nine point seven miles and he wasn't even out of breath. He didn't even see them, so engrossed was he with his journey. The first blow with the steel dumb bell knocked him clean out. A further flurry of blows left him slumped over the handlebars with the meter just on ten miles. What brains he had were splattered on the gym floor. Sean Joseph Henry died in McFee's saloon bar drinking a pint of Guinness and listening to his favourite music.

Sam was stuck in traffic, minutes away from the Post Office containing Owen Price when the mobile rang. A driver to his right looked across, disapprovingly, as Sam put the phone to his ear and moved the car slowly forward.

'Mr Carew?'

'Speaking.'

'Hello Mr Carew, it's Roger Constant. I've just had a phone call from Wakefield Jail.'

'Look, sorry, you're breaking up. I'm in traffic at the moment, can I ring you back?'

The staccato voice at the other end seemed to understand, so Sam clicked the phone off and indicated left.

Sam had been sitting in his car for nearly an hour, when the tap came on the window. He was trying to assimilate what Roger Constant had just told him. Sean was dead. On the very day they'd uncovered evidence which could free him, someone inside the prison had murdered him. Sam tried to remember what Constant had told him. The details. But the shock of the news had blanked everything out. He rang him back.

'Apparently, Sean had beaten up his cellmate. Put him in hospital,' said Constant.

Sam remembered Sean talking about straightening this man out. He'd warned him not to do anything stupid.

'The men who did it were all members of some sort of prisoners' gang. No one inside messed with them. Sean's cellmate was one of the gang, apparently. Sean didn't know about this.'

'I doubt if it'd made much difference if he had,' commented Sam.

'They've all been rounded up and charged with murder. It was all captured on video. A concealed camera had just been installed in the gym and the prisoners hadn't twigged.'

Anger arose within Sam. Anger at the unfairness of it all. He turned off the phone without saying goodbye and sat back, his mind racing.

Another tap on the passenger window again, more urgent this time. Traffic Warden, small, female, pinch-faced. Sam knew the type. He pressed the window switch, but it didn't work because his ignition wasn't on. Leaning over, he opened the door.

'Yes?' he enquired, belligerently.

'You're parked on a yellow line, sir. Is something wrong with your ... vehicle?' She hesitated over the last word, not knowing whether to call a Range Rover a car or something else.

'No, just with me, that's all.'

'Oh, are you ill?' She seemed genuinely concerned.

'No, I'm not ill. Oh, never mind, I'm going.'

'And your tax disc is out of date sir.'

'Is it really? Well I'll have to do something about it, won't I?'

She was cooling to his attitude. It was her who was supposed to be snotty. They'd sent her on a sort of customer relations course. How to be charming as you're giving someone a ticket. Sod that! Her manner hardened to match his.

'It's over two months out of date sir. Tax dodgers such as you are subsidised by the honest motorist.'

Sam exploded. 'If the government is so worried about tax dodgers, why don't they just stick a few pence on the price of petrol and do away with the tax disc altogether? No discs, no dodgers. No dodgers, not as many traffic wardens. It's us dodgers that keep you people in work. So bugger off and stop biting the hand that feeds you!'

The last sentence was shouted through the window, after he'd slammed the door. He drove off before she could get her act together. Not to worry, she'd keep an eye out for him.

16

Sam and Sally turned up just as the Requiem mass ended and joined the procession of mourners following the coffin to the burial plot. Four pall-bearers wearing dark suits, all of which seemed to have been tailored for someone else. These weren't suit-wearing men – more likely suit-borrowing men. Those who knew it were singing:

'Faith of our fathers living still,

In spite of dungeon fire and sword ...'

One pall-bearer belched loudly, earning a rebuke from his wife, a few paces behind. The wake had begun the night before and the men were recovering, to prepare for the forthcoming funeral tea which was to be held in the Dog and Gun.

As the procession reached the graveside, Sam and Sally stood a respectful distance away, watching the coffin being lowered into the ground as a priest sprinkled holy water on it. Something was amiss, but Sam couldn't put his finger on it. Around the grave stood Sean's family. Dozens of them. Father, mother, sisters, brothers, cousins, aunts, uncles. Bridie and his son and daughter. Mick and Curly and what seemed like half the members of the Unsworth Shamrock Club.

Bridie's face held a look of resignation. She'd never been a beautiful woman and the years had not been kind. The son had inherited his father's lumpy looks, whereas the daughter favoured the mother. An uncomely trio, glumly throwing earth on Sean's coffin. Lips moved in silent song as they followed the priest's requiem dirge.

'I wonder where that priest is? You know, the one who came to talk to us in the pub the day Sean was sentenced?' mused Sally.

'He's standing behind Sean's wife,' pointed out Sam, now realising what was amiss. Surely Father Michael Donnelly should be officiating.

'Why hasn't he got a dog collar on?' wondered Sally. 'He said he was Sean's parish priest.'

The two of them stood back to allow some of the mourners past as they came away from the grave, leaving Sean's immediate family to pay their final tearful respects. Sam caught Michael Donnelly's eye, causing the Irishman to turn away.

'Father Donnelly?' he called out.

Donnelly froze, then hurried over to where Sam and Sally were standing. A few questioning stares followed him. He took Sam's arm and bustled him out of everyone's earshot. Sally went along with them.

'I, er, I'm not actually Father Donnelly!'

Just for a second it occurred to Sam that he might be a twin brother. 'Who are you then?'

The man shuffled his feet, uncomfortably, waving a respectful hand to the priest who was walking away from the grave.

'I'm Sean's uncle. Michael Donnelly.'

'Not *Father* Donnelly?' inquired Sally.

He shook his head. Sam was mystified. 'Then why ... ?'

Donnelly shrugged apologetically. 'It was me own foolish way of persuading ye that Sean didn't do it. I figured that if I convinced ye, then ye'd get on the case. Ye were the lad's only hope.'

'You mean all that stuff about hearing his confession wasn't true?'

Donnelly gave a guilty wince and a slow grin appeared on Sam's face. He shook his head, impressed with the man's effective subterfuge. 'Well, it worked,' he said.

'It did indeed,' replied Donnelly. 'An' the family are grateful to ye for clearing his name. Even if it was a bit late in the day.'

'It's not exactly clear yet,' warned Sam.

'It is in the eyes of his family,' said Michael, 'and that's the most important thing. He was a disreputable gadget was yer man, but I had some affection for him. There was a lot of good in the feller.'

Sam nodded his agreement and added, 'I'm confident he'll be completely exonerated.'

'The law will take its own course,' Michael said, 'it usually does.' He winked at them. 'After which, there should be some compensation flying around.'

Sam gave him a disapproving look. 'If I thought that was all it's about I'd pack it in here and now! His wife buggered off back to Ireland as soon as things got tough.'

Sally tugged at his arm. 'Sam, remember where you are!'

'It's okay, miss,' said Donnelly. 'It looks a lot worse than it is. Ye know, Sean led her a dismal life. She'd nothing to thank him for. Yer man'd try the patience of a saint – and he often did. She's a good woman is Bridie, but she'd no option but ter go back home. The family knew he didn't do it, but there's more than the family to consider. There's so-called friends – neighbours and schoolfriends and workmates an' all sorts o' stuff.'

He took out a packet of cigarettes and offered one to each of them. Sam and Sally refused, there was something disrespectful about smoking in a graveyard. Donnelly lit up then cupped the cigarette inside the palm of his hand, shielding it from disapproving eyes.

'If Bridie gets some compensation out of this, it'll be the only good that ever came out of that marriage.' He looked over towards the grave, where the son and daughter had left their mother on her own. 'The kids are a pair of pillocks,' he added, confidentially.

Sam nodded his agreement. He'd met the kids and couldn't stand either of them. Bridie was okay. Long suffering, with never a kind word to say to, or about, her husband. She'd always been genuinely pleasant to Sam though. It had surprised him when she went back to Ireland, but what Donnelly said made sense.

'She should get compensation for his murder through the Criminal Injuries Compensation Authority,' said Sam. 'Then if his appeal's successful she can apply for compensation for the time Sean spent in jail. It should all come to a tidy sum.'

'Criminal Injuries Compensation Ortority,' repeated Michael. 'I'll tell her that shall I?'

'Her solicitor already knows. As for the appeal side of things,

I'm sticking with it until I find out who did it,' Sam said. 'The police are a bit half-hearted at the moment. Can't make up their minds.'

'Ah! Now I knew ye would. Yer a good man, Sam Carew.'

'And you're a crafty old sod, Michael Donnelly!'

17

'Is Firefighter Thornycroft on this watch?' enquired Sam, of an attractive female firefighter writing up some notes in the downstairs office. It was late afternoon and Sam was paying a long overdue visit to the Unsworth Fire Station.

'Pete? Yeah. I think he's playing snooker. Top of the stairs, facing you.' She looked up and gave him a smile of recognition. 'You're Sam Carew, aren't you?'

'Do I know you?' he responded, with a smile of his own.

'Not personally. I helped drag you into the street before the house went up.'

'Ah, no one told me.' He shook her hand. 'I actually came round to thank Firefighter Thornycroft for saving my life. Looks as though I need to thank you as well.'

'Kathy Sturridge. You could thank me by buying me a drink. I'm off in half an hour.'

Sam was taken aback, then flattered at being propositioned by such a pretty young woman. 'How can I refuse? I'll just pop up to see – Pete? Did you say his name was?'

'Yes, Pete won't turn down a free drink either, nor will the rest of the lads.'

Sam gave a disappointed grin, some things were too good to be true.

Pete Thornycroft was trying to clip the blue into the middle pocket to make a personal record break of thirty-seven when Sam called out his name from the door. Distracted, he missed the pot.

'You pillock!' he shouted, whirling round on Sam.

Sam grimaced and held up his hands in apology. What he'd done was unforgivable.

'Sorry mate, I didn't realise.'

Pete's scowl gave way to an easy smile. 'Forget it. I was on a personal best. What do you want me for?' He stared at Sam. 'Sam Carew, isn't it?'

Sam nodded. Pete turned to the other men in the room. 'Hey, this is the bloke I was telling you about – Mad Carew!'

Sam winced. *How come people never forget the stupid things?* The *Unsworth Observer* had latched on to the soubriquet whilst Sam was still on the force. He'd once disarmed a deranged man, who was threatening to shoot all and sundry with what had looked to Sam like a replica gun. Ordering police marksmen to hold their fire, he'd walked out from behind the cover of a police car, shouting and cursing and gesticulating wildly at the man, who was so gob-smacked by the irrational behaviour of this lunatic policeman that he allowed Sam to walk right up to him and take the gun away. Paradoxically such an action did little to further his police career, but it probably saved the deranged man's life. Sam had taken a couple of days sick leave when he found out the gun was real.

'I prefer Sam,' he said, in response to the grinning men. He turned back to Pete. 'And I'd like to thank you personally for saving my life.'

'All part of the job,' said Pete.

'The woman in the office reckons you'd join me in a drink.'

'That's very kind of you,' chorused the men, who'd done this before.

Red Watch stayed for just one drink, leaving Sam alone with Pete and Kathy, who had gone to the bar to get the next round in.

'I used to be in the building trade,' mentioned Pete – 'trainee Quantity Surveyor, bored the pants off me.'

'A job's what you make it,' said Sam. 'It's a bit like accountancy. You have to be a certain type.'

'Tell you what, though,' said Pete. 'I learned enough to know that the Starlight Club contravened a few regulations – building and fire.'

'I noticed,' said Sam.

'How they got planning permission beats me,' said Pete. 'Still, it's all academic now.'

Kathy returned with the drinks. Sam was wondering if there

was anything between the two of them. Why he wondered, he didn't know. Normally he wasn't curious about people's relationships. No harm in asking.

'Are you two ...?' He gave what he hoped was a knowing look.

'What? – brother and sister?' guessed Pete.

'No, you know what I meant.'

'We are, actually,' said Kathy.

'Are what?'

'Brother and sister,' she laughed. 'I'm divorced, hence the different name.'

'And she's available,' added Pete, 'but only if you're really hard up.'

She slapped her brother on his arm. 'Watch it, Thornycroft! You're not too big for a good hiding.'

Sam grinned, not quite sure why Kathy being available made him feel good. After all, he was engaged.

'What about you?' asked Kathy. 'Is there a Mrs Carew?' Her interest seemed more than casual.

'There's an *ex* Mrs Carew,' replied Sam, arousing more interest from Kathy. 'Apparently I wasn't cut out for marriage.'

'Few men are,' she said. 'Marriage seems to go against all male instincts.'

'Oh yes, and which particular instinct do you have in mind?' asked Pete.

'The instinct of infidelity, for a start,' replied Kathy. 'Men are easily led. A standing willy has no conscience.'

'I've been faithful,' pointed out Pete.

'You've only been married six months. Wait till you've been married six years.'

'Now then children, no arguing or it's off to bed without any supper,' admonished Sam, feeling he ought to change the subject. He looked at Pete. 'What was that you were saying about Chisel Joo's club contravening building regs?'

'Go back and take a look yourself. It might help with any damages claim you care to make. How he got it insured beats me.' Pete looked at his sister and explained, 'Sam used to be a copper,' then back at Sam, 'and I gather you're still keeping your hand in.'

'My word, you are well informed,' said Sam. 'At the moment the only case I'm interested in is one involving a murdered girl called Nicola Fulbright. My dad was killed at the same time.'

Pete and his sister gave sympathetic nods. They knew all about it, most people in Unsworth did. Sam returned to the subject of Chisel's business methods. 'Chisel had a lot of people in his pocket.'

'His money would have been better spent on doing the job right,' said Pete.

'That's not the way his type operate,' Sam said. 'Not having to obey rules and regulations is a way of life to them. The Chisel Joos of this world like to make their own rules.' He made a mental note to revisit the scene of his near death. Somehow he knew the late Chisel Joo had been connected with the killing of Nicola Fulbright. He owed it to himself, to his dad, and now to Sean to find out how.

'I'll come with you if you like,' volunteered Kathy, almost reading his mind. 'You never know, a fresh pair of eyes. I always fancied being a Private Eye.'

'She used to fancy Magnum,' said Pete. 'She only got married because the bloke had a moustache.'

This time the slap was harder. Sam almost felt it himself. He finished his drink and got to his feet. 'Right,' he said. 'Thanks for everything, especially for saving my life.'

'Hang on, I'll come with you,' said Kathy. 'That's if you're going straight there – to the Starlight Club?'

'Well, yes.'

Sam hadn't actually planned on going there right this minute, but he felt disinclined to turn down this slightly pushy lady.

'When you get there, keep an eye out for the single step in the entrance to the bar. I nearly tripped over it,' said Pete as they got to their feet.

'Gotcha,' said Sam, holding up an index finger to say the

143

information had been received and noted. Single steps contravene most building regulations. Two steps are okay. People are ready for two or more steps, but a single step is an accident waiting to happen. It indicated that someone hadn't been doing their job properly and Sam needed to find out why.

Kathy was pleasant and chatty as he drove her there. She was a woman he felt comfortable with. With Sally he always felt as though he'd done something wrong and was about to be caught out. More often than not that was indeed the case.

It was weird looking at the scene of his near death in broad daylight. Many of the terraced houses in the street had For Sale signs outside, all with the same agent – Dwyer Estates. The two end houses were completely burnt out and a third had its ground floor windows boarded up. Sam gave a shudder that Kathy picked up on.

'Someone just ran over your grave?' she asked.

Sam nodded and expelled a long breath. 'If it hadn't been for your brother, some of those ashes would have been me. There were a few seconds when I knew I was going to die. I thought my heart was going to burst.'

She took his hand and squeezed it, comfortingly. 'That's an experience I've never had, and I hope I never do have.' She looked at him, quizzically. 'Is it true then? You know, about your life flashing before your eyes?'

Sam went quiet, reliving the moment. 'I prayed,' he recalled. 'For the first time in years, I said the Hail Mary. "Once a Catholic", as they say. I just got to the bit about Pray for us sinners, when your brother turned up.'

'Right on cue, then,' she laughed, but Sam didn't laugh with her. Pulling his hand, she added, 'Shall we have a look inside?'

He led her down the steps and through the entrance to the cellar club. Dusty light filtered through the upstairs windows and gaping holes in the roof, down through the burnt out floors. Only the outer shell was left. Pigeons fluttered about, perching on blackened joist ends, sticking from the walls in uniform rows, like rotten teeth. Bird droppings already contrasted with the charcoaled joists, knee deep in parts on the cellar floor. They picked their way gingerly through the crumbling black debris towards the bar area, coughing and spitting out the burnt black dust disturbed by their feet. As Pete had noticed, there was only one step in the entrance, partially concealed by the charred timber. Sam only spotted it at the last minute.

'Watch out for the step,' he warned. Too late, she tripped and fell down, grazing her shin.

'Shit! Shit! Bloody shit!' she cursed. 'Oops! Pardon the French. Banged my shin. It hurts like buggery. Oops!'

'Who's down dere, man?'

The voice had a distinct Caribbean patois. Sam had heard it before, coming through the speakers inside the club that night. This time it came from outside.

'Fire Officers,' he called back.

'Okay man. Thought it was kids.'

Kathy was limping badly when they emerged. She sat down on a low wall. A small black Rastafarian, with his dreadlocks hidden under a voluminous knitted hat, came from round the back of the house.

'Fire officers ya tellin' me? Ya don' lookin' like no fire officers ta me, man.'

'I'm not a man, I'm a woman,' said Kathy, sharply. 'If you can't tell a man from a woman, how can you expect to know what a fire officer looks like.'

The man neither expected nor understood her answer. His brow lowered in puzzlement.

'Who are you?' asked Sam, brusquely.

'I'm da feller what own da houses, man.'

Sam didn't press for a name, he didn't want to scare the man off.

'Really? I thought Chisel Joo owned the houses.'

'Chisel Joo?' The man gave a hollow laugh. 'Chisel Joo never put his name ta nuthin', man. Him jus' arranged things an' took all da money – an' meself took all da shit, man.'

'Who's name was the club insured in?' enquired Sam, who had a vested interest in this.

The man gave a loud, toothy laugh. 'Insurance? Ya mus' be jokin' man. Mister Chisel Joo was his own insurance. Me houses was insured because am told me got to insure dem because o' da mortgage money, innit? Da mortgages is all in my name, man, but Chisel he made all the payments – at least he did when tings was goin' well. Me guess that tings ain't goin' too well wid him any more – wid him bein' dead for sure.'

'Things could be better for him,' agreed Sam. 'Seems he left you in a pickle. Still, at least the houses were insured.'

The rastafarian gave him a sad-eyed look. 'Me insurance company ain't goin' pay me shit, man, because dey never knowed 'bout what went on in da cellar. An' now dey *do* know, dey don' wanna know. So me financially very fucked up, man!'

'You and me both, by the sound of it,' said Sam. 'I was hoping for a few quid myself.'

The man shrugged, not having a clue what Sam was on about. Kathy had pulled up the leg of her jeans to reveal a nasty bruise developing. Sam was more interested in what the man was saying.

'How did Chisel get a licence to operate the club?' He asked.

The man rubbed his fingers against his thumb, indicating money. Then gave a cruder mime indicating something more base. 'Money an' women, man. He got some o' dem official fellers so jazzed up, dey do anythin' for him, man.'

'What about police? Did he have any of them er, jazzed up?'

The toothy smile returned. 'Sounds ta me like dis information worth some bread, man. An' bread is what me needin' right now. Me need ta get me black ass back ta Jamaica before da bank fellers start asking where me insurance money comin' from.'

Sam took out his wallet. 'I've got forty quid. Tell me some names and it's yours.'

'Me got some great names for ya man. But dem worth more dan ya forty quids. Worth a long note at least, man.'

Sam turned to Kathy, who was rubbing her shin, slightly irritated that Sam had lost interest in her injury.

'Kathy, you can't lend me sixty quid can you?' he asked.

'I don't believe this,' she said. 'I've known you two minutes. On our first date you bring me to a burnt-out house, I practically break my leg and now you want me to give you money!'

'Date? This isn't a date. Anyway, you asked to come, I didn't invite you. Does it hurt?'

'Yes, it damn well does hurt, thanks for asking.'

'It's only till I get to a hole in the wall. You can have it back.'

'Okay, okay. I've got some money. Have you seen what I did to my leg?' She addressed her question to the Rastafarian, who displayed more sympathy than Sam. He took off a coloured silk neck-scarf and gave it to her to wrap around the bruise. 'Thank you,' she said gratefully. 'At least someone cares about me.' She counted out sixty pounds from a man's wallet she had in her jeans' pocket and gave it to Sam, who waved it under the Rastafarian's nose.

'Well?' he asked.

The man mimed a man drawing back a bow. Sam twigged straight away.

'Bowman?' he couldn't believe his luck.

The man nodded his head and gave another toothy smile.

'What about Bassey?' queried Sam. In truth, he held out little hope that Bassey was bent.

The man shook his head 'Jus' know da Bowman feller. Hey! Mebbe that's why dey call him Bowman, cos him bent.' He laughed at his own joke. Sam waited patiently until he'd finished.

'What did Chisel give him?'

The man rubbed his fingers and thumb. 'I guess he gave him bread, man.'

'No women?' asked Sam, hopefully.

'No, man. Never knowed him go with no woman. Maybe him prefer small boys, man.'

Sam would have loved proof of this. The Rastafarian's eyes were glued greedily on the wad of notes in Sam's hand. Sam took his hand away.

'You said names. That means more than one.'

Disappointment in the man's eyes. 'Him de only one me remember, man. Him a big shot, gotta be worth a long note, man.'

It probably was. No harm in trying for the jackpot though. Sam waved the money again. 'Okay, you get the money if you tell me all you know about Nicky Fulbright and what she had to do with Chisel.'

The man took on a worried look, as though Chisel could somehow reach him from the grave. 'Look, man,' said Sam. 'He's dead. He can't hurt you now.'

The Rastafarian didn't seem entirely convinced of Chisel's mortality – a measure of the hold he'd had over people in life. But the money in Sam's hand was also very persuasive.

'He didn't own Nicky no more. Gave her to some official dude, who help wid his property business.'

'Gave her?' said Kathy in disgust. The silk scarf was neatly wrapped around her shin. She pulled the leg of her jeans gingerly back down. 'What was he? Some sort of White Slave Trader?'

'Who was this official?' enquired Sam. 'Did you know his name.'

The Rastafarian looked from one to the other, wondering which question to answer. He chose the easier option.

'Never know no one's name, only Bowman. Him arrest me on a framed up charge, man.'

'Was he old? Young?'

'Never seed him, man. Jus' know him had somethin' ta do wi' da plannin' fellers. Dem fellers who *approve* what ya do. He musta been very high up in the *approvin'* department to approve that shit, man.'

He dwelt on the word 'Approve' as though it more or less pin-pointed the official in question. It didn't. Sam figured this was the extent of the man's information. He held out the money, the man snatched it, looked around warily, then hurried off round the back of the houses. He turned, just before he disappeared.

'See ya man, bye lady. Hope ya leg get better soon, man.'

'Thank you,' called out Kathy. 'Hope everything works out for you.' She held out an arm for Sam to pull her up. 'You can take me home now, please.'

'Drink?' said Kathy, turning to him as she opened the door to her flat. It was on the ground floor of an old converted house, not far from Sam's place.

'Just a quicky.' Sam watched her limp into the spacious hallway. 'It's a lot bigger than my rabbit hutch,' he commented, grudgingly.

'I thought you were a rich builder. What's a builder doing living in a rabbit hutch?'

'Well, it's not for much longer, thank God. I'm just waiting for a land sale to go through, then I'm buying something a bit bigger. Is your leg going to be okay?'

'It'll have to be. If I take time off work because of a bruise on my leg, the men'll never let me forget it.'

'Quite right too.'

Sam never pandered to feminism. If they handed it out they should be able to take it. That's equality.

She looked at him, sharply, then smiled. 'You treat women the same as you do men, don't you?'

'Not all the time,' he grinned. 'But if she's doing a man's job, earning a man's wages, then why not?'

'Scotch, beer?' she asked.

'Beer please. Having said that, I believe there's a certain respect due to women which men don't qualify for.'

'Ha, you know all the right things to say.'

Her flat was far better appointed than his. Tastefully decorated and carpeted. Un-matched easy chairs somehow matched the décor, Sam could never have made that work. There were paintings on the wall which didn't feature galloping horses or green-skinned Oriental women. The woman had class. 'It's a nice place,' he said. 'Wouldn't mind living here myself.'

She looked at her watch. 'I've known you for just over two

hours and you want to move in with me. Aren't there some formalities we should go through first?'

Sam laughed and said, 'Do you take anything seriously?'

'Everything,' she answered. 'Everything but men. Then I'm never disappointed.'

'That's a relief. Being a disappointment is my speciality.'

She handed Sam a can of Fosters.

'This isn't beer,' he pointed out, 'it's lager.'

'Have what you're given and be thankful.'

He found himself liking this woman – liking her a bit too much. She sat down in an old fashioned, high backed arm chair, obviously her favourite. He sat opposite on a two-seater settee.

'I rather fancy there's a woman in your life,' she said, challengingly. She held his gaze with an amused look in her eyes. 'I'm right, aren't I?'

'Spot on,' he replied. 'Engaged to be married.'

He said this as a form of self protection against this woman who was captivating him. Women with her sort of power over men spelled trouble. Men are far better off with the Sally Grovers of this world. It had taken him thirty six years to learn this lesson and he wasn't going to throw all that experience down the drain.

'Isn't that supposed to be the triumph of hope over experience?'

'It's more an engagement of convenience,' he admitted, dropping his guard under her gaze. She had beautiful eyes, dark brown and sparkling. Her hair was thick and glossy and almost black. She undid a tie at the back and let it cascade over her shoulders. It was as though she was doing it on purpose.

'You look very young to be divorced,' he commented.

'Twenty-six. Married at twenty three, separated at twenty-four, divorced last year.'

'I'm thirty-six,' he informed her. Half hoping the age gap might switch her off him.

'You look younger.'

He needed to get away to give himself time to consider the

implications of a relationship with this woman. Relationship? Who was he kidding? She was probably just being nice to him. Patronising even.

'Sorry about your leg,' he said. 'I ought to make it up to you somehow. Maybe a meal sometime. That's if you fancy it.'

'Hmmm.' She thought long and hard, teasing him. 'Dining out with an older man. Not good for my image. Perhaps we could go somewhere where no one knows me.'

'The Tomato Dip on Penny Pot Lane's out then,' he retaliated. 'This time next week okay?' He was giving himself plenty of time to consider things.

'Sounds good. Better not bring your fiancée, she might get the wrong idea.'

'Perish the thought,' said Sam, getting to his feet. 'See you next week then. I'll pick you up about this time.'

He left her flat with an excitement fluttering inside him that he hadn't felt since he was sixteen years old and had landed a date with Molly Openshawe – two years his senior and the object of many of his sexual fantasies. Fantasies which had sadly remained unrequited as they'd bumped into twenty year old Barry Whitaker in the picture queue and she left the cinema on the older man's arm. Sam allowed himself a small smile of triumph at the memory. Time had wreaked its own revenge on Molly – now a bulbous divorcee with three of unemployed Barry's children to cope with.

Kathy Sturridge would never become bulbous or unlovely. There was a permanence about her beauty. And a danger.

18

It was 7.30 am and Sam had arrived on site a few minutes before Alec. Last night's confidential phone call from Chalky White, the Building Inspector, was bringing them out early.

The mid-August sun was already warming the site up, which made a pleasant change from the unseasonal gloom of the past few days. A straggle of crows flapped across the sky and a black-bird, perched on top of the scaffold, whistled cheerfully. An hour from now the birdsong would be replaced by the monotonous grind of the mixer and the shouting and swearing and hammer-ing and sawing and singing of the men. Sam sat on a pack of bricks, lit his first of the day and surveyed the work of the past couple of months. The first phase of the short road was in, kerbed and constructed up to basecoat. The top course, or wear-ing course, of tarmac, would be laid after all building work was finished. At the moment it was being used as a site road. Beneath it were the new foul and surface water sewers, already connect-ed to the sewers in the main road next to the site, and ready for connection into the houses. Service ducts had been laid beneath the proposed footpath and would, in time, provide the dwellings with gas, power, water and telephones.

One house was up to roof level, awaiting delivery of the roof trusses. A second was five feet out of the ground, awaiting the scaffolders to put up the first lift of scaffold. A third house had its foundations in, awaiting the arrival of another two-and-one bricklaying gang. Two brickies served by one labourer. Sam drew great satisfaction from what he saw. Three months ago this had been a brown field, no use to man and of little interest to beast.

The construction business offers a unique job satisfaction. Day by day the workers see their efforts taking gradual shape before their eyes. Like watching the picture emerge from within a fairly substantial jig-saw puzzle. And the best time is now, during the first few weeks, whilst the buildings are rising rapidly from the ground, higher and bigger every day. At some time during the course of a day everyone on site, from the site manager to the humblest labourer will take a few seconds to stand back and view the progress, knowing that they played their part in it. It's a very good thing to do. To know that people will be living inside the houses, or working in the offices or driving down the roads. The ones they helped to build.

And in years to come they'll drive past and tell people with them, 'I worked on that job,' and they'd know that their work might well still be there long after they've gone. Not many jobs provide that sort of monument. Like Sir Christopher Wren once said: *If you seek my monument, look around you.*

Sam watched the blackbird fly away, leaving the site oddly quiet. He had much on his mind. Kathy Sturridge mainly. Last night he'd made love to Sally thinking about her. Gone to sleep thinking about her and woken up thinking about her. The woman disturbed him. An urban fox padded across the site, seemingly unaware of Sam. Its mind concentrated on the piece of meat in its mouth, hanging out of a grease-proof paper wrapping. Sam was amazed. Where on earth would a fox get that from at this time of a morning?

His thoughts moved on. The official to whom Chisel had "given" Nicky Fulbright, needed tracking down – he could be the key to it all. Could even be the killer. Must chase that up PDQ. Maybe once he'd resolved this crime, he'd get this whole detective nonsense out of his system and concentrate on becoming a millionaire builder. Which brought his mind back to current matters.

He was flicking his cigarette stub towards a water butt when Alec's pick-up crunched to a halt beside him.

Sam got to his feet, rubbed the imprint of Halifax Buff Rustics from his backside, and grinned at his partner.

'Sorry to get you out of your pit, but I can see a big hold up if we don't sort it out now. Chalky said she'd applied for a TPO yesterday. He reckons she's likely to come charging down here sometime this morning. First thing, knowing her.'

153

'Best do it then,' grinned Alec, through the pick-up window.

Mrs Quarmby arrived at nine, looking out of place in a Ford Escort, driven by a small, bespectacled, young man. After the car stopped, she waited for a while, hoping someone would open the door and offer her a guiding hand. Her companion was engrossed within his briefcase, unaware of her requirements. She opened the door herself and gazed around, with some distaste, at her surroundings.

A large boned, formidable woman, of sixty something, Mrs Quarmby was a wealthy widow and part-time eco-warrior. Her current mission was to save a flourishing mountain ash growing in the path of a proposed sewer connection. Mrs Quarmby had somehow caught wind of this and applied for a temporary Tree Preservation Order. She'd lose in the long run, but not before she caused an expensive delay. She was already in the site hut as the young man was still getting out of his car.

'This is Mr Smithson from the Parks and Gardens ... ' she began, waving her arm in the direction of an absent Mr Smithson.

'Who is?' enquired Sam, looking round. He could only see her.

She went back to the door and gave the young man an exasperated shout.

'Do hurry along, Mr Smithson!'

Mr Smithson hurried along, slightly embarrassed at her attitude. He walked into the hut behind her.

'This is Mr Smithson, Parks and Gardens' said Sam, introducing the young man to Alec.

Mrs Quarmby looked irritated. Mr Smithson was *her* man, it wasn't up to Sam to introduce him. Mr Smithson seemed unsure of himself.

'Alec Brownlow, pleased to meet you, Mr Smithson,' greeted Alec, shaking the man's hand.

'Sam Carew,' said Sam. No hands were offered to Mrs Quarmby. She was well known to them.

A pregnant pause followed, as Mrs Quarmby waited for

Mr Smithson to do his job. He suddenly seemed to realise they were waiting for him.

'Oh, yes ...' he handed Sam a document. 'It's a Tree Preservation Order.'

'Backed up by Law,' added Mrs Quarmby, threateningly.

'Really?' mused Sam. He handed it to Alec. 'It's a Tree Preservation Order.'

Alec took it and read it carefully, as the three of them looked on.

'He hates trees,' said Sam, conversationally, inclining his head towards Alec, as he browsed the document.

'I do not!' protested Alec, looking up from his reading. 'I've got one in my back garden, as a matter of fact. A sycamore. The kids have built a tree house up –'

'This is not for a *sycamore*,' declared Mrs Quarmby, in a manner that suggested sycamores were unworthy of her attention. 'Sycamores are little more than weeds.'

'It's a very nice tree,' protested Alec.

Sam chose to side with Mrs Quarmby. 'I wouldn't give a sycamore house room,' he said.

She looked him up and down as though he were an idiot. 'The preservation order is for the mountain ash, growing over there.' She waved a vague hand towards the window.

'Also called a rowan,' said Mr Smithson. 'It says rowan on the order.'

'So it does,' confirmed Alec.

'Mountain ash is its more widely used name,' insisted Mrs Quarmby.

'What's in a name, eh?' smiled Sam. 'And where would you like this mountain ash-stroke-rowan tree, preserving?'

She looked at him as she would an idiot once again, then addressed herself to Alec, believing him to be a superior type. 'Does he always talk in riddles?'

Alec nodded. 'He's at a funny age.'

'Where is it, exactly?' enquired Smithson.

'On the back of that wagon,' replied Sam, cheerfully. He

pointed through the door at a wagon with the chopped up, red- berried tree on the back. 'Where do you want it taking?'

Mrs Quarmby was apoplectic. 'Ring the police!' she shouted to Smithson. 'They're in defiance of a court order.'

'Wouldn't it have been better to have given us the order a bit earlier?' asked Sam. 'Like three months ago when we first came on the site, instead of leaving it until after we'd chopped the tree down. Smacks of inefficiency, if you ask me.'

'I only found out about it yesterd – why did you cut it down?' asked Smithson, more perturbed by Mrs Quarmby's reaction than by the loss of a tree.

'It was on the line of a sewer connection,' explained Sam. 'No other way we could go. We did agree to plant three new ones, or didn't they tell you?'

'Oh really? Well fair enough then.' He took the order back from Alec and put it in his briefcase.

'How do you mean? *Well fair enough then*!' screamed Mrs Quarmby. 'Damn well do something!'

Sam had always found such women hard to deal with, so he left Alec to it. As he walked out, he jabbed a thumb in the direction of his partner.

'It's him you want to play hell with, missis,' he said. 'He hates proper trees, him. He only likes sycamores.'

He closed the door behind him and winced as Mrs Quarmby set about the two men left inside. A few minutes later, she emerged, still cursing loudly. Work had stopped. The men never missed an opportunity to see a gaffer getting a roasting. Sam had quickly filled them in on the details.

'You tell him, missis!'

'He wants lockin' up! Bloody sycamore lover.'

Mrs Quarmby was getting plenty of support from the men, Sam included. An ashen faced Smithson came out, darted past her and swiftly got into his car. Alec shut the door quickly behind them both but not before giving Sam a venomous glare. The irate woman turned and aimed a hefty kick at the side of the hut, to loud cheers from the men.

'Go back and gerrim, missis! He's growin' illegal sycamores in there.'

She waved, uncertainly, at her supporters on the scaffold. Smithson couldn't get away fast enough, dust and stones flew from under his spinning wheels as he accelerated away, leaving Mrs Quarmby without transport.

With arms akimbo she stood there and concentrated all her venom on the vanishing car. To no one's surprise, a minute later Smithson came back, got out and meekly opened the passenger door.

Only after the car had gone, taking Mrs Quarmby with it, did Alec emerge from the hut with a face like thunder. He marched forcefully across to the men, who all turned and went about their work, Sam included.

'Thanks a lot, you bastards!' he shouted. 'Next time, just keep it shut! She needs no bloody encouragement from you lot! And I'm including you in this, Carew!'

Not a sound came from the men, although a few shoulders heaved when Sam was included in the bollocking.

Sam stood on the top lift of scaffold. He and Arthur were removing wooden templates the joiner had made for the window openings. It was always easier to build the windows in as the building went up, but the window manufacturer was behind schedule and the job couldn't wait for windows.

A truck pulled onto the site with uPVC windows tied on to its sloping sides.

'About bleedin' time! Where were you when we wanted yer?'

This was Arthur, who hated walling around templates even more than Sam did. Now they had to hope that the windows fitted properly and that there'd be no cutting or re-building to fit them into the openings.

'Hey! I'm only t' fitter. I don't make the bloody things!' shouted the man getting out of the truck. He walked over to where Sam was standing, several feet above his head. 'Do you know, I'm sick of all the crap I get from you lot.'

'To be honest, Trevor, we're sick of all the crap we get from you,' returned Sam. 'Your gaffer reckons the windows were ready on time. He says it's you who's the hold-up!'

Trevor Hughes was a sub-contract window fitter who had taken too much on. He realised Sam was on to him, so he wisely discontinued the argument and began to unstrap the windows from the side of the truck. A pale youth got out the other side to help. Spiky-haired, with metal rings adorning his ears, lips and eyebrow. He was stripped to his waist, with an assortment of tattoos littering his scrawny body, including the highly unoriginal *Made In England* around his navel. It occurred to Sam that he ought to have another tattoo saying: *It Seemed Like A Good Idea At The Time.*

Trevor was a hard-looking, middle-aged man, who'd been in the plastic windows business since its infancy. In his time he'd been a handy middle-weight boxer; one of the few with enough wisdom to pack the game in before he took one punch too many.

A thought occurred to Sam. He put down his trowel and swung down the scaffold. Sometimes it was easier and quicker than using the ladder.

'Trevor,' he enquired. 'Didn't you used to work for old Fred Castle?'

Fred had returned Sam's call with information about his window fitters, but as Sam had feared, he'd used several different ones – mostly sub-contractors who tended to disappear off the face of the earth when things got tough. Trevor's name had cropped up, though.

Trevor turned round, surprised at Sam's friendlier manner. 'Fred? Aye. It were him what got me started in t' game. He came round ter fit some winders in my house. I'd just packed boxin' in and I were lookin' for a trade. We got talkin' and Fred took me on. I worked for him for a couple o' years, then I went on me own.'

Sam considered the possibility of Trevor being a suspect. He hoped not – the thought of tackling someone as hard as Trevor didn't appeal to him.

'When was this, then?' he asked, chattily.

'Nineteen seventy five I started wi' Fred,' recalled Trevor. 'Started up on me own in seventy seven – CAREFUL! Yer clumsy little shite'awk!'

His final words were for the benefit of his assistant, who had almost dropped a £500 window on the floor.

'Left him in the lurch, eh?' teased Sam. 'I bet old Fred wasn't too pleased.'

Trevor paused to recall the time. 'Nah, he weren't bothered. Fred had plenty on, but he started using subbies. He didn't need me. I did a bit o' sub-contracting for him meself. That's when I started making proper money.'

'Subbies, eh?' grinned Sam. 'Bane of my life. They try to screw you for every penny you've got.'

'Eh!' protested Trevor. 'I were never like that.' He grinned, 'Not wi' Fred any road. Not like some.'

'Oh? Who?'

'Gary Johnstone for one. Did yer ever come across him?' Sam shook his head. 'Yer don't bloody want ter neither,' warned Trevor. 'I worked wi' Gary meself for a bit, but he were allus on t' bloody fiddle. I reckon he fiddled owd Fred out of hundreds, an' that's when a hundred were worth summat. Fred never twigged.'

'Gary Johnstone?' It wasn't a name familiar to Sam. 'Is he still fitting?'

Trevor ruminated, squeezing his unshaven face between gnarled thumb and fingers. 'Nah,' he decided. 'Not round 'ere, any road. I'd 'ave known. Must be doin' summat though. I still see him about.' He nodded to himself to reinforce his theory. 'He's got a better motor than me, so he must be doin' summat.'

'Do you know where he lives?' Sam had forgiven Trevor his tardiness. He was convinced this Johnstone was his man.

'Up on t' Robertstown somewhere. He's got a white ...' He turned to the youth, now staggering under the weight of a six by

159

four window. 'Hey, shit fer brains! What sort o' motor were Gary Johnstone driving?'

'Peugot 307,' said the youth. 'Give us an 'and, Trev. I can't carry these bastards on me own.'

19

'Is PC Price there?' Sam tried, unsuccessfully, to disguise his voice.

'Sam?' said PC Johnnie Slattery.

'Yes, keep your voice down. Is Shirley within earshot?'

'Keep your knickers on Sam, Shirley's out, so is Owen for that matter. He's in a panda with Biggles.'

Biggles was PC Melia, who'd failed in his ambition to become an RAF pilot due to being too thick. This wasn't the official reason, just the reason his colleagues in the force had deduced.

'Can you give him a message to ring me?' asked Sam. 'It's important.'

'We're not supposed to pass on private messages. You know that.'

'It's police business,' Sam assured him. 'To do with the burglaries.'

Slattery laughed. 'I heard about your plastic window theory. Kept us amused for weeks.'

'What's the official theory then?' enquired Sam.

'How d'you mean?'

'I mean,' explained Sam, 'how do the police think the burglars get in?'

'You know better than to ask that Sam. We can't go revealing our information to all and sundry.'

'You don't have any information. I could solve that case in a couple of days, if I put my mind to it.'

'Oh really?' Slattery didn't even try to conceal his scorn.

'Yes, really,' responded Sam.

'Well I've got a hundred quid that says you can't.'

'You're on,' said Sam. He regretted this as soon as he said it. Two days might be nowhere near long enough.

'Forty eight hours from ...' he was obviously looking at his watch. 'Four fifteen, oh, and Rod wants a bet.'

'Tell Rod he's on for a hundred.'

'Hang on.'

Slattery put the phone down on the desk and Sam could hear chatting and laughing in the background. Slattery came back on.

'There's three more. Janet Seager from CID, Stan and Sergeant Bassey.'

'I thought you said Shirley wasn't in.'

'He just walked through the door.'

'Tell 'em they're all on. Two days from now I want five hundred quid from you lot. Now can you get a message to Owen for him to ring me?'

Half an hour later, Owen rang him. It was late afternoon and Sam was pointing the afternoon's brickwork. The day had been warm, with plenty of work done, including foiling the redoubtable Mrs Quarmby and digging out the information about Gary Johnstone. Sam was feeling pleased with himself. The only downside was the reckless bet he'd just taken on.

'Owen, thanks for ringing.'

'What's all this I been hearing about you taking bets from the lads down at the station?'

'Oh, that. It was that smug bugger Slattery winding me up. He was laughing about me saying the burglars got in through the windows.'

'They've all been laughing. Mainly at me. What you go an' do a daft thing like that for?'

'Daft? How d'you mean daft? It's only daft if I can't prove him wrong.'

'Do you know who the burglar is?'

'I think so.' The more he thought about it the more unsure Sam got about Gary Johnstone being the culprit. He certainly wasn't sure enough to gamble five hundred quid on him. Still, it was done now.

'Really?' Owen's tone went from critical to curious. 'Who is it then?'

'What time are you off?' enquired Sam.

'Eight.'

'Clog and Shovel, half past eight.

Owen turned up in corduroy and twill. Why he hadn't been sin-gled out for CID, baffled Sam. No one would ever take him for a copper. 'Did you ever have an urge to join plain clothes?' he asked. Owen picked up the waiting drink and did it more than justice.

'Never, not proper policing, see. Too fine a line to be drawn between criminal and copper.'

'I take your point,' agreed Sam, thinking of Bowman.

'Take you, for example,' went on Owen. 'Now you trod a very fine line, if you don't mind me saying.'

'As a matter of fact I do mind,' protested Sam. Owen opened his mouth to prolong the discussion. Sam put an end to it. 'Look, I brought you here to talk about your burglaries. I reckon I know who's doing them.'

'You know? You mean you're sure?'

'Absolutely,' confirmed Sam, who was good at hiding uncer-tainty. He took a large gulp of his pint in an attempt to catch up with Owen.

'And you have proof?'

'Ah, that's where you come in.'

'You don't have proof.' Owen's face dropped. 'And you've bet half the station you can solve the crime within two days.'

'Owen, I know how it's done and I know who's doing it. It's a bloke called Gary Johnstone. He used to be a window fitter for Fred Castle.'

'Gary Johnstone? Never heard of him. Does he have any form?'

'No idea. I'm sure you can chase that up. All we have to do is catch him at it.'

'Is that all? What do we do, set up an obbo? I'd have to approach Bassey for that and he'd need authorisation, and for authorisation he'd need a sound reason, not the hunch of a disgraced ex-cop. I gather he's bet a hundred quid as well.'

'Excuse me, Constable Price. I wasn't disgraced, I left of my own free will. Anyway, I take your point. Bassey's not going to help me win money off him is he?'

'See, your stupid bet's backfiring on you already. When was the last time you did anything sensible?'

Sam ignored him. Owen was like an old woman at times. Were it not for the five hundred quid, he'd forget all about the burglaries. Why should he bother? He'd enough problems of his own to worry about. A germ of an idea which had entered his brain earlier in the day began to take shape.

'Owen,' he said. 'I can give you this on a plate if you like, but if you don't like, just tell me now!'

'Oh dear! Don't get so bloody touchy, look you. It's always been my lot in life to go along with your hare-brained schemes, it doesn't mean to say I have to like them. What do you want me to do?'

Sam slid his empty glass across to him. 'Get me a pint while I think.'

Owen disappeared to the bar as Sam tossed his idea over in his head. A whiff of strong perfume disturbed his thoughts. Sam looked up into the eyes of Mandy Jackson.

'I never got a proper chance to thank you for saving my life,' she said.

He gave an awkward smile. Mandy's occupation was rather obvious, being seen talking to her might give people the wrong impression. What the hell? He didn't know these people anyway. Had he turned round, he'd have noticed the woman at the bar with the tattoo of a black cat's head, giving them a curious look. He pushed out a chair with his foot and said, 'Be my guest.'

Owen was also doing a double take from the bar, uncharacteristically allowing someone to get served out of turn. He was now in no rush to get back.

'How have you been?' enquired Sam.

'Oh, you know,' she shrugged and smiled. 'Trying to get back to normal. What about you?' Her accent was local, marred by an attempt to sound posh. It rarely worked.

'Me? I never was normal,' grinned Sam. He studied her, forcing her eyes to drop.

'Sorry, I didn't mean to stare. It's just that you're such a pretty girl for ...'

Her eyes came back up, flashing. 'For what?' she challenged. 'For someone who's on the game?' She made to get up, but Sam held out a restraining hand.

'Yes,' he said. 'Exactly.'

She sat down again.

'It's my guess,' ventured Sam, 'that you didn't go into it voluntarily.'

Her eyes looked up at him. Bright hazel, shining out from within a veil of dark make-up. She said nothing, waiting to hear what Sam had to say. He pressed on.

'Drugs is usually the key to girls like you falling in with the likes of Chisel Joo. Drugs or some sort of blackmail. Which one was it with you?'

He had a stab at answering his own question. 'Drugs?' he guessed.

Her eyes were damp now, making Sam feel uncomfortable. One of his many ideas came to the surface. 'I know a Model Agency in Leeds,' he suggested. 'You should go there. Just show up on the doorstep. They'll do the rest.'

'I've thought of that meself, but I could never afford to get the photos done.'

'I reckon if Maggie likes you, she'll organise that.' She gave him a dazzling white smile that told him he was giving the right advice. 'The Maggie Jones Agency,' he went on. 'Tell her Sam Carew sent you.'

He took out his wallet and wrote the name on the back of one his business cards. 'Let me know how you go on,' he said, handing it to her.

She examined both sides of the card. 'Maggie Jones,' she nodded her recognition of the name. 'I've heard of her. Thanks mister, I'll give her a try.'

'You might give the Lister Lane de-tox centre a try, while you're at it,' he added.

She shook her head and gave a rueful grin. 'I'm already on that wagon, mister. Now Chisel's gone, I need to re-build. I'm trying to get off the game as well. A job'd come in really handy.'

Sam figured now was payback time. 'I don't suppose you knew Nicky Fulbright, did you?'

'I went to school with Nicky, of course I knew her.' She looked at the card again. It was one of his Carew Investigations Bureau cards. 'I reckon you're on the track of whoever killed her,' she guessed. 'That Irish bloke didn't do it, did he?'

Sam nodded. The newspapers had published the new forensic evidence. Sam had seen to that – much to Bowman's annoyance. The police had come out of it in a bad light, especially Bowman. It hadn't inspired him with any enthusiasm to re-investigate the case.

'It's an unofficial investigation, but it's personal,' Sam said.

She frowned. 'Personal? You mean you knew her?'

'No, but I knew two people who are dead because of what happened to her. One of them was my dad.'

A memory stirred within her. 'Oh right,' she said. 'I heard about that.'

'I gather Nicky had a boyfriend,' said Sam. 'So far I haven't been able to track him down. Did you ever meet him?'

She went instantly on the defensive. 'Why?' she asked, almost belligerently.

Sam regarded her closely. 'You know him, don't you?'

'Why should I know him?' She was on her feet.

'I don't know. Why should you get upset when I talk about him?' pressed Sam.

'I'm not upset. Not about him, anyway. I never even met him. I just get upset when I think about Nicky. Look, I've got to go, and thanks again for, you know.'

She was gone just as Owen arrived with the drinks. Sam was gazing after her shapely form walking out of the door.

'You dirty old man, Carew,' said Owen. 'She can't be more than eighteen.'

'She knows who killed Nicky,' said Sam, turning his attention to Owen. 'Maybe she's not aware of it, but I'm sure she knows.'

20

It was now only five days to his date with Kathy. God, he was beginning to count them off. He'd never been like this with any woman. How sad, especially at his age. Sam was driving round the Robertstown estate looking for a white Peugot 307. It should stick out like a sore thumb. Anyone in this area with a nice car would be well advised to keep it in a garage at night, only bring it out during the day and stand guard over it with a bazooka. Sam grinned, there it was, shining like a tanner on a sweep's arse. Parked alongside an overgrown grass verge, behind a rusting Austin Maestro that had one wheel propped up on bricks. He stopped in front of it. A man was coming out of an adjacent house, possibly heading for it. Sam waited until the possibility turned into a probability, then shouted through his car window.

'Mr Johnstone?'

His question brought a guarded look to the man's face.

'Gary Johnstone?' called out Sam. He suddenly realised he sounded like a bailiff trying to identify a debtor. He got out of the car and walked towards the man with an outstretched hand.

'Who wants to know?' asked the man, thereby positively identifying himself as Gary Johnstone.

'Fred Castle told me where you lived.'

The man's guard dropped at the mention of Fred's name. 'Old Fred?' he grinned and shook Sam's hand. 'By the heck! I haven't seen him fer years. How is the old bugger?'

Sam joined him in his grin. 'He's still ticking along.'

Johnstone's smile turned quizzical, wanting to know what this friend of old Fred Castle was doing here. Sam introduced himself. 'Sid,' he lied. 'Sid Charlesworth. I were talking to Fred yesterday,' he said. 'He reckoned you might be able to fit me some windows.'

Johnstone didn't seem keen, he shook his head. 'I packed that game in last year,' he said. 'Me back started playing me up. The specialist told me not to do no more heavy liftin'. Yer've got ter do what them fellers say, haven't yer?'

Sam nodded. 'Fair enough. It's just that I got these windows on the cheap and I need somebody to fit 'em. It's all cash, no bills or vat or nowt.'

Johnstone still wasn't interested but Sam pressed on. 'Maybe you could give me a price. The problem is there's a lot of burglaries in my area and I've got a house full of expensive electrical gear – stuff I daren't insure, if you get me drift. I need decent windows for security.' He had now got the man's full attention.

'How come yer know Fred Castle?' enquired Johnstone, clicking open his car door locks.

It was time for Sam to play his ace. 'I've known him years. He built our house. Well, it was me dad's house originally. It's already got plastic windows, but to tell the truth I always thought they were a bit crap. I didn't tell old Fred that, I told him they'd been in for twenty odd years and they needed replacing. He gave me your name.'

He was reeling the man in like a fish on a line.

Johnstone grinned. 'Yer mean yer've got some knocked off winders and an 'ouse full o' knocked off gear and yer want someone who knows how ter keep his mouth shut ter fit yer winders for yer.'

'The windows aren't knocked off,' protested Sam. 'They're all made to measure, only the feller who measured 'em isn't in a position to fit 'em.'

'I'll bet,' smirked Johnstone. 'Look, I'm not an idiot. I've been up to all them tricks meself.'

'If yer don't want ter do it, fair enough,' Sam turned to go.

'Hang on,' said Johnstone. 'No harm in givin' yer a price. If me back feels up to it I might give it a go.'

'Fair enough,' said Sam. 'I live at 48 Chapel Fields Drive. Bob round when yer like. If no one's in, stick yer price through t' letter box. It's dead straightforward. I'm replacing all the downstairs windows and the front and side doors.'

'48 Chapel Fields Drive,' repeated Johnstone. 'Yeah, I know where that is. I might pop round sometime today.'

'Sooner the better,' urged Sam. 'The quicker they're in, the safer I'll feel. Tell you what, to save wasting each other's time, if I don't hear from you today I'll know you're not interested and I'll see if I can get someone else tomorrow.'

'Fair enough. Hey! Yer don't want anyone nicking yer knocked off gear,' chortled Johnstone.

Sam grinned sheepishly. 'When yer doing your price,' he said. 'Remember I'm paying cash. I don't expect to be paying top whack.' He turned to get back in his Range Rover.

'Nice motor, Sid,' called out Johnstone. 'Get it from a Main Dealer?'

Sam tapped the side of his nose. 'Sort of,' he grinned. Johnstone laughed out loud.

'Come in.'

Maggie Jones was expecting an averagely pretty young lady. She was slightly annoyed at Sam for forcing her to see someone without first seeing at least a photograph. But she owed Sam. Her parents lived in Unsworth and Sam had been on the case when they'd been robbed at knifepoint in their home. He'd managed to put them at ease when she couldn't, because she'd been too distraught. He'd also gone round to a certain pub and bought all their stolen valuables back for them before they disappeared into thin air as stolen goods tend to. After which he apprehended the villains and forcibly retrieved his financial outgoings in the car on the way to the station. An action which had caused a protest from the villains at their civil rights being abused, but Sam had denied everything. Maggie's parents thought the sun shone out of him, so she had to treat him right.

But he was just a cop-cum-builder, so what the hell did he know about real beauty? The type that jumps off the page at you and not just Page Three. Mouth too wide, nose too long, eyes slightly hooded. A happy combination of marginally imperfect features, all of which can be found on the plainest of faces. But sometimes nature has a way of randomly juxtaposing all these within the contours of the face in a way that makes it all very pleasing to the eye. Just the luck of the draw, the spin of the wheel. Another spin of the wheel might re-position the same features to produce a real plug ugly.

Artists have tried for centuries to conjure up such beauty from their imagination. But none have succeeded in turning out anything more than a bland image that looks like nobody because it is nobody. Even the great Leonardo needed a model to create the Mona Lisa. Such beauty is created by nature, not by man. Mandy Jackson, erstwhile prostitute, drug addict and nude dancer, was one such beauty.

Maggie's eyes were transfixed as the girl walked in. Everything about her was right. The walk, the posture, the attitude, the face. Especially the face. Maggie's assistant, Tony, looked from one woman to the other and knew they'd found the girl they'd been searching for to bring their agency into the big time.

He took a Polaroid of Mandy before she sat down. Maggie walked round her desk and shook the girl's hand. She rarely took the trouble to do this. What was racing through her mind now was the condition she'd agreed to with Sam. A condition she thought she'd have little problem complying with.

'You're everything Sam said you were,' smiled Maggie.

'And more,' agreed Tony.

'Take no notice of him,' smiled Maggie. 'He's a only man.'

'Maybe – but I'm an animal when I'm roused!' There was a pronounced lisp to his voice that Mandy hadn't caught straight away.

'You're safe with him,' said Maggie. 'This is Tony. He likes his vice versa.'

Mandy laughed and felt instantly at home among these people. Maggie's mind was already made up, she wanted this girl on her books before anyone else snapped her up. Her face went serious. Whenever she had something on her mind she needed to unburden herself as quickly as possible.

'Look, Mandy,' she said. 'After I spoke to you yesterday, I rang Sam. He's a good friend of my family and I made him a promise. I said I'd only take you on if you gave him certain information about some sort of case he's investigating. I understand you know what I'm talking about.' She tried to gauge Mandy's reaction. 'Is this a problem?'

Mandy's face dropped. Unaware that Maggie had already made up her mind to ignore her promise to Sam if it was too much for Mandy to agree to. Girls like her just didn't come along every day.

'Are you saying you'll take me on?'

Tony looked at Maggie as if she was mad to impose conditions. Maggie ignored him and nodded.

'I'll sign you up here and now. You'll have a portfolio of photographs by tomorrow and be working the day after.'

Mandy breathed deeply. This was what she'd been waiting for. 'Can I use your phone?' she asked.

Sam was driving away from Gary Johnstone's when his mobile rang.

'Mandy?... How're you doing? ... That's great. No, not tonight, I've got something else on. Tomorrow's fine. Clog and Shovel, one o'clock. You won't regret it. Don't worry, Maggie knows all about that – as much as she needs to know anyway. Put her on ... morning Maggie ... told you. Yeah, I'll take her word for it. You sign her up. See you, bye.'

He clicked off his phone, happy that he was going to solve two cases within the next twenty-four hours. And he had a date with Kathy in five days. Prospects were good, but what should he say to Sally?

21

Sam put the question of Sally to the back of his mind. The way to handle problems is one at a time, don't let them crowd in on each other, causing confusion. It was Sam's guess that Gary Johnstone would make his move tonight, before Sid Charlesworth got someone else to fit his new windows. Hence the thinking behind Sid's apparent hurry to get the job done.

He had parked his Range Rover outside Trevor Hughes' house for authenticity and he, Owen, and a reluctant Alec were cramped in the cab of Alec's pick-up. Owen belched for the fourth time – loud and unapologetic. He shook a couple of Tums from a box and stuck them in his mouth, crunching.

'If he starts farting, I'm away,' said Alec, to Sam, as though Owen wasn't there. Owen looked offended but said nothing. Neither did Sam. You can't argue with a threat like that.

Alec looked at his watch for the umpteenth time. 'Half past bloody twelve!' he grumbled. 'This is the last time I'll let you talk me into something like this. Does this Trevor Hughes bloke know he's going to be burgled?'

'Of course he doesn't. That's the beauty of it.'

'And he's an ex-boxer? Liable to get violent?'

'Stop moaning, Alec!' remonstrated Sam. 'You're like an old woman. This is excitement. This is what gets your adrenalin flowing. I've only invited you along because you lead such a boring life.'

'I get enough adrenalin surges fighting off the Mrs Quarmby's of this world,' retorted Alec. He turned to Owen. 'Did he tell you what he did?'

Owen gave a fifth burp which he had the decency to try and conceal. He shook his head, but he knew that nothing Alec was going to say about Sam would surprise him.

'He wound this old battleaxe of a woman up, who was moaning about a manky old tree being chopped down. He only tells her it's all my fault because I hate trees, which is not true. Then he just buggers off and leaves me with her. Can yer believe that?'

Owen crunched and nodded. 'I believe it.'

'It was like being locked in with Attila the bloody Hun. On top of which he got all the lads to encourage her.'

Sam was grinning and received a dig in the ribs from Alec. 'See!' he said to Owen. 'He still thinks it's bloody funny!'

A dark Ford Transit drove past, slowing down outside the house, then picking up speed and driving to the end of the road where it executed a three point turn. Its lights went out as it cruised back, drawing to a silent halt in front of Sam's Range Rover. Two figures got out, one of them unmistakably Gary Johnstone. He opened the back doors to the van, then followed his partner around the rear of the house.

'Give them five minutes to get the window out. I'll go first and give you a wave if it's all clear.'

The other two nodded, petty differences forgotten in the excitement. Alec was still very uncertain as to the wisdom in him being here, but he felt he owed Sam a favour or two and Sam was never backward in calling in favours.

Mandy was unhappy at having to break the news to her boyfriend. *Boyfriend?* Hardly a fitting description. Up to Chisel Joo's death she'd been paid to attend to Isaac's every need. But now Chisel's money was no longer forthcoming it was time to make the break. Pity in a way. Isaac was a nice enough bloke – not bad looking in a boring sort of way. Nicky, her predecessor, had tried to talk him into leaving his wife. She had it bad for him did Nicky. Mandy couldn't see why. She didn't know who had killed her friend but it wasn't beyond the bounds of possibility that Chisel had been behind it. That had worried her. Chisel's death had come as a great relief to her.

Isaac was okay, but that was all. Tonight they'd have some fun, she'd tell him about her modelling job and they'd go their separate ways, still friends. That's how she liked things.

She'd arranged to go with him to one of Chisel's many houses which were used for such purposes. Some of the girls had gone freelance and in the absence of any claimants, were using the houses on a rota basis they'd organised themselves. Before much longer, another pimp would come along and claim the territory, but until such time the girls were making hay. Mandy had booked a flat in Ragley Terrace for the night. Isaac was due to arrive at around midnight and stay a couple of hours. She knew Isaac wasn't his real name, his middle name maybe, but not his everyday name. She even knew what his real name was. It suited him a lot more than Isaac, but she went along with his subterfuge just to humour him.

She hadn't made up her mind what to tell him about Sam, if anything. And vice versa. No way was Isaac connected with Nicky's death, he just wasn't the type. If the police started sniffing round, questions would be asked about his association with Chisel Joo. He'd lose his job at least, and Mandy wouldn't want that on her conscience. On the other hand, if Sam had been able to see her tonight the story might have been different. Just a farewell call to Isaac and spill the beans to Sam – she certainly owed him. Tomorrow she'd be starting a whole new life. Maggie had made it sound brilliant. The money seemed unreal. A knock on the door told her Isaac was here.

Alec and Owen got out of the van on Sam's wave. They were round the back of the house in a few seconds. Leaning against the wall was a double-glazed window panel about five feet by four, recently removed by Gary and his crony. Without a word, Sam and Alec picked it up and put it back in its frame. Owen stepped forward and held it in position as the others fitted the plastic beading back in place. The whole operation took two minutes. The three of them waited until the two burglars reappeared carrying a television and a video recorder. Sam took out his mobile phone and stabbed a number out.

'Mr Hughes? ... I believe you have burglars in your house.'

He switched the phone off and stood at the back of the garden with Owen and Alec as an upstairs light went on. Gary

175

stood for a second in front of the window, conducting a hurried conversation with his accomplice, which brought them to the conclusion that they were in the wrong room. They put down the TV and video and tried to open one of the sashes, but found it was locked, so they dashed out and appeared in the kitchen, trying the window. Locked again. By this time Trevor Hughes had appeared on the scene and mayhem began. His absence from the boxing ring hadn't robbed him of his aggression and what skill and strength he had left was more than enough to deal with the intruders. The three onlookers cringed as they witnessed the carnage.

'I think I'd better put a stop to it,' said Owen, moving off down the side of the house. He gave a loud clear knock. Trevor stopped punching long to enough to shout, 'Who is it?'

'Police.'

Sam saw him fire once last blow at Gary then disappear out of the room. He and Alec waited a few seconds before going along to join the policeman.

Owen was putting handcuffs on Gary, a younger man was on the floor, moaning, as Owen read them both their rights. Sam and Alec walked in.

'Sam?' said Trevor, surprised.

'Sam?' said Gary. 'I thought your name was Sid.'

'Sorry,' admitted Sam. 'I lied.'

Trevor was massaging his bruised fists. His wife was standing at the bottom of the stairs armed with a large kitchen knife.

'What the hell's going on?' she demanded.

'I'm arresting these men for burglary,' said Owen, inadvertently stumbling over a fallen chair. Under Mrs Hughes' disapproving gaze, he picked it up and placed it back on its feet, then took Sam's phone from him and called the station.

'Sergeant Bassey? Owen here. I've just apprehended the burglars we've been chasing for the past few months, I need a van ... 48 Chapel Fields Drive. It's the home of a Mr and Mrs Trevor Hughes. Yes Sarge ... It was Sam's idea. They were doing it just like he said ... He's here now. I think he wants a word.'

Sam took the phone from Owen. 'Hello Sergeant. Now before you start heaping praise on me, I want some of the credit to go to Owen. After all, he was the only one who had the sense to realise what I was telling you was true. I'll pop round tomorrow to collect the five hundred, be a good lad and make sure they've all got it ready.'

He clicked off the phone and found himself confronted by Trevor.

'You set this up, yer bastard!' he fumed. 'You were asking me about Gary Johnstone yesterday.'

'If I'd known it were you, Trev, I'd never have done it,' whined Gary, through a bloodied mouth. 'I thought it were his house.'

Gary's accomplice lay semi-conscious on the floor, bruised and bemused by the whole pantomime; as was Alec, standing beside the handcuffed Gary, who spotted the baffled expression on Alec's face and saw an ally.

'It's not right what he did yer know, setting us up like that.'

'He does it to everybody,' sympathised Alec.

'See,' said Gary. 'Even yer own mate agrees wi' me.'

'Just shut it you, yer thievin' bastard!' yelled Trevor.

'And you just you watch your language, Trevor!' scolded Mrs Hughes. 'You're not at work now!'

A slightly chastened Trevor jabbed an angry finger in Sam's direction. 'Sorry love, but this bugger set me up. That's why he rang yer up today to ask if we'd got proper locks on us winders. I thought there were summat fishy about it. I mean, what's it got ter do with him if we've got proper locks on us winders?'

Sam flinched under Mrs Hughes' angry stare. 'He told me he'd got some cheap locks left over and he wanted to get rid of them,' she informed her husband.

'As it turns out, your locks seem quite adequate,' Sam assured her.

'He wanted ter make sure the buggers couldn't get away,' complained Trevor. 'He wanted me to do his dirty work for him.'

'Is this true, Sam Carew?' she demanded.

177

'Well, your Trevor's so good at it, love. And we all have to do our bit for law and order.'

'It's you what wants locking up,' grumbled Gary. 'Tricking people like tha –'

A cuff from Trevor ended his contribution to the discussion.

'And I won a few quid from the lads down at the station,' added Sam. 'I'll split it with you to compensate you.'

'Won a few quid?' Trevor was flabbergasted. 'How'd yer mean, *won a few quid*? Watcha been bettin' on? Whether the buggers beat me up or not. I don't believe this!'

'No, nothing like that,' soothed Sam. 'I just had a sort of hunch they'd come round here, so we had a friendly wager.'

'Hunch?' whined Gary. 'It weren't a hunch, it were a bloody set –!'

Trevor silenced him with a glare and a raised fist. 'How much?' he enquired.

'Two hundred, that's a hundred each.'

'I just heard yer say five hundred,' Trevor remembered. 'That's two-fifty each.' He held out a large, grazed hand, perhaps expecting payment.

Sam shook it. 'Two-fifty it is then. And, may I say, a job well done. I'll be round with it tomorrow.'

Mandy stretched out her nude body on the bed. A haze of post-coital cannabis hung in the air. It was a functional room. Deep-pile pink carpet, a king-sized bed, television, video, porno tapes galore, en-suite bathroom, mirrored ceiling, little else.

The love-making was over, and all in all it had been worth-while. Isaac was an attentive lover, not the most imaginative she'd ever had, but by no means the worst. And now he was going home, back to his woman, hopefully with enough life left in his loins to cope with her immediate needs.

As he pulled on his trousers, he looked down at her naked form and smiled. 'Mandy, don't keep doing that to me. I've got to save something for when I get home.'

She pouted, coquettishly, drew up a seductive brown

knee and ran her tongue around her lips. 'I'm in no rush, mister.'

He turned away to avoid weakening. 'Anyway,' he said. 'You've got a busy day tomorrow. I hope you'll remember me when you're a supermodel.'

His words brought a smile to her face. 'I still can't believe it,' she said. 'They really like me. Maggie Jones reckons I can be earning as much as a grand a day when my face gets known.'

'If Chisel had still been around, he'd have put a stop to all that,' remarked Isaac.

'That bastard had a hold over us all in one way or another, including you,' Mandy reminded him. 'I reckon whoever topped him did us all a favour.'

Isaac said nothing, but he showed no disapproval of her condemnation of Chisel, no disapproval whatsoever. It had started with him doing Chisel a small favour for which he'd been rewarded with pick of any of Chisel's girls he wanted. It was the gangster's way, to draw him in. Very soon he was in too deep to get out. The rewards were fine but the risk too great – especially for someone in his delicate situation. Now it was over he was as relieved as Mandy.

'If it's any consolation,' Mandy went on, 'your secret's safe with me. I don't want anyone to know about my past any more than you do. Maggie Jones knows about me, but she'll keep it to herself. Sam thought it best to tell her from the outset.'

'Sam?' he asked, 'Sam who?'

'Sam Carew. He's the bloke who put me on to Maggie Jones. The bloke who pulled me out of that fire. I thought you knew about him.'

'I wasn't around at the time, how the hell could I know?' His mood had changed to confrontational.

Mandy sat up and began to get dressed. 'I didn't know who he was meself at the time,' she said, pulling on her panties. 'I was so popped up on drugs, one day just drifted into another.'

The humour had gone from Isaac's face. His eyes became unfocused.

'He's a really nice bloke you know,' she said. 'You'd like him.'
Still half naked she lit another joint and offered him a drag. He
took it and drew nervously on it as Mandy continued dressing.
'I'm meeting him tomorrow,' she said. 'And I've got to tell him a
few porkies. I feel bad about that. All for your benefit an all.'

'My benefit? How d'you mean for my benefit?'

She took the cigarette from him. 'He's investigating Nicky's
murder and he wants to know who her boyfriend was.'

'And you told him you knew?' There was worry in his eyes.
Panic almost.

She grinned and shook her head. 'I told him nothing and
nothing's what I'm going to tell him. So don't get your knickers
in a twist. What Sam doesn't know won't harm him. His dad
was killed at the same time, you know. Weird that.'

'And you've got this meeting with him tomorrow?'

'Clog and Shovel. One o'clock. He reckons I'm going to spill
the beans.'

'And you feel guilty about not telling him what he wants to
know?' Beads of sweat appeared on his brow.

'Sort of,' she replied, absently, pulling her sweater over her
head.

Isaac was pacing around the room, arms gesticulating. 'Have
you told him anything about me? My name or anything?'

She checked her make-up in the mirror and spoke to his
reflection. 'He knows absolutely bugger all about you, no name,
no nothing,' insisted Mandy, amused at his consternation.
'Besides, your name's not Isaac is it?'

He took her by her shoulders and swung her round. 'It is
actually – one of them anyway.'

She held up placating hands. 'Fair enough.'

He stared at her for a while, as though trying to make up his
mind about something, then asked, 'What if he tries to – to persuade you?' His voice was quieter now, more controlled. 'What
if he tries to talk you round. I've heard he's a very persuasive
man.'

Perhaps sedated by the cannabis, Mandy had failed to see the change in his manner – his voice. She smiled, closed her eyes and took a deep drag on the joint. 'You'll just have to trust me,' she said.

Isaac's hands closed around her throat and made her open her eyes. At first she thought he wanted a second helping, but the unbalanced look on his face spoke of anything but sex. Fear paralysed her body, she fought, maniacally, for several seconds but his grip was too tight. She felt the air closed off – to and from her lungs – fighting for breath that just wasn't there. Lungs bursting, intense distress, then blackness, then nothing.

'Sorry about this Mandy, love,' he said, with genuine remorse. 'I can't afford to trust you.'

He kept the pressure on long after she died, taking no chances. Slowly releasing his grip he lowered her to the floor, then he sat on the bed, his heart thumping with decreasing ferocity. He had time to calm down, unlike last time, when he'd had to think fast to avoid capture. His quick thinking had saved him then. Something to be proud of. Foxed the police. Even Sam Carew hadn't worked it out. This time there was no rush. He sat there as the bedside clock ticked away quarter of an hour, allowing his mind to absorb the enormity of what he'd done. Not as much guilt this time – the second time. In fact he sensed a perverted pleasure, a sexual pleasure. In the struggle her sweater had risen up to reveal her breasts. He turned his head to one side to study her, and necrophilic thoughts crossed his mind. He put them to one side and lit a cigarette – not one of the funny ones they'd been smoking earlier – and paced the room. Clear thinking was needed now. DNA – not much he could do about that. They'd figure out she was killed by the same man who killed Nicola but they'd need to have cause to suspect him first in order to make a match, and they had no cause. What about fingerprints? It hadn't mattered so much with Nicky. It wasn't unusual that they found his prints in Greerside Hall, they only fingerprinted him then for elimination purposes, after which they were supposed to destroy them. But were they to be trusted? No point taking chances. He meticulously went round the room polishing everything he'd

181

touched and everything he might have touched. He looked down at Mandy. He'd touched her. There were very few parts of her he hadn't touched. Can they get fingerprints off someone's skin? Unlikely, but who knows? Lifting her off the bed, he carried her into the bathroom, laid her in the shower tray and turned on the water at its hottest; enough to scald away all traces of his fingerprints, and any other bits of him that might be stuck to her body. It was all he could do but it should be enough.

Owen knew about Sam's meeting with Mandy. He'd even been invited along, but he had other, more mundane police duties to attend to, mainly involving the paperwork concerning the Gary Johnstone arrest. Sam had called in the station and duly collected his winnings. Owen had had a pat on the back from the superintendent and his kudos had risen somewhat, mainly due to a certain sheepishness some of his colleagues felt at poo-pooing his suggestions about the burglaries. All in all, Owen felt good that morning. Until the call came in from the girl who'd booked the Ragley Road flat for a morning session.

Owen had taken a welcome break from his duties to go out on the call with Segeant Bassey. No identity had been offered by the caller. Two officers were already on the scene.

Mandy's naked and discoloured body was lying in the bottom of the now switched off shower. Hair bedraggled, covering her face but not the livid contusions around her neck. Bassey and Owen looked down on her, both experiencing the same sense of revulsion. Bassey went back into the hallway and spoke to a weeping young girl.

'Are you the person who made the call?' he asked.

She nodded, tearfully.

'Do you know who she is?'

Another nod. The girl collected her breath. 'It's Mandy, Mandy Jackson!'

Owen did a double take of the dead girl. 'Oh heck!' he exclaimed.

'Oh heck?' enquired Bassey. 'Why, *Oh heck*! Do you know this woman?'

Owen hesitated to answer. He knew Bassey wouldn't be pleased.

'Sam Carew was supposed to be meeting her this lunchtime to ask her about Nicky Fulbright.'

Bassey shook his head, despairingly. 'Sam Carew! I'm sick to death of Sam bloody Carew!' He glared at Owen. 'I want you to go find Carew and bring him down to the station. We'll start this case by finding out what he knows.'

Owen was clattering down the stairs as Bassey was making a call to invite forensic and any other interested parties onto the scene. It was a CID case but he'd insist on sitting in on an interview with Sam.

'Interview with Samuel Carew, commencing at,' Bowman looked at his watch. 'Fifteen thirty hours. Present are DI Bowman, Sergeant Bassey and Samuel Carew's solicitor, Mr Armitage.'

'For the benefit of the tape,' said Sam. 'I wish to point out that I've been arrested simply because Sergeant Bassey lost a hundred pounds in a bet with me this morning, when I solved a simple crime that he and Detective Inspector Bowman were too thick to figure out.'

Bowman looked questioningly at Bassey. 'For the benefit of the tape,' added Sam, who was livid at being arrested, 'Inspector Bowman is giving Sergeant Bassey a very funny look.'

'Can we get on with the interview, please?' snapped Bowman.

Sam's solicitor, Derek Armitage, gave Sam a warning glance.

'Where were you between the hours of midnight and two this morning?'

'With PC Price, solving one of your crimes for you.'

'PC Price tells me you left him at one-twenty. Where did you go after that?'

'I went home.'

'Straight home?' enquired Bowman, who'd already interviewed Sally.

Sam knew he'd have spoken to her and that she'd have had no cause to lie. He hadn't arrived back at his flat until half past two.

The intervening hour or so had been spent trying to work out his personal life. He was on his way home to sleep with Sally when his heart was elsewhere. His turmoil was centred around Sally. She didn't deserve this. He thought just too much about her to do this to her. Maybe he should tell her. That was the right thing to do. Tell her, but not just yet.

'I asked you if you went straight home,' repeated Bowman, impatient at Sam's delay in answering.

'No, I drove around for a while.'

'Drove round for a while?' said Bowman. 'Where did this drive take you? To your girlfriend in Ragley Terrace, for a quick shower maybe? She *is* your girlfriend, isn't she? The one you pulled naked out of Chisel Joo's club. The one you had a meeting with today. I understand she was a friend of Nicola Fulbright, who just happened to be murdered in very similar circumstances on one of your building sites. Now, apparently we're not very good at figuring things out. Perhaps you could do it for us?'

Sam didn't like where this was leading. 'She's not my girlfriend, as well you know,' he retorted. 'She's someone who was paid by Chisel Joo to perform certain favours for his friends. A bit like yourself, Inspector!'

Sam was pitching in the dark here, but his annoyance had caused him to throw what sense he had out of the window. Bowman coloured visibly.

'What's that supposed to mean, Sam?' snapped Bassey. 'You know better than to make accusations like that.'

'Unlike you lot, I wouldn't dream of making a false accusation,' responded Sam. 'It's common knowledge on the streets that Bowman was one of the many people in Chisel Joo's pocket.'

'Interview suspended at fifteen thirty-four,' snapped Bowman, switching off the tape. 'Mr Armitage, I'm going to leave you with your client and I suggest you have a word with him and persuade him to co-operate.'

'I can but try,' sighed Armitage.

The two officers left Sam alone with Armitage and a lone police constable.

Bowman led Bassey into his office, sitting down at his desk and leaving his uniformed colleague standing, looking uncomfortable.

'I'm inclined to throw the book at him,' fumed Bowman. 'Accusing me of corruption. You know what CIB are like. They get a whiff of anything like that and they come sniffing round.'

'They're hardly likely to take notice of the ravings of a madman, sir.'

Bowman smiled. 'He is, isn't he? God, we're well rid of him.'

'Mind you, the *Unsworth Observer* seem to think he's some sort of Simon Templar.'

'Tomorrow's fish and chip paper,' grunted Bowman.

'Very true, sir,' agreed Bassey. 'Although I don't think we've got much on him.'

'You don't think I should have arrested him, do you, Sergeant Bassey?'

Bassey shifted uncomfortably. He was regretting getting involved with the plain clothes lot. 'CID have their own way of doing things, sir. I wouldn't have thought we had enough to charge him with.'

'Not yet, we don't, Sergeant. But the girl is a prostitute and a friend of the girl who was murdered on Carew's building site. Mandy Jackson probably had sex with whoever murdered her and the odds are it was the same man who had sex with the girl on the building site. Carew was never eliminated from the Nicola Fulbright investigation, I think we should hold him here until he's eliminated from this one. Don't you agree?'

'He was in hospital when the Fulbright girl was killed, sir,' Bassey reminded him.

'I take full responsibility, Sergeant.'

Too bloody right, you do, said Bassey to himself.

Sam looked up at the constable leaning awkwardly against the wall.

'Any chance of a cuppa, Mark?'

The constable disappeared, leaving Sam and his solicitor alone.

'There appears to be an unaccountable forty minutes in your story, Sam,' said Armitage.

'I know,' said Sam. 'The truth is that I was driving around. I've got a few personal problems.'

'I think you'd better sort out what you're going to tell them when they come back.'

'Come off it! They can't hold me on this flimsy evidence,' said Sam, irritably. 'You know that. There's not a single scrap of evidence to connect me to the crime. Once forensic have finished, they'll have to let me go. The CPS will think they've gone barmy. Maybe I'll sue for wrongful arrest. Spite's got a lot to do with this, you know. He hates me, does Bowman.'

'I can't understand why. You're so sweet to him.'

Sam grinned. 'I had him going, didn't I? It's true, you know. He was in Chisel's pocket. It was written all over his face.'

'True or not,' warned Armitage. 'Say no more about it. It's a separate issue, nothing to do with this.'

The constable arrived with the tea a minute before Bowman and Bassey.

'I wish to make a statement,' said Sam. Armitage rolled his eyes upwards. *Here we go.*

'Go on,' said Bassey.

'Mandy Jackson was killed by the same person who killed Nicky Fulbright,' began Sam. 'They had a common boyfriend whose identity I would have discovered by now had she not been killed. He was an associate of Chisel Joo, one of many who Chisel paid, or provided sexual services for, in return for favours.' He looked directly at Bowman as he said this. 'There will be no evidence, forensic or otherwise, connecting me with the murder, because I didn't do it. I suggest you stop wasting your time with me and get after the real killer.'

'Where did you go after you left PC Price?' asked Bowman coldly.

'I've said all I need to say. As far as I'm concerned the interview is over,' replied Sam.

'If you've no more evidence than this, I suggest you release my client,' requested Armitage.

'Not until we've had a full forensic report. We need your client to submit a blood sample,' said Bowman. 'Your client can go as soon as he's been eliminated. Which won't be tonight.'

'If you're thinking of holding my client for more than twenty four hours,' said Armitage, sharply, 'then I suggest you charge him now. You certainly won't get any DNA results within that time.'

'We'll just have to see about that.'

Bassey caught the petulance in Bowman's tone just as much as the other two did. He looked at his superior, whilst trying not to reveal his reservations to Sam and his solicitor.

'I'm advising my client to make a formal complaint about this,' said Armitage, getting to his feet.

Sam leaned forward until his face was inches from Bowman's. 'Your pal Chisel's no longer around to cover up for your incompetence. He'll be handing no more villains your way in exchange for you leaving him alone. That was the deal, wasn't it?'

Bowman's control snapped, he drew back a fist and aimed a punch, which Sam easily avoided.

'For the benefit of the tape,' said Sam. 'Inspector Bowman just tried to hit me.'

Bowman got to his feet and stormed out, closely followed by Bassey, who paused at the door to say to the bemused constable, 'Put Mr Carew back in a cell, Mark.'

The constable shrugged and went round the table to place a hand on Sam's shoulder.

22

Sam emptied the plastic bag containing his belongings onto the desk and looked up at the custody sergeant. He'd spent a totally unnecessary night in a cell.

'Tell Bassey and Bowman I'm making an official complaint for wrongful arrest. If I learnt nothing else in the force, I learnt they can't do this. They had no more cause to arrest me than the Man in the Moon.'

Sam's anger at what had been done to him was more than apparent. The sergeant wisely chose not to argue with him.

'I'll tell them what you propose,' he replied, officiously. 'If everything's in order, would you sign here please?'

'You'll be well advised to keep your nose clean, Sergeant,' snapped Sam, signing his name. 'When the shit hits the fan, you don't want any dropping on you!'

Sam was aware that the young constable in the interview room had heard his accusation against Bowman and would be unlikely to keep it to himself. Rumour, whether true or false, was sometimes a powerful ally. Bowman's behaviour would now come under close scrutiny.

Owen timed his exit to coincide with Sam's. "Biggles" Melia was already in the Panda, awaiting Owen.

'Need a lift?' enquired the Welshman, quietly, despite being out of earshot of everyone in the station. He felt guilty about bringing Sam in for an informal interview, only to see him being arrested by Bowman as soon as he set foot inside the station.

'Bloody Judas!' growled Sam. He knew it wasn't Owen's fault, but he wasn't in a forgiving mood.

'Come on, Sam! How was I to know he was going to arrest you?'

Sam walked silently to the car and sat, almost petulantly, in the back seat. The car drove out of the station yard into Dunsford Road.

'After all I just did for you as well,' complained Sam. 'Wrapped up a whole case for you and that's the thanks I get. What do you reckon to a bloke like that, Biggles?'

'My name isn't Biggles!' objected Melia, who owed Sam nothing. 'Since you left, no one calls me that anymore.'

'Oh dear! I do beg your pardon. I thought they only let the grown-ups join the police!' retorted Sam, scornfully.

A late summer downpour hammered against the car windows. PC Melia slowed the car down and looked across at Owen. 'I don't care if he is a mate of yours, Owen. If he doesn't shut his gob, he gets out here and now!'

'Fine by me,' agreed Owen, who could stand just so much of Sam.

Sam looked through the window at the downpour and considered his options. He'd had a depressing twenty-four hours. Beginning with him being told about Mandy's murder. This had hit him hard. According to Maggie Jones, the girl had had a glittering career in front of her. If only he'd arranged to meet her the previous evening, she'd still be alive. She was dead because of him. Another "If Only". His life seemed to be full of them.

He sat back in his seat. 'Don't mind me, fellers. I'm going through a bad time, that's all.'

Owen turned and looked at him and felt suddenly sorry for this maddening man. Sam's face was creased and care-worn, perhaps on the verge of tears. All this bluster was just a front to cover his inner frustrations.

'The girl had had sex with someone just before she died,' he informed Sam. 'Probably the man who killed her.'

Sam was miles away. His blank gaze was fixed on the saturated urban landscape moving past the window. The downpour matched his mood. There was a bloke out there killing people. It had to be the same bloke who killed Nicky. What the hell was Mandy doing with him? Sam had warned her about him. No, he hadn't. He just asked her about him. She probably thought he was okay. Killers can be very plausible people. But why had he killed her? Maybe Mandy had mentioned to him, in all innocence, that Sam had been asking questions about him. She'd have told him about the meeting they arranged. Probably assured him that she'd lie to Sam on his behalf, but the killer wouldn't be able to rely on this. Not if his freedom depended on it. It was only because of the modelling job that Mandy agreed to go along with it. Because of the conditions that Sam had imposed on her. What right had he to do that? He looked up at Owen and asked, 'What did you say?'

'Apparently Mandy had sex just before she was killed,' repeated Owen. 'Probably with her killer.'

Had sex with him! This depressed Sam even more. He felt tears welling up. Rubbing his forehead to hide his eyes he said, 'Let me out here, I'll walk.' He managed to get the words out without revealing his out-of-control emotions.

'Don't be daft, it's pissing down!' argued Owen, but Melia had already stopped the car.

Sam got out, said a vague 'Thanks' and disappeared into the wet morning. His thoughts were confused and meandering. The rain disguised his distress. He strode through the streets trying to regain his composure. Think about something else. At least he hadn't lost a day's work. The lads would all be rained off any-way. Alec might wonder where he was, though. Good bloke, Alec. It'd be wise not to wind him up so much. His thoughts switched to Sally. She'd be at work now, wondering about Bowman's questions. What had the bastard said to her? Maybe he should ring her up and explain his side of things. He stopped in a shop door and took out his mobile. The screen lit up, telling him to re-charge the battery.

'Shit!'

He put it back in his pocket. The chances of finding an unvan-dalised phone box in that part of town were slim to nil. The rain had eased off so he set off walking once again. No destination in mind. Just walking and thinking. A passing car drove through a roadside puddle, completing the job the rain had begun. Drenching him from head to foot. As mornings go, Sam was having a bad one.

The man known to Mandy and Nicky as Isaac drew a heart in the condensation on his bedroom window. Then drew an arrow through the middle, stopping it off halfway across the heart and re-starting it at the edge to make it look as though it went through the middle, like he used to do as a boy, when he made his home-made Valentine cards. He wrote *Nicky* next to the flight and *Mandy* next to the tip, then hurriedly erased it as he heard her coming up the stairs. She was older than him, quite a lot older, but she was still easy on the eye and had a need for regular sex, which suited him. He was no good at emotional relationships. Marriage was for suckers, being stuck with the same woman all the time was not for him. The variety in his sex life had come from the occasional prostitute. The occasions became quite frequent when Chisel started fixing him up in exchange for favours. All that was finished now. Everyone from that side of his life was dead. Which was good.

'You could have gone in today, you know,' she grumbled as she entered the bedroom. 'I could well do without you under my feet. I only took today off so I could give the house a good going over.'

'I'll give you a good going over, if you don't watch it,' he retorted.

'The first time will be the last time, sonny,' she replied, coolly.

He backed down. 'Anyway, have you seen the weather?' he said. 'How much work do you think I'd get done on a day like this?'

'About the same as me, if you don't get out of my way,' she grumbled.

'Get stuffed!'

'Charming!'

He pushed past her and went downstairs. If he thought he could get away with it she'd go the same way as Nicky and Mandy. He had things to think about. What had Mandy told Sam Carew about him? According to her, nothing, but was she to be trusted? He allowed himself a grin. *She was now.*

The police weren't going to be a problem, not with Bowman on the case – one of Chisel's many unofficial employees. Both girls were connected with Chisel, and Bowman would very be wary of opening that particular can of worms. He knew about Bowman, despite Chisel's rule about keeping everyone's identity secret from each other. It had been Bowman who'd got him off the speeding charge, the one that would have put him over the twelve points and lost him his licence, which would have made it very awkward for him to do his job. Impossible in fact. He wasn't supposed to know who had done it, but he'd seen Chisel with the inspector once, just before Bowman had his picture in the paper for catching a rival drug dealer. Chisel must have shopped the dealer to Bowman. *Honour among thieves?* What idiot thought that one up?

Sam Carew. Now he was the one to watch. Far more dangerous than Bowman. Nowhere near as much of a clown as he appeared on the surface.

Sam cut a pathetic figure as he stood, bedraggled, on Kathy's doorstep.

'Can I use your phone?' he asked. 'My battery's flat.' She was in her dressing gown. 'I hope I didn't disturb you,' he added, apologetically.

'No, I was getting up anyway,' she said, 'I'd had my four hours.'

Sam didn't catch the gentle sarcasm as he walked past her. 'Good,' he said. 'It's a bit damp out there. I need to ring Sally.'

He took off his coat and looked round for somewhere to hang it. Kathy took it from him and put it over a chair.

'I was arrested last night,' he said. 'The police seemed to think I'd murdered someone. A girl called Mandy Jackson.'

'Mandy Jackson?' mused Kathy. 'Rings a bell.'

'She was the girl your brother pulled out of the fire.'

'Oh my God! What happened?'

'She was murdered last night. The police thought I might have been with her. Silly sods locked me up.'

He picked up the phone and racked his brains to remember the number of the building society where Sally worked as the manager's secretary. 'Do you have a directory?' he asked.

She bent over to look under the telephone table and picked up a phone book. The movement caused her loosely tied dressing gown to fall open, momentarily revealing her naked breasts.

Sam's eyes dwelt on the tantalising image, the picture imprinted itself on his memory, even after she covered herself up. He tried to shake it out of his head and opened the directory but the distraction of what he had seen was making it difficult to concentrate.

'Coffee?' she asked.

'Great.'

His eyes were on her, bustling around in the kitchen. He had to force his attention to looking up the number. After several wrongly dialled attempts he got through to Sally.

'Sal? ... hiya. Look, I gather Bowman was round yesterday asking questions about what time I got home ... No, it's okay now ... Well, a slight problem. I couldn't account for about an hour of my time ... before I got home. It cost me a night in the cells, can you believe that? ... What? Come on Sally, not you as well. I was driving around, I do that sometimes ... because I bloody felt like it! ... Jesus Chr ... well if you really want the truth I nipped round to Mandy Jackson's, shagged her, then killed her, satisfied?'

He slammed the phone down, knowing he was in the wrong for losing his rag with her, but he couldn't help it. There's just so much you can take in one day.

Kathy came through with the coffee. 'It didn't go well, I take it,' she said.

'I lost it,' admitted Sam. 'She was only asking me why I was driving around on my own at two o'clock in the morning and I chewed her head off.'

She handed him a cup. 'Care to tell me, or would you chew my head off as well?'

Sam looked at her and managed a wry smile. 'No, I'd never chew your head off.'

She returned his smile with interest. 'After you've finished your coffee, get out of those wet things and get in the shower.'

'Do I smell?'

'Let's just say you'd have a hard time seducing me in your present state.'

The phone rang before Sam could figure out what she meant. Kathy picked up the phone.

'Kathy Sturridge ...'

No answer.

'Hello ... Kathy Sturridge.'

The line went dead. Realisation hit them both at the same time. Kathy put the phone down and gave a slight grimace. Her eyes were saying, *Oh dear,* to Sam.

'Sally?' she guessed.

He nodded and dialled one-four-seven-one to identify the number of the last caller – as Sally probably had. It confirmed his fears. He could have rung her back to explain the innocence of his location, but he wasn't sure just how truthful that would be.

Kathy sat down on her favourite chair. Knees modestly together, her gown pulled across her front. Revealing nothing. He sat down opposite and sipped his drink under her gaze. She was such a comfortable person to be with. A similar phone conversation with her wouldn't have ended with him slamming the thing down. He was sure of that.

'Why *were* you driving round at two in the morning?' she asked, gently. It was as if she was reading his thoughts.

'Oh, you know. Things to think about.'

'Anything I might be interested in?' She was fishing.

He looked up at her. Kathy was the only good thing about his world at the moment. 'Well ... you know, a lot's been happening to me lately. I'd just helped an old pal of mine capture a local villain.'

'Yes, I heard about that. It was in the *Observer*. Along with a very old and handsome photo of you.'

'Was there? I didn't see it.'

He'd rung the *Observer* the morning after Gary Johnstone's

arrest with a full account of the story. Good publicity for the Carew Investigations Bureau, if ever it took on another case.

'Then there's all the other stuff,' he went on. 'My dad was killed, Sean was killed, Nicky Fulbright, Chisel Joo.' He shook his head, as if suddenly realising the extent of the mayhem surrounding him. 'And you know, it all seems to be centred on me, somehow. I can't figure it out. Now Mandy Jackson.'

'You certainly have a lot on your mind.'

He looked up at her, deciding to come clean for once. 'None of that was on my mind the other night.'

'Oh?'

'Sally was on my mind.'

Her eyes betrayed a glimpse of disappointment.

'Yeah,' he continued. 'I think she's great, a lovely woman. But she deserves better than me.'

He had noticed an absence of ashtrays on his last visit to her flat, so he'd then refrained from smoking. He needed one now.

'Mind if I smoke? I gather you don't.'

'You gather correctly. I won't ask how you know, I've no doubt it's somehow obvious.'

Sam smiled. 'No ashtrays. No tobacco smell about the place. I intend giving up when I move. I want my new place to smell as fresh as this.' He held up a cigarette. 'May I?'

'Oh, sorry – please do. You look as though you need one.'

Walking over to a cupboard, she brought out an ashtray, phrasing her next question in her head as she did so. 'Why does Sally deserve better than you? It sounds as if you've been a naughty boy.'

Sam tapped his head with his forefinger. 'In my mind, maybe. I haven't been naughty yet. I'm actually not very good with women. When I was a lad I was totally useless at pulling. That's why I ended up getting married. Sue sort of singled me out for marriage and I went along with it. Mind you, the fact that she was pregnant moved things along a bit.'

'So, why does Sally deserve better than you?' Kathy persevered.

Sam looked across at her. He was thirty-six years old and still embarrassed to reveal his true feelings. Jumping into bed with a woman was one thing, but this was different. In the past he'd never had any feelings as true as these. He took a deep breath and said, 'It's because of you.' Damn! His voice had let him down – it came out as a croak.

'Me?' she said, innocently.

He cleared his throat. 'Yes, you. I'm er ... I'm very much attracted to you.'

He reserved any stronger declarations for later – covering his retreat in case his feelings weren't reciprocated. There was a pause as she digested his words. Welcome words. He held his breath waiting for her reaction. She leaned over and took his hand.

'As luck would have it, Sam Carew,' she said, quietly, 'I feel the same way about you.'

'Really?'

'Really,' she confirmed.

'In fact,' he went on, 'I *was* going to say "I could fall in love with you" but I didn't want to embarrass you, just in case – you know.'

'That pretty much describes my feelings,' she confirmed.

He put down his cigarette brought her to sit beside him. Kissing her tenderly at first, then gradually with more passion. She pushed him gently away.

'Sam,' she said. 'The first time we do this, I'd prefer you not to be smelling like the inside of a fireman's boot.'

'Fair point,' he acknowledged. 'A shower it is then.' He got to his feet, then looked down at her. 'Care to join me?'

23

Dear Sam,

I've no doubt you knew it was me who rang back to check where you were ringing from. The fact that you didn't call me to explain who the woman was, told its own story. In many ways you're a coward, Sam.

Goodbye,

Sally

It had been waiting for him when he got back to his flat. The truth of the last sentence in the letter made Sam wince. He'd been hoping she wouldn't be there when he got back; that's why he'd left it so late – give her time to pack up and go. She hadn't disappointed him. He picked up the phone to dial her parents' number. That's where she'd be. True to her assessment of him, he put the phone down. Best leave it till she'd calmed down. A tearful earful from Sally was the last thing he needed. Kathy had picked him up over the last few hours and he intended to stay picked up.

They'd spent ten solid hours in bed. Really getting to know one another. Talking, laughing, loving. Everything but sleeping – and that's what he needed now. Sleep. The previous night he'd been locked in a cell, and only drunks and hardened villains get any sleep in those places. The phone rang. He looked at it for several seconds, knowing it might well be Sally. Taking a deep breath, he picked up the receiver.

'Has she gone?' asked Kathy.

'Yes,' replied Sam.

'Good. I want you to myself.'

The phone clicked off, causing Sam to smile at it. They hadn't discussed their future together. Only the past and present. That was all that mattered. Amazingly he'd found a soul-mate, he didn't think there was one out there.

But there was.

* * *

The roofers were lathing and felting when Sam arrived on site the following morning, having slept for twelve solid hours. They were laying the second line of defence lest any of the tiles let in water. This was never done in the 'good old days' when people reckoned houses were built properly. Modern roofs rarely let in water.

A wagon load of Double Roman tiles were being off-loaded and hoisted up the scaffold, ready for the roofers. Elsewhere the site was buzzing. Alec was waiting for him at the cabin door.

'Mornin'' he greeted.

'Morning Alec. Sorry about the last couple of days. I was a bit, er, pre-occupied.'

'Locked up, you mean.'

The term "shacked up" was actually on Sam's mind, but he didn't reveal it to Alec. 'Yeah, they reckoned I killed Mandy Jackson on the way home from catching Gary Johnstone. By the way, thanks for your help in that.'

'I hope you think it were worth it,' said Alec. 'The cops obviously weren't very impressed.'

'Are, but the papers were. Nice bit of publicity, see.'

'For you, not for me,' pointed out Alec, sharply. 'Don't ask me ter do it again, Sam. Once were enough.'

'Fair enough. What's on the agenda for today, boss?'

'A nice little surprise for a start.'

'Oh really? What?'

'Fosdyke's back on the job!'

'Alec, you've ruined my day.'

A morning laying bricks and concrete blocks down in the footings did much to bring a sense of normality back to Sam's world. The warm sun was drying the mud of the previous day, making work progressively easier. A muddy site is a slow site. Familiar sounds all around him. Mixer rumbling, a wagon tipping sand, Arthur, knocking at a brick with his brick-hammer to create a half bat to complete the bond at the corner of a wall. Banging, shovelling, sawing, drilling, swearing, singing, shouts of instruction and derision criss-crossing the site. Sounds of men doing a proper job. A worthwhile job. Not locking innocent people up, depriving them of their liberty. No job satisfaction in that.

Sam climbed out of the trench and surveyed his work. The footings were up to DPC level. After dinner they'd fill the cavity with mortar and lay a roll of damp course, the barrier to prevent moisture being drawn up from the ground, through capillary action, through the pores of the bricks. The building inspector would be called to inspect this stage of the work, then the joiner would lay the ground floor joists on top of the damp course. The joists would then be walled in and the brickies would proceed to bring the house up out of the ground.

'A work of art, that,' he said to Jacob, his labourer, as he checked for visual imperfections. 'It's frightening, how good I am.'

'What I like about you,' said Jacob, 'is your modesty.'

'A lot of people say that,' commented Sam. 'There must be something in it.' He looked at his watch and called out to whoever was listening. 'Right lads. Dinner!'

The ones without wives or girlfriends to pack them sandwiches, which was most of them, headed for the Station Road Café, where Melvin, the proprietor, tended to overlook hygiene in favour of value for money. In any case, building workers had a built-in immunity to germs of all kinds. The state of the average building site tea mug was testament to that. Dish of the day was written on a blackboard. *MEAT AND POTATOE PIE, MASH AND PEA'S, TREECLE PUDDING, MUG OF TEA – £2.30p. SECOND MUG OF TEA, 25p.* Every calorie and more would be worked off that afternoon. Curly sat back, belched his compliments to the chef, picked at his yellow teeth with a grimy finger and asked, 'Has anyone got a match?'

Tim, Alec's gullible lad, produced a lighter and handed it across the flimsy formica table to the Irishman, who examined it carefully, before looking up at the young joiner and asking, 'An' how am I goin' ter pick me teeth wid this?'

Tim took the lighter back, vowing never to do Curly any more favours.

The conversation drifted back and forth. The craic. Filthy jokes; loose women; piss-taking; mindless, shallow talk, covering nothing of any importance – until one of the roofers on another table piped up.

'Have they got any further findin' out who killed that lass what got murdered on t' Greerside job?'

'Nah, they locked poor old Sean up for that. It were never him what did it, not in a million bloody years,' said Alec, trudging back to the counter for a fill-up of tea.

'Dey locked yer man up,' observed Mick, 'because dey figured he was the only one what could possibly have done it. Because there was no way out of de place apart from the front door an' no one but Sean came out the front door so the polis fingered yer man for the job. It's a bit of a mystery how de actual killer got out, but it was never yer man what done it.'

In café conversation terms this was an erudite piece of logic, which produced many nods of agreement.

'It's no mystery ter me!' said a roofer.

Sam turned in his chair to face the grimy man behind him. Roofers somehow always manage to look filthy.

'How d'you work that out?' he asked, fully expecting the man to spout the usual rubbish, roofers never having been renowned for their erudition.

'If it'd been me, I'd have gorrout through t' roof,' said the roofer. He jabbed a fat finger skyward. 'Straight out, no bleedin' messing.'

Sam shook his head and turned away, satisfied that the man had nothing new to offer. 'There was no access to the roof,' he said, over his shoulder. 'No skylights, no roof windows, no holes in the roof, nothing.'

'If it'd been me,' persisted the roofer, undeterred by Sam's logic. 'I'd have whipped a few slates out and crawled through. Easiest thing in t' world ter put 'em back so it dunt look as though they've been disturbed.'

Others in the café were muttering their agreement to this theory. Sam could now see some merit in it. He heard himself saying 'Shit' under his breath. How could he have missed this?

'Then he climbs down t' scaffold an' buggers off,' continued the roofer 'Christ! Me bleedin' granny could've done that. Yer not telling me t' police never thought o' that.'

'They never thought of that,' said Sam. 'And I must admit, I never thought of it.'

The roofer shook his head despairingly at the thought of the so called experts missing something so obvious. His two colleagues smirked their agreement. 'Hey! They reckon us roofers are thick,' commented one of them. 'We can't be as thick as them bleedin' bobbies.'

'Hang on!' said Alec. 'Why would he waste time putting the slates back?'

There was a silence as both tables sought an answer. Sam came up with the obvious. 'Because he was stuck on the roof – it was only scaffolded at the front and somebody might have seen him climbing down. He could have hidden up there, behind a parapet wall, all day if necessary. Then climbed down when it was all clear. That's why he put the slates back. So no one could see how he'd got out.'

'I tell yer what,' decided Alec. 'He'd need ter be in the trade ter work all that out.'

Many heads nodded their agreement, including Melvin.

'That's if he got out that way,' said Sam. 'It makes two possibilities now.'

He thought back to all his efforts in trying to discover an escape route for the killer. Looking for tunnels, culverts, secret passages. Everything but the patently obvious. Sam shook his head, silently castigating himself. Pity he hadn't worked all this out before Sean went to trial. They certainly couldn't have convicted him on circumstantial evidence then. And that's all they had.

Sam and Jacob were in the process of laying the damp course when Fosdyke's van arrived on site. He swung his legs out of the van and proceeded to take off his shoes. There was enough undried mud on the site to merit rubber boots, especially down the trenches.

'Morning Mr. Fosdyke,' greeted Sam, cheerily. 'Leg okay now? Bad do that.'

Fosdyke grunted something unintelligible and walked around the newly built footings. Searching for a fault. He'd grown a moustache which didn't suit him at all. Sam chose to ignore it and made a mental note to warn Curly not to make any untoward comments.

'We're laying the oversite and putting the joists in as soon as you've given us the all clear,' said Sam, jabbing a thumb in the direction of a neatly stacked pile of seven by two timber.

'Polythene under the oversite and I want it a hundred mil thick. Don't try and get away with two inches, like some I know.'

'We're not like some you know.' Sam was trying hard to be civil. The oversite is the rough concrete covering the bare ground beneath the ground floor joists. Its main purpose is to keep out damp and stop the weeds growing through the floorboards.

'I assume you'll be treating the joist ends.'

'Already done,' Sam assured him.

Fosdyke stared at the joists to make sure the ends were treated against damp with creosote or the like.

'Air bricks every two metres,' said the building inspector.

'Yes, we know,' said Sam. Fosdyke was beginning to irritate him. 'They're over there beside the joists.'

Fosdyke did one more complete circuit then walked to the next block where Mick and Curly had dug the trench for the concrete foundation. The ground was clay, ideal for foundations but no good for drainage. The trench still held some of the previous day's rain. Sam followed him across.

'The bottom's sound,' Curly was assuring the inspector. He'd spotted the moustache.

'It should dry out before we concrete tomorrow,' Sam assured the sceptical inspector, whilst glaring at Curly, whose eyes were firmly fixed on Fosdyke's upper lip.

'If I had a nose like yours, Mr Fosdyke,' commented Curly, cheerfully, 'I wouldn't underline it.'

Sam glared at the Irishman. Fosdyke's mouth tightened. 'I want the trench bottomed out and six inch of stone put in, properly compacted with a mechanical tamper,' he instructed Sam, petulantly.

Sam opened his mouth to protest. It was an unreasonable request. He decided against it. They had a tamper on site. He'd make Curly do it in his own time.

'I'll be back first thing in the morning,' said Fosdyke. 'Don't pour the concrete until I've been.'

Chalky White would have trusted him, this is what annoyed Sam about the Fosdykes of this world. There was no give and take. Alec was standing in the hut door as Sam hurried to catch Fosdyke up after delivering a hasty rebuke to Curly.

'Everything okay?' smiled Alec, hopefully.

'Mr Fosdyke reckons he's never seen such tidy work in his life,' said Sam.

'Plot four's okay up to DPC,' said Fosdyke. 'I'm coming back first thing tomorrow to re-check the excavation on plot five.' He uttered the word "re-check" with some relish.

'There's a bit of water still in the trench bottom,' explained Sam to his partner, who nodded.

'Hey!' lied Alec. 'I like the tash. How long have you had that?'

Fosdye looked uncomfortable. 'I grew it while I was off sick.'

'Suits you,' lied Sam. He glanced through Fosdyke's van window at a small pile of large envelopes on the passenger seat. Cheekily he took a closer look.

'Hello – it's someone's birthday if I'm not mistaken.'

Fosdyke coloured slightly. Sam had him at a slight disadvantage.

'Yes, it's mine,' he said quickly, walking round to the driver's side as Sam and Alec offered their congratulations.

Behind Fosdyke's back, Alec mimed *going for a drink*, pointing first at Fosdyke and then at Sam, then nodding his head encouragingly. Sam glared at him then accepted the possible advantage in such a move. He leaned in the passenger window.

'Have you eaten, Mr Fosdyke?' he enquired.

'Pardon?'

'I er, I was wondering if you fancied a pie and a pint by way of celebration. It's the least we can do.'

Fosdyke hesitated at this unexpected turn of events. 'Well I, er – ' He didn't know what to say.

'In a way I feel guilty at you breaking your ankle,' added Sam. 'You'd be doing me a favour if you'd come.'

'Where were you thinking of going?' enquired Fosdyke.

Alec felt a surge of pride in his partner. Sacrificing so much for the good of the company. This would earn Sam many Brownie points.

'Clog and Shovel, I'll meet you down there,' said Sam, making up Fosdyke's mind for him.

Fosdyke nodded his acceptance of the venue and drove off. Sam looked across at Alec. 'This makes up for a lot of stuff,' he said. 'Stuff I haven't done yet.'

Fosdyke was still sitting in his van in the car park when Sam arrived. As if he didn't believe Sam had been serious. Sam knocked on his van window. The building inspector was looking at his cards, Sam turned his head to one side to read one of the messages. "Happy Birthday, Jiff. Mick".

'Jiff?' queried Sam, as Fosdyke got out of the van. Fosdyke gave an embarrassed grin.

'It's a nickname I had when I was at school,' he explained. 'JIF are my initials. You know what kids are like.'

'I know,' agreed Sam. 'All my mates called me Mad – as in Mad Carew. Then when I left school, I thought I'd got rid of it until some bright spark at the *Unsworth Observer* dug it up again.' He looked at Fosdyke's blank face, 'It's from that monologue – *The Green Eye of the Little Yellow God* – you must have heard of it.'

'No,' said Fosdyke.

'Right,' said Sam leading the way to the bar. The woman with the cat's head tattoo was there, touting for lunchtime trade. Her eyes dwelt on the two of them, Sam was conscious of it and looked the other way, at Fosdyke.

'Bitter?' he enquired.

'Just a half, Mr Carew,' decided Fosdyke. 'Is there a menu?'

Sam passed him a bar menu and ordered a pint and a half of Bootham's bitter. Fosdyke decided on a Ploughman's and Sam, having already eaten, settled for a cheese and ham toastie.

'Look,' he said, placing the drinks down on a table. 'I can't keep calling you Mr Fosdyke, any more than you can call me Mr Carew. I'd prefer you to call me Sam.'

'James,' said Fosdyke.

'Jim?' ventured Sam.

'I prefer James.'

'Quite right. There's too much of this shortening of names. Mind you, I'm not struck on Samuel.'

'Our parents tend to inflict these things upon us,' agreed Fosdyke.

'Go on,' said Sam, struggling to make conversation with this dull man. 'What's the 'I' for?'

Fosdyke hesitated, then said, 'Isaac – my parents read the bible a lot.'

The conversation flagged for a while, then Sam thought of a subject of mutual interest. 'I worked out another way the killer could have escaped from Greerside Hall.'

Fosdyke was taking a drink as Sam said it. He almost choked. Was Sam up to some sort of subterfuge? Tricking him to being alone with him, then making an accusation?

'Are you okay?' enquired Sam, solicitously.

Fosdyke gave several loud, throat-clearing coughs, attracting looks from all around the room, including the woman with the cat's head tattoo.

'Yes, thanks,' he replied at last. 'Went down the wrong way that's all.'

Sam tried to remember what he'd been talking about. 'What was I saying?' he asked.

Sam's memory lapse gave Fosdyke some relief. Had it been important to him, he wouldn't have forgotten. 'You were talking about how the killer escaped from Greerside Hall.'

'Ah, right,' said Sam. 'You see, he could have hidden behind the stairs when Dad came in the door, then sneaked out just before you arrived.'

'I always thought that was a bit unlikely,' said Fosdyke.

'I agree,' said Sam. 'But it was a possibility, and a possibility that could have got Sean off the hook.'

'I was sorry to hear about him,' said Fosdyke. 'It was a terrible thing to happen to an innocent man.'

'Terrible,' agreed Sam. 'But now I've come up with another alternative.'

'Oh?' Fosdyke's apprehension returned.

Sam jabbed a finger skyward. 'The roof,' he said.

'The roof?' repeated Fosdyke, relieved.

'Yes, don't you see? The killer went up into the roof space, prised out a few slates and crawled out, intending to climb down the scaffold. Then he realised he couldn't because there were people about, namely you and Sean and then the police and a site full of men, so he stayed up there until everyone had gone. He was probably up there all day. In the meantime he covered his tracks by replacing the roof slates.'

Sam looked for a reaction to his theory. Fosdyke nodded his head slowly, then looked up, admiringly, at Sam. 'Do you know,' he said. 'I think you're probably right.'

Alec was just putting the phone down when Sam arrived back on site, slightly bloated from his extra lunch.

'How did it go?' enquired Alec. Keeping the grin off his face with great difficulty.

'He's hard work,' said Sam.

'We must all do our bit. My bit was Mrs Quarmby, if you remember.'

'Lovely woman. Who was on the phone?'

'Mr Broughton.'

'What, from Manston Holdings?'

Alec had a grin on his face. 'He likes the way we work and wants us to put a price in for renovating an empty multi-storey office block in Market Street. By the sound of it the job's ours if our price is anything like reasonable.'

'Doing two jobs for the same firm?' pondered Sam. 'All our eggs in one basket.'

'Sam,' said Alec. 'All our eggs are in one basket now, it's just a bigger basket that's all. They're a publicly quoted company.'

'Is renovation up our street?' queried Sam.

'Why not?' said Alec. 'From what I remember the place has stood empty for a couple of years and it needs upgrading from top to toe. Six months work, regular payments. Ideal for winter, no rained-off time.'

'We'll be tied up here all winter,' pointed out Sam.

'No harm in running two jobs at once,' argued Alec.

'We'll need extra working capital,' said Sam. 'The bank won't be interested in funding a contract job. Not if we can't give them some security.'

Alec said nothing. Sam knew what he was thinking. 'You want me to put my land up as security?'

Alec shrugged. 'It'd only be for a couple of months until the job starts to pay us back.'

'Alec, the profit won't show up until the final payment.'

'Well, six months then,' conceded Alec.

Sam's face dropped. 'You know I was going to buy a house with the money. I'm sick of living in that squalid little flat.'

'Rent a bigger place,' suggested Alec, who knew he'd won the argument.

Sam accepted defeat but struck the best deal he could.

'I want you to go into my flat and renovate the hell out of it and don't come out until it's fit for the Queen to live in.'

Alec held out his hand.

'You've got a deal, Your Highness.'

24

'Sal, it's me.'

'Oh.'

Sam was ringing from his flat. His pokey little flat. Sitting in his only chair. Wondering if he was doing the right thing with his life. The woman he'd just got used to coming home to, wasn't there any more and it was his fault. Sally was decent, kind, funny, sexy, attractive and she loved him. So why was he doing this?

Sally took up the conversation. 'Who is she?'

'Her name's Kath – '

She jumped straight in with, 'I know her damn name – she's already told me that!' There was a sharp edge to her voice that Sam didn't know if he could cope with.

'She's a firefighter,' he said, more lamely than he intended.

This information drew no comment from Sally.

'She helped pull me from the fire at Chisel Joo's.'

'I thought that was a man.'

'It was – Kathy's his sister.'

He realised how odd this sounded, so he added, 'She was there as well.'

'So was Mandy Jackson,' retorted Sally. 'The girl the police thought you'd been with, the night she was killed.'

'I wasn't with Mandy Jackson.'

There was a long pause. Sam detected tears at the other end.

'Do you love her?'

A quick answer to this would have somehow been insulting to her. Insulting what they'd had together, which had been good. Better than most people experience. That's why Sally couldn't understand what he was doing.

'Do you?'

He waited another few seconds before answering.

'Yes.'

The phone clicked. The conversation was over.

James Isaac Fosdyke parked his van in the short, concrete drive-way and wondered if she was in – it would make a change. Beverley had packed her job in a week ago and since then had scarcely been at home.

Even at forty-three she was a good looking woman. Insatiable in bed. That's how they got together. He was seventeen and still at school, she was thirty-seven and just divorced. He'd gone round to do some gardening – one of his many and varied sum-mer jobs. It was a warm day and she'd invited him in for a drink of orange juice. She made all the moves. Seduced him. There was no other term for it. What else could you call swanning around in a tee shirt and nothing underneath? Not the longest T-shirt in the world either. Fosdyke was an enthusiastic victim. When you're a seventeen-year-old virgin, a good looking divorcee in a T-shirt and no knickers is hard to resist. It went on for two years, then he moved in with her. A relationship based on lust.

Her suitcases were in the hallway. Three of them, all packed. She heard him come in and walked through from the lounge to confront him.

'What's this?' he asked.

'I'm leaving you, James,' she said. 'I was going to leave you a note, but I thought you deserved more than that.'

'Leaving me?'

He wasn't expecting this. He'd often thought of leaving her, but apart from going back to his mother's, he'd nowhere to go, and no one to go to.

'Why?' he asked, huffily.

'Because you and I have come to the end of our particular road, James. We're arguing, we're being nasty to each other, and I think it's time to quit, simple as that. Unlike you, I haven't many good years ahead of me.'

Fosdyke gave a petulant snigger. 'You, you haven't got *any* good years ahead of you.'

She walked back through to the lounge, determined not to rise to his bait. He followed, convinced he could talk her out of it. He wasn't going to grovel, that wouldn't be necessary. All he had to do was switch on the charm and in five minutes they'd be in bed.

'Sorry about that,' he said. 'I didn't mean it.'

'That's the trouble, James. You *did* mean it. Anyway, what you think doesn't matter anymore. You can stay in this house until it's sold. I want to get on with my life.' She looked at him, steadily. 'By the way, the moustache doesn't suit you. You look like one of the Village People.'

He fingered the insulted hair. 'Did you purposely wait for my birthday to tell me all this, or hadn't you remembered?'

'Oh damn! Sorry about that. Mind you, you forgot mine.'

'Where will you go?' He still wasn't convinced she was serious.

She took in a breath and let it out slowly. 'Actually, I've met someone else!'

This totally threw Fosdyke. He didn't know how to handle this. 'Someone else? You're going to live with another man?'

She nodded. 'Don't look so badly done by,' she said. 'You haven't been exactly pure and innocent recently. Over the last six months you've been coming in late, smelling of at least six different types of perfume. You don't need me.'

'So what? We had an understanding. You went your way, I went mine. So long as we eventually came back to the same b –'

She stopped him with a wave of her hand. 'Okay, I know, it's just that, well I'm getting too old for all that.'

'I don't want you to go.'

She ignored him. 'And if you don't mind my saying so,' she added, 'you've been acting very odd lately.'

'Odd?' he protested. 'Bev, I've had a broken bloody ankle, or hadn't you noticed?'

'It's more than that. Anyway it's all academic now. You're not my problem any more.'

'I don't want you to go,' he repeated.

'James, I'm going. Whether you want me to or not. Please don't make it difficult. I'm met a lovely man called Dave. He's my age and I want to spend the rest of my life with him. You and I were good while it lasted, but our relationship was only based on sex. We never had anything else in common.'

'Please, Bev. I don't want you to go.' He was grovelling now.

She made to walk past him, but he blocked her path.

'James, I'm ringing for a taxi.'

'Wait!' It was half command, half plea.

She shook her head and sat down. 'It won't do any good.'

He sat down opposite her, his mind in a turmoil. Bev was his, no one else's. She'd no right to leave him. They belonged together until he decided otherwise. No one else had the right to split them up. Christ, he'd killed Nicky because of her! She'd wanted him to leave Bev and go with her. Nicky couldn't understand what he saw in a woman as old as Bev. She'd threatened to tell her he'd been going with prostitutes. Beverley wouldn't have liked that. That's what the fight had been about. Chisel had loaned Nicky to him in exchange for him taking a relaxed attitude towards Chisel's house renovations. Nicky had decided they were an item. No way did he want a prostitute as a steady girlfriend. The argument had got out of hand. A night together inside a sleeping bag in Greerside Hall had ended with him killing her. Basically he was simply trying to shut her up, stop her strident yelling. He could hear someone outside and that someone would be bound to recognise him if they came into the house.

And now all this was for nothing. He'd killed Mandy to stop her blabbing about Nicky. That's two murders he'd committed because he didn't want to lose Bev, and two more dead on top of that. Now she was leaving him. Where was the justice in that? There wasn't any. He'd have to make his own justice. He found himself grinning. He'd no idea why.

'Before you leave, I've got something I want to tell you,' he said.

She looked at her watch, impatiently. 'Will it take long?'

He didn't seem to hear her. 'I went for a drink with a builder today, a bloke called Sam Carew.'

'Yes, I remember him. His father was killed at the same time as that girl –'

Fosdyke spoke across her answer, as if she wasn't there. She found it slightly odd.

'He was telling me how the killer got away. He had two theories. One that the killer hid behind the stairs and ran out just after his father came in – but before I arrived – and another that the killer escaped by breaking through the roof slates and putting them back afterwards to cover his tracks. I prefer the second one. What do you think?'

'What the hell does it matter what I think, James? I'm ringing for that taxi.' She stood up, but he pushed her back down, scaring her.

'Wait, I haven't come to the best bit yet.' His grin was scary now. 'You see, neither theory was correct. The killer just walked out of the back door. He had a key, you see. The owners had given him one when the job started.'

She didn't like this one bit. 'This is fascinating, James, but I want to leave right now!'

'Not until I've finished.'

Fosdyke stood over her, a hand on each of her shoulders. She wasn't a big woman and he held her down with ease.

'The killer let himself out the back door, got in his van and drove round to the front, where he found a mad Irishman standing over two bodies – the girl he'd just killed and Ernest Carew, the builder, who for some inexplicable reason had just been killed by the mad Irishman.'

'James, please, let me go. You're frightening me.'

Fosdyke looked at her, as if surprised that she wasn't dying to hear the end of his story.

'No, no. You must hear the rest,' he said, in a hurt voice. 'This is absolutely fucking brilliant.'

'Okay,' she tried to smile. 'I'm listening.'

Fosdyke increased the pressure on her shoulders and continued his story.

'This man – the killer – rang for the police, and while he was waiting for them, he walked through to the back door and bolted it from the inside. Then I picked up the sleeping bag Nicky and I had spent the night in, and put it in my van.'

He grinned sheepishly, like a naughty boy who's just been caught fibbing. 'Oops! Gave myself away. Never mind. I never could fool you for very long. You were always too clever for me.'

Beverley was crying and shaking with fear now. The realisation had struck home. Fosdyke ignored her tears and continued with his story: 'Anyway, the mad Irishman was feeling far too sorry for himself to notice me covering my tracks. Unfortunately for him, I made him the prime suspect for both murders. That was cool-headed don't you think? I bet your new feller's not as cool-headed as that.'

'Please James, please let me go.'

'But I can't, can I? You know too much. That's why I had to kill Mandy.' He was smiling as he spoke, as if trying to get his point home in the nicest manner.

'Oh my God, James! You're sick, you need help.'

She didn't say any more. His hands, experienced now, were squeezing the life out of her.

Sam tried Kathy a couple of times, but he'd no idea what shifts she was working, that was something they'd have to sort out. One of many things. It even crossed his mind to ring the Fire Station, but he sensibly restrained himself. God! He was besotted, get a grip Carew. He needed a friendly voice. Someone who didn't think he was a pillock. The list of candidates was small. Darren Feast was pretty much at the top. He'd never turn his back on him. Sam shook his head at his unfortunate choice of phrase and dialled his pal's number. An answering machine told him that Darren Feast was out, but if you'd care to leave your name, number, age and colour of eyes, he may, or may not, get back to you.

Sam shook his head once again at his pal's outrageous behaviour, and him a schoolteacher as well. He dialled Sue's number, she wasn't a candidate, but he knew two who were.

'Hello it's me.'

'Who's me?'

'Sam.'

She recognised his voice all right and was only saying *who's me?* for effect, to emphasise how unimportant he was in her life. But he let it go.

'I was wondering if the boys fancied going to the pictures,' he asked, cheerfully. 'I haven't seen them for a while.'

Sue put the phone down on the table and, after a discussion that Sam couldn't quite make out, Tom came on the line.

'Hiya, Dad. Where're we going?'

The boy's decision had already been made, much to Sam's delight. If only grown-ups could be as uncomplicated. Sam's empathy with children had much to do with his own juvenile mind – although he would be the last to admit it.

'Wherever you like. I fancy seeing the latest *Lord Of The Rings* myself.'

'Seen it twice.'

'What about Jake? Has he seen it?'

'Twice.'

'Fair enough. What else do you fancy?' asked Sam, hiding his disappointment. He could a hear a discussion taking place, Sam's own preference was being taken into consideration, which he thought was very decent of them.

'We'll go see *Lord Of The Rings* again if you like.'

'Great,' said Sam. 'Put your mum on.'

Another discussion and Sue came back on. 'I gather they're taking you to see *Lord Of The Rings*. Honestly Sam, they've seen it twice.'

'It was their choice, I had nothing to do with it!'

God! She was moaning about which picture he was taking them to see now, no wonder they didn't get on. 'Tell them I'll call round about seven.'

Having a garage with door directly into the kitchen is a tremendous asset to a murderer who needs to dispose of a body without arousing the neighbours' suspicion. Fosdyke turned his van round and backed right in, closing the up-and-over door behind him.

His ultimate plan hadn't formed in his mind yet, but his preliminary action was obvious. To get the body out of the house before darling Dave calls round to see where she is. Fosdyke figured he'd probably phone first, but he couldn't take any chances. He loaded her into the back of the van with some ease, threw her suitcases in after her, then he went back inside to wait for dark.

He knew he couldn't keep her in the van for long. Vague threads of ideas were beginning to knit themselves together in his mind. She must be buried where no one would find her, ever. Never mind these shallow graves that bone idle murderers always seemed to settle for. He could never understand the mentality of someone who'd risk their future freedom by killing someone, then couldn't be bothered digging a deep enough hole to hide them in.

He mentally pictured the various sites in his area. Who was doing groundworks? How could he bury a body without anyone spotting it? The grin returned. Providence had provided him with the perfect place. The phone rang just once. He picked it up, apprehensively, it could be Dave. It was his mother.

'Just ringing to wish you happy birthday, love.'

'Thanks, Mum.'

'Are you having a nice time?'

'Not bad.'

'Are you and ... Beverley, going anywhere nice?'

His mother forced the name "Beverley" from her lips with obvious distaste. Mrs Fosdyke didn't approve. The woman was a hussy, much too old for her boy. She never visited them, apart from just once, out of curiosity. Her boy would be much better off at home with his mother.

Fosdyke paused, thinking quickly. 'Beverley and I have split up, Mum.' He smiled to himself as he said it. It was the right thing to say under the circumstances.

'Really? When did this happen?'

'About three hours ago.'

'James, I'd be lying if I said wasn't pleased. But on your birthday? She could have shown a bit more consideration.'

'It was mutual, Mum. I'm okay.'

There was a knock at the door which saved him from going into detail.

'There's someone at the door, Mum.'

'Probably one of your friends, come to take you out.'

'Probably, I'll ring you tomorrow, bye.'

He put the phone down on all her usual farewell platitudes and went to the door. Behind the obscure glass he made out the shape of a man. Steeling himself, he opened it.

The man was tall, middle-aged and obviously middle-class. Soberly and expensively dressed in a dark suit, with an open neck shirt, his only concession to a warm summer evening. He looked like a man who was usually very sure of himself, this occasion being the exception.

'I'er – is Beverley in?'

Fosdyke hesitated before answering. 'Are you Dave, by any chance?'

'David Renishawe.' David didn't offer to shake hands, he didn't think it appropriate. 'Well?' he enquired.

Fosdyke conjured up a sigh of annoyance. 'You'd better come in.' He turned and led the way through to the lounge where he'd killed Beverley just over three hours ago.

'Look,' said David, following him in, his self-confidence back in place. 'I know this is probably awkward, but would you mind telling me what's happening. Beverley was supposed to meet me three hours ago.'

'Good old Bev,' grumbled Fosdyke. 'Dropped me in it again! She told me you might phone – she never mentioned anything about you coming round.'

'I don't understand.'

Fosdyke turned to face him. His face a mixture of annoyance and embarrassment. 'As she no doubt told you, Bev and I split up. All very amicable. It's been coming on for a while. Anyway, she decided to leave this evening. A sort of twisted birthday present to me.' He inclined his head to the cards on the dresser. 'It's my birthday today. I appreciate it in a way. She said I could stay in the house until it's sold, which I thought was very good of her.'

'You haven't told me where she is!' said David, impatiently.

'That's the point,' said Fosdyke. 'That's why it's so embarrassing having to face you like this. When she went out of the door, her parting shot was, "If Dave rings, tell him I'm sorry." Then she cleared off, just like that.'

David sat down, baffled and saddened. 'I don't believe this.'

'I thought you wouldn't. Can I get you a drink?'

David waved away the offer with a confused hand. 'Have you any idea where she went?'

'She wouldn't say. But I'm pretty certain she was going abroad. She had me searching for her passport for her.'

There was a look of complete disbelief on the man's face.

'Look,' offered Fosdyke. 'If you don't believe me and you think she's changed her mind and she's hiding from you, feel free to have a look round. She's taken all the good stuff from her wardrobe.'

Prising himself up from the chair, David shook his head. 'None of this makes sense,' he said. 'I loved her. Christ, I left my wife and kids for her. She knew that. She bloody knew that, and she does this to me – why?' He was looking to Fosdyke for an answer.

'Look, I'm sorry, I don't know. What do you want me to say?'

'She just isn't like this.' David looked questioningly at the younger man. 'Is she?'

Fosdyke gave him what his mother would call an "Old fashioned" look, his expression implying a knowledge of Beverley that David perhaps wasn't party to. 'Do you mind me asking –

how long you've actually known her?' Fosdyke asked the question with an appropriate degree of hesitation.

David didn't answer at first. He was treading on tricky ground here. Still, there was no harm in telling the truth at this stage.

'About four months,' he said. 'April the second, actually. It's one of those silly dates you tend to remember.'

Fosdyke nodded his understanding. 'Ours was July the nineteenth. I've known her six years and I still can't weigh her up. She's the most unpredictable person I've ever come across. On top of which, I couldn't trust her as far as I could throw her. But with us it didn't matter all that much.' He looked at David's crestfallen face. 'It'd matter a lot to you though, I suppose.'

David turned to go. His world had collapsed. Fosdyke followed him to the door, which he opened for him.'Look Dave, er, David. I feel bad about this – which is bloody annoying, because it's not my fault.'

Nodding his acceptance of this, David stepped out of the door. Fosdyke called after him.

'If I hear from her I'll let you know. Even if she makes me promise not to. I think what she's done to you stinks.'

'Thanks,' said David, half turning. 'I'd appreciate that.' He took out his wallet and handed Fosdyke a card. 'Ring me if you hear anything.'

'I'll do that.'

Fosdyke closed the door and felt a wave of triumph envelop him. No sense of bereavement at the loss of his partner, just satisfaction in the knowledge that she hadn't got away with doing the dirty on him. She'd got her just desserts. There was an added bonus to all this – he could now live here as long as he wanted. Who was going to kick him out? This was a definite improvement on waiting for her to sell it from under him. He was so good at this, getting rid of Bev's body would be a piece of cake.

As they drove home, Tom and Jake were having an in-depth discussion as to the relative merits of the latest *Lord Of The Rings* compared to the previous ones.

'I thought the first was the best,' said Tom. 'By the time you get to the third you lose track of what its all about.'

'The special effects were far superior on this one.'

'How could they be superior? All three films were made at the same time.'

'What difference does that make?'

'Stands to reason,' said Tom.

'*We* were made at the same time, but I'm superior to you,' Jake pointed out.

'In what way?'

'In every way.'

'You fart louder than me,' Tom conceded. 'I'll grant you that.'

'Now then children,' said Sam. 'Hey, I bet old Tolkien never imagined anyone could do this with his book. I bet he'd be well chuffed.'

'Tom hasn't even read it,' said Jake.

'I've read *The Hobbit*,' said Tom, 'same difference.'

'No, it's not.'

'It isn't, is it, Dad?' Jake said, trying to recruit Sam on his side.

'No idea,' Sam admitted. 'I haven't read either.'

'You're both philistines,' said Jake, who had battled his way through both books.

Sam grinned at the banter. He felt comfortable in the boys' company. Not wanting to go straight back he decided to drive past the Fletchers Field site. It was slightly out of his way, but it did no harm to have a quick look. They'd hired a security firm, who looked in on the place from time to time during the night, but they couldn't stop the continuous thieving of bricks and bags of cement. Anything that wasn't nailed down.

He slowed down as he passed the site and squinted up the short road. Nothing unusual. Picking up speed he passed a familiar van – Fosdyke's van – with the man himself driving, all on his own on his birthday night. It didn't surprise Sam. Fosdyke was a real oddball. He put the building inspector out of his mind and returned his attention to the discussion, which now involved both boys talking like Gollum. It had Sam laughing out loud and wondering where the boys had got their talent as mimics from.

Fosdyke had spotted Sam's Range Rover. Which was why he drove straight on. He didn't want Sam looking in his rear view mirror, wondering why he was turning into the site. Pulling up further along the road, he drove slowly back. A sign at the entrance caught his eye, he hadn't noticed this before:

This site is regularly patrolled by Farrah Security Ltd.

It would do no harm to wait and find out how regularly they patrolled.

It was a good hour before a small white van arrived and drove onto the site. A man got out and shone a powerful flash-light all around for a few seconds, then got back in the van and drove off.

Fosdyke waited until he was definitely gone and wasn't try-ing to catch any hidden thieves out by coming straight back. He waited ten minutes, leaving him at least fifty minutes to do what he had to do – loads of time. He drove the van as near to the foundation of plot five as he could, then taking a shovel with him, he jumped into the shallow trench, at the bottom of which was the six inches of crushed limestone stone he'd ordered Carew and Son to lay earlier in the day. Working by the light of a bright moon, it scraped away easily. He cleared away the stone for a five foot length of trench, then started to dig another foot out of the exposed clay. It was a job that Curly would have done in ten minutes. Fosdyke took half an hour and was totally exhausted. Climbing out of the trench, he belatedly realised he was going to need all of the time available. He picked up Beverley's body, now wrapped in a bin-liner. It seemed to have put on weight. He struggled to the edge of the trench dropped it in, slipping in himself and landing prostrate on top of his former mistress's corpse. His breath was coming in short bursts. If any-one came on site now, it would all be over for him. They'd prob-ably tie him up with all three murders. Stop thinking like that, James! Keep your head. Take a breather. You've got plenty of time yet. He sat on the edge of the trench for a few minutes until his breathing returned to something like normal, then he curled Beverley's body into the newly excavated hole. Rigor mortis was setting in, forcing him to dig the trench a little longer to accommodate an outstretched leg, protruding through the bottom of the bag. He then shovelled the limestone back to cover her, using additional stone from a pile near the trench. Levelling it and stamping down on it in an attempt to compact it – as per his own instructions. He took a torch from his pocket and shone it along the length of the foundation. As far as he could tell the trench bottom looked okay, level up to the point where it was stepped up to accomodate higher ground. He scattered the extra clay he'd just dug out, then got back in his van. Tomorrow would see whether he was in the clear or not.

Preferably he'd like to be many miles away when the concrete was poured. But common sense told him he should be there, using whatever influence he had to make his plan work. That night he didn't sleep.

Sam was surprised to see Fosdyke's van following him on to the site. He looked at his watch, eight o'clock. Fair play to the bloke, he said he'd be here first thing.

'Morning James,' he greeted his new pal.

'Morning, Sam,' Fosdyke was slightly more hesitant with this new first name familiarity.

Alec was standing at the door of the hut, impressed at the camaraderie between the two of them. 'The concrete's ordered for half past eight,' he called out to Fosdyke. 'I'd appreciate it if you'd have a quick look at the trench. If there's a problem I'll have to put the concrete back.'

'There won't be a problem,' grinned Sam. 'This is Carew and Son, not Bodgit and Scram.'

Fosdyke forced a smile as he walked to the trench, desperately hoping no one would come with him. Sam shattered this particular hope. The inspector walked all around the excavation, then looked up at Sam.

'This is fine,' he said.

'Good,' said Sam. 'Fancy a brew? You look knackered.'

'I've felt better,' admitted Fosdyke, walking away from the trench. He didn't want anyone near it until the concrete was poured.

'Out last night?' enquired Sam. Wondering whether to mention that he'd seen him. Fosdyke beat him to it.

'You might say that. I was driving around trying to get my act together. My girlfriend left me last night.'

'On your birthday?' said Sam with genuine sympathy. 'Jesus, that's rough.'

They reached the site hut. 'I wouldn't mind a cup of tea,' Fosdyke said. 'I didn't sleep much last night.'

'Alec!' shouted Sam, through the door. 'Put a brew on.'

'Has he okayed it?' asked Alec.

'Course he has.'

'Good. He can have a brew then.'

The concrete arrived early, which is not unusual for the first load from a concrete plant. Later loads are not so punctual. Curly directed the reversing wagon up the site, his instructions ending with a loud "Whoa," as the wagon reached its nearest proximity to the excavation. He swung out the chute and helped the driver clip an extension on to it, so the concrete could be delivered directly into the trench, in which Mick, Curly and Jacob were waiting, shovels at the ready. Fosdyke's heart almost stopped as Curly shouted out.

'Dere's a bit of a soft spot here!'

He was standing directly above Beverley's body, stamping his foot to demonstrate the problem area. Sam glared at him. What a time to find something like this out!

'How come you didn't notice this yesterday? Or were you too idle to dig it out then?'

'I tell yer boss,' protested Curly. 'There was no soft spot here yesterday. If there'd been a soft spot I'd have dug it out for sure.'

Sam turned to Fosdyke. 'Sorry about this. We'd better dig it out before we pour the concrete. Better safe than sorry.'

Fosdyke panicked. 'I said it's okay! Carry on with the concreting. I can't wait here all day!'

Sam could scarcely believe the transformation in his attitude. One day he's the world's worst nitpicker, the next day he's lax to the point of incompetence. Sam's own common sense prevailed.

'I can't do that, James. You know as well as me that a building's only as strong as its foundation. For what it is, we'd better dig it out.' He looked at the building inspector, who was sweating profusely. The man wasn't well, nor was he thinking straight. His personal problems were clouding his judgement. The concrete wagon was revving up impatiently, in readiness for pumping it out.

'Hold it a minute!' ordered Sam. 'We'll have to dig that soft spot out first.'

'I'll have ter charge waiting time!' warned the driver, who was in a hurry. Drivers are always in a hurry.

'We're allowed fifteen minutes standing time on site,' Sam reminded him, looking at his watch. 'Up to now you've had less than five!'

'It'll take more than any ten bloody minutes ter dig yon out,' grumbled the driver. 'I've three drops ter make afore dinner.'

'What do yer want me to bloody do?' snapped an irate Sam. 'We can't start concreting till we've dug the bloody soft spot out! Show a bit of sense!'

'I could ring base up and ask if I can swap deliveries,' suggested the driver, who owned his own wagon and made precious little by standing on site. 'I'd be back here afore ten o'clock.'

This sounded reasonable to Sam. The only problem was Fosdyke, who obviously wasn't well enough to give them the go ahead once the excavation was ready. He looked as if he belonged in bed. Of all the building inspections, this was the one that needed to be done correctly. The last thing a builder needs is for the someone to complain that he hasn't had his foundations checked properly. The ramifications can be far reaching.

Fosdyke couldn't believe what was happening. The one and only time he didn't want builders to be conscientious and they were doing this to him. It was a conspiracy, as if everyone knew what was down there. Sweat ran down his face, he was struggling for breath, quaking with fear. He might as well tell them about the body and be done with it. There was no way out of this. The bastards had got him.

'Jesus! Yer man's shivering like a shitin' dog,' commented Curly to Mick, but loud enough for Fosdyke to hear, had he been listening.

'Are you okay, James?' enquired Sam, genuinely concerned. Fosdyke looked as though he was about to pass out.

The building inspector didn't hear him, his world was collapsing. He was going to jail.

'We could put some reinforcement across it,' suggested Alec, who had appeared behind them.

Fosdyke heard his voice vaguely through his inner panic. The suggestion taking some time to register in his brain. He turned round and said, 'What?'

'We could put some reinforcing over the soft spot to make a reinforced beam,' said Alec.

'I never thought of that,' grinned Sam. 'Course we can. Or we could bridge over it with a long lintol.'

'Either or,' agreed Alec. 'What do you think, Mr Fosdyke?'

Fosdyke was breathing great sighs of relief, which everyone took to be some sort of chronic virus he'd picked up. He'd have thought of this himself had his mind been right. 'Have you any reinforcing bars?' he asked, between gasps.

'We've got some nine millimetre mesh,' said Sam, pointing to a pile of steel mesh.

'Right, put some of that right across the soft spot to form a reinforced beam,' instructed Fosdyke, his breathing easier now.

'That'll do fer me, mister,' said a delighted Curly. He was already out of the trench, grabbing a pair of bolt croppers on his way to the pile of mesh.

'You can start pouring now,' said Sam to the relieved wagon driver, who pressed the switch that sent the lumpy grey mixture flowing down the chute and oozing into the trench above

Beverley's body, to be pushed and paddled all round the perimeter by the busy shovels of Mick and Jacob. Curly arrived with a piece of four-inch-square steel mesh, ten feet long and eighteen inches wide, which he pressed deep into the concrete, directly above Beverley's body.

'I think we'll have another length on top of that,' ordered Fosdyke, looking at Sam. 'I don't know what I was thinking about earlier.'

'You're not thinking straight, that's what's wrong with you,' observed Sam. 'Women do that to you. To tell the truth, I had a bit of it myself recently. Mind you, it was my fault, so I've only myself to blame.'

Fosdyke wiped the perspiration from his forehead with the palm of his hand, which he then wiped on his coat. 'I suppose I was a bit to blame myself,' he admitted.

'We're none of us squeaky clean where women are concerned,' grinned Sam. 'I reckon you should go straight to that phone, ring in sick, go to the pub at dinner time and get totally rat-arsed.'

'I think I'll just do that. I might as well wait till you've finished concreting first.'

'You know what your trouble is,' said Sam. 'You're too bloody conscientious. You want to lighten up a bit.'

25

Fosdyke had been through every item in each of her three suitcases. Checked every garment for personalised labels. He wasn't aware that she had any such labels, but he was eliminating every possibility. Satisfied, he then put the contents back in the cases and stuck the suitcases into drawstring dustbin liners, which he took to the White Cross Road Household Waste and Re-Cycling Centre and threw them into a skip. He'd already burnt her passport and all the contents of her handbag in the garden incinerator, before carefully shovelling up the ashes and placing them into a bin bag, which went the same way as the suitcases. Chalky White had almost sounded sympathetic when he rang in sick that morning.

'Take as long as you like, lad, we'll manage.' Chalky almost added "Like we have for the last three months". But he didn't.

Come lunchtime, Fosdyke had finished. Wiped away every trace of Beverley McAndrews. If anyone came looking for her, he could prove she'd left of her own accord, or was planning to. If push came to shove, Darling Dave would have to back him up. He grinned to himself. Darling Dave, the Unwitting Accomplice. If only he knew.

Thinking clearly now he realised that not reinforcing the concrete over the top of Beverley's body would have been potentially disastrous. In time the concrete would have subsided, causing cracks in the wall, causing a structural investigation which would reveal the body of his mistress. What the hell had he been thinking of? Providence had come to his rescue. It was up to him now to capitalise on his luck and to make sure the Fletcher's Field houses were built to last. He didn't want some future demolition contractor having to knock down a jerry-built development, unearthing a fifty year old skeleton and tracing her back to him. Carew and Son wouldn't be putting a foot wrong. No corners would be cut. He'd see to that.

26

Curly knelt beside the trench and leaned into it, placing a three foot spirit level on top of the hardening concrete. The bubble settled dead centre. He looked up at Mick.

'That's near enough, fer me,' he reported.

'Near enough's not good enough, it has to be dead on,' said Mick.

'It is dead on.'

'That's near enough,' said Mick.

They re-commenced stacking concrete foundation blocks in handy piles around the plot, in readiness for the brickies to start on the footings the following day. Sam came over to have a look at the foundation.

'Have you checked it for level?'

'It's near enough,' reported Curly.

Sam knew the rest of the routine but he couldn't be bothered. He knew it would be dead on. Mick and Curly had their faults but they knew the job inside out. Skilled labourers. A man approached. Forties, pale, unshaven, watery eyes lined in black.

'Are yer setting men on?' he asked.

'We might have something for a skilled labourer,' said Sam.

'I've done a bit,' said the man.

'Such as?'

The man shrugged. 'Nowt clever. Yer know. Diggin', loadin', bit o' this, bit o' that. Turn me hand to owt, me.'

He looked down at the foundation just completed by the two Irishmen. 'I can do all that. Layin' cement an' stuff.'

'What about mixing?'

'I can work a cement mixer as good as anybody. Handy lad me.'

Sam regarded him, steadily. 'I wish I could help, mate. But I reckon you've just been laid off from the pit. You're not in the trade are you?'

The man's face dropped. 'That bloody obvious is it?'

'Sort of,' admitted Sam. 'It's round your eyes, mate. No colour in your face either.'

'They laid twenny off this mornin'' admitted the man. I thought I'd come straight here afore anyone else turned up.'

'Jimmy Dickinson's looking for lads,' Sam advised.

The man nodded and turned to go. Dickinsons were building a large development not far away. Sam shouted after him.

'Word of advice. It's not cement, it's concrete. And nobody in the trade would ever call that a cement mixer.' He pointed to the mixer rumbling away in the distance.

The man grinned and raised a finger of acknowledgement. 'Concrete mixer?' he checked.

'Just a mixer. Best of luck, mate.'

He looked down at Mick and Curly, glorying in their new status as skilled men. He deflated them with, 'It could have taken days to train him up to be a fully fledged shit-kicker, like you two. I just haven't got the time.'

He walked back to where he'd been laying facing bricks on plot two. Life here was normal, why was he making things hard for himself by trying to do the police's job for them? Then he thought of his dad and Sean and Mandy Jackson – even Nicky Fulbright whom he'd never met – and then of Bowman, bent as a nine bob note and in charge of the investigations. He'd just answered his own question.

Sam and Kathy took a week off work to get to know each other. He drove her down to St. Ives in Cornwall to add to his fond memories of the place. Still unspoiled, everything where it had been when he'd last visited as a teenage boy.

September sunshine warmed their pale bodies as they basked on tiny Porthgwidden beach and surfed on Porthmeor, Kathy amazing Sam with her skill on the board. They rented a miniscule fisherman's cottage on The Digey, from where they emerged each lunchtime for a drink in The Sloop.

To her mock annoyance, he laughed at the caricature of her, drawn by the ancient artist on the harbour wall and she bought him a painting of The Harbour by Moonlight, probably the hundredth version by the artist who, by this time, had perfected his technique. Sam bought Kathy a gold ring depicting the St. Ives skyline. She slid it onto the third finger of her left hand, saying it was the only ring she'd ever want from him. Soppy, sentimental stuff. Happy people. A happy week. Their love firmly cemented in this quaint old place.

The next three months turned up no clues, nothing to go on. According to Owen, Bowman was only making token noises whenever he felt pressure from above. The murder of a known prostitute didn't present a high priority, especially when the investigation might prove awkward for him. Until Sean's appeal was heard, the other two murders were resolved cases.

Sally had made a dignified exit from his life, unlike a lot of women, who would have sought revenge and retribution. Not Sally. In a way it made Sam feel worse. She placed herself beyond criticism, even from Kathy.

Summer turned into Autumn, rain soaked the site with seasonal regularity and Alec was chomping at the bit to get into the Market Street job. He'd submitted his price and followed it up with several phone calls. Mr Broughton assured Alec that all was well, but he must remember that Manston holdings is a multi-national company and the Market Street job is just one of many demanding their attention. However, the contract wasn't being put to anyone else at the moment. They were simply awaiting certain planning consents, which were a foregone conclusion.

Fosdyke was back to being a pain in the arse. Then he mentioned something to Sam about moving out of his girlfriend's house and renting a small place for himself.

'There's a flat to let below mine,' suggested Sam, wondering why on earth he'd said it; he could do without a prat like Fosdyke living underneath him. Still, he'd be moving out himself soon. Moving in with Kathy was the obvious next step. Alec might be a bit miffed at just having spent good money making

Sam's flat fit to live in, but his bachelor days were well and truly over, Kathy was the light of his life.

Living in Beverley's house was proving awkward for Fosdyke. Friends and relatives turning up, ringing up, letters arriving for her, bills, bank statements. He could do without all that. He'd lost his rag a couple of times when people insisted he must have some clue as to her whereabouts. To cap it all, some relative reported her missing, meaning he had the police snooping round asking stupid questions. Where was she? When did you last see her? How the hell should he know? She'd left him for God's sake. All he knew was that she'd gone to live abroad with some Latin toy boy. She had a thing about Italians.

'The owner left me a key in case of emergency,' said Sam. 'I'll show you round if you like.'

'Isn't there an estate agent?' enquired Fosdyke who liked to do things by the book. Even murder.

'Hartley's,' said Sam. 'I'm sure they won't mind.'

'Fair enough, I'll call round this evening. Seven o'clock all right?'

'Seven it is. Forty-three Burroughs Walk.'

'Forty-three, right.'

David Renishawe had had a tortuous time. He'd slunk back to his family in Leeds, cap in hand. There was nowhere else to go. He'd lost the trust of his wife and the respect of his two teenage children. 'There's no fool like an old fool, Dave,' his colleagues had said, as much out of embarrassment as anything else. 'There but for the grace of God,' many of them thought, especially the ones who'd been introduced to Beverley McAndrew, and at least one who'd taken full advantage of the introduction behind David's back.

Sam went down to meet Fosdyke. He'd been keeping an eye out through the window and saw the van come down the street. He didn't want him coming into his flat. No way did he want

Fosdyke as his friend, no matter how much this would please Alec.

He watched as Fosdyke got out of his van and stared at the flat for quite some time before making his way over to Sam.

'How old are these places?'

Sam shrugged. 'Pre-First World War, couldn't say exactly.'

'What is it? One house divided into two flats?'

'More or less. There's a floor above me, but the owner hasn't done anything with it. They're not much to shout about inside, but that's pretty much reflected in the rent. I've just had mine done out, so it's just about habitable. You'd need to do the same.'

He let Fosdyke into the ground floor flat and followed him from room to room. A short journey.

The living room was dominated by an old five-seater settee. Odd patches of latex foam were visible through the worn, maroon moquette. An old dresser stood in a corner, heavy and scratched and ugly with a three panelled mirror – all three panels cracked. The dining table and chairs looked to have been bought at the same furniture auction. Given away for peanuts when no bids were offered. The ubiquitous wood-chip wallpaper clung tenaciously to the walls, thinly painted with magnolia emulsion. A carpet, once expensive, probably laid in the fifties when the house was still respectable, was now wafer thin and worn through to the lino beneath. A house clearance man would have baulked at offering two balloons and a goldfish for the lot.

Sam saw the expression on Fosdyke's face. 'It'd make good firewood,' he grinned.

'Wouldn't it just,' agreed Fosdyke. 'It looks as though squatters have been living here. Phew! Smells like it as well.'

Sam grinned, ruefully. 'Next best thing. A bunch of weirdos. Forever burning incense and candles and stuff. If this place had gone up in smoke, I'd have gone up with it. I was glad to see the back of them. My bedroom's directly above here.'

Fosdyke looked up at the ceiling. At ornate cornices, hung with cobwebs, and an elaborate plaster ceiling rose, from the centre of which hung a single dusty bulb, now attracting a noisy, fluttering moth. The original lathe and plaster ceiling had obviously been replaced with the more modern plaster boards.

'By rights that ceiling should be double boarded to give one hour fire protection.' Fosdyke was reciting fire regulations.

'Tell me about it,' agreed Sam, lighting a cigarette. 'Do you ...?' He offered Fosdyke one. His offer was brusquely refused.

'Never touch the things.'

'I shouldn't really,' Sam said. 'But every time I vow to give them up, something arrives to worry me into carrying on.'

Fosdyke looked at him, curiously. 'Did you ever get anywhere with that Greerside Hall – thing?' He chose the last word for want of a better description of what had gone on that day.

'Not really.'

'I suppose you've given up on it, have you?'

Fosdyke asked the question with disguised hope. His words injected a sense of guilt into Sam for his recent lack of momentum over the whole business. It was all right him criticising Bowman for his apathy. He was just as bad himself.

'As a matter of fact,' said Sam, 'I'm determined to get to the bottom of it, if it's the last thing I do.' Somehow, just saying the words to someone helped with his commitment. 'The police,' he added, 'are a total waste of time. They haven't fully accepted Sean Henry's innocence. It could be another two years before his appeal's heard. Until that time he's technically guilty.'

'So, as far as the police are concerned, there isn't a crime to solve?' Fosdyke was contriving to sound more polite than actually interested.

'Correct,' agreed Sam, appreciating Fosdyke's polite interest. Maybe he wasn't such a bad bloke after all. 'Although it's all tied up with the Mandy Jackson murder, which Inspector Bowman is following up with his usual diligence.' He found it hard to keep the sarcasm from his voice when he spoke about Bowman.

'Sounds to me like you're the only person likely to get to the bottom of it.'

'You're not wrong there, James,' said Sam. 'Sometimes it takes a bloke like me, who's constantly got the job in mind, to pick up a clue that no one else would. Sometime, somewhere, maybe next week, maybe next year, I'll spot something or hear something that'll point me in the right direction. It'll be a clue the killer doesn't even know he's left.'

Fosdyke looked around for another few minutes, saying nothing, deep in thought. Sam waited by the door, twiddling the key in his hand, allowing the man his own space.

'It needs work,' said Fosdyke. 'A lot of work.'

'Ah, you mean you don't like it,' perceived Sam, hopefully. 'Look, it's no skin off my nose.'

Fosdyke laughed, thinly – all he was capable of. Sam's determination to one day solve the murders had rattled him. 'Well, I'll have to give it some thought,' he said. At that particular moment a very different thought was running through his head. Yet another plan was forming. 'Thanks for showing me round. I, er – I wondered if I could return the compliment by buying you a drink?'

Sam was taken aback. He'd planned on an early night. A certain person might well be calling round after her shift finished at six in the morning. He wanted to be able to give her his undivided attention. But it seemed curmudgeonly to turn down Fosdyke's offer. The man probably had few friends, it'd do no harm to be nice to him. Alec would appreciate it. Perhaps it might get Fosdyke off their backs for a while.

'I wouldn't mind a swift half, thanks very much.'

'Right, I'll er – see you at the Clog and Shovel.'

'Hmm, Friday night. I suspect it might get a bit noisy in there,' said Sam. 'I'm a bit long in the tooth for that sort of racket.'

'Anywhere to suit you,' said a surprisingly amenable Fosdyke.

'How about The Pear Tree?' suggested Sam. It was Owen's regular haunt. It'd do no harm to share the boring young bugger with the Welshman.

'Fine,' said Fosdyke. 'Come in my van if you like.'

'Right, I'll get my coat.'

The Pear Tree was a drinkers' pub as opposed to a poser's pub or a music pub – if the noise battering the senses in the name of house, garage, anthem, rap etc. can be classed as music. Sam had a catholic taste in music, which ranged from Whitney Houston through to Aerosmith via Meatloaf and Billy Joel, but it didn't include the mechanical sounds purely designed for jumping up and down. Such sounds belong in a club or a mental institution, not in a pub. Hence his aversion to the Clog and Shovel on an evening.

Owen was already ensconced at the bar, engaging the young barmaid in a conversation about his digestive system. She seemed relieved when Sam and Fosdyke arrived.

'Evening Pauline,' greeted Sam. He inclined his head towards his Welsh pal. 'He hasn't been discussing his bowels, has he? He's a martyr to his bowels is Owen. And you'll be a martyr to them if you get downwind of him.'

Owen coloured. Sam never failed to embarrass him. 'Pauline knows I never do that, see!' he protested. 'Breaking wind is far more common in the building trade than in the constabulary.' He looked at Fosdyke, awaiting an introduction.

'This is James,' said Sam. 'He's thinking of moving into the flat below me.'

'Pleased to meet you, James.'

Both Owen and Pauline held out polite hands of greeting to Sam's friend. Fosdyke responded as warmly as he knew how.

'Can I buy you all a drink?' he enquired.

'That's very decent of you, James,' smiled Owen. 'I'll just have a small pint.'

'Whisky please,' said Sam, who didn't want to be up all night, peeing. He needed his beauty sleep before Kathy arrived.

The conversation flowed, with Fosdyke not contributing a great deal. He stuck it out until he was confident that Sam was firmly entrenched until closing time. He'd already supplied him with two double whiskies, on top of which, the pints were now flowing. Sam's bladder was now a forgotten priority. Fosdyke, who had, in the main, restricted himself to low alcohol drinks, looked at his watch – 9.35.

'Do you mind if I shoot off?' he asked, politely. 'If I stay with you, I'll be over the limit and I daren't leave the van in a pub car park overnight.'

'Very sensible, boyo' said Owen. 'Unusual for Sam to have sensible friends.'

'That's very true Owen, me old friend,' agreed Sam. 'I'll get a taxi back, James.'

Fosdyke's departure was no great loss. Owen watched him as he went out of the door. 'Bit quiet, your friend,' he commented.

'I wouldn't go so far as to call him a friend,' said Sam. 'He's a building inspector. Bit of a pain in the arse really. Sorry Pauline, didn't know you were listening.'

Pauline grinned. 'He did seem a bit of a hanger-on,' she observed. 'Not much in the way of personality. Shame really – he's not bad looking, apart from the nose. Same again?'

Sam handed her his empty glass, he wouldn't be leaving before closing time.

Fosdyke was banking on Sam being in the pub until closing.

He made a detour via his own – or rather Beverley's – house, picking up a few items before he drove back to 43 Burroughs Walk. A back window was open, as he'd left it earlier in the evening. Pulling on a pair of rubber gloves, he climbed in silently, not wishing to arouse any suspicion from the occupants of the adjacent houses. Once inside he made his way to the living room, where he closed the heavy curtains and switched on the dim light.

From a sports bag he took a can of paraffin – originally bought to fuel the heater in Beverley's garage – a claw hammer, a chisel, a candle and a roll of bandage. He pulled a dining chair into the middle of the room and climbed on to it, hammer in hand.

'Bollocks!'

The ceiling was much too high for him to reach in such a way.

He'd need to stand on the dresser at least. It took him several minutes to drag it into the middle of the room, walking it from side to side. Nothing lost here, he needed it in the middle of the room anyway. Two birds killed with one stone. He grinned to himself – *two birds and a builder, in fact*. After tonight it would all be over.

Standing on the dresser he punched a hole in the ceiling with the hammer, then he hooked the claw into the hole and eventually managed to pull down a four by three sheet of plaster board. Once one was out it was easier to strip a few more. Within half an hour most of the ceiling in the centre of the room was down, revealing rows of dusty joists running at right angles to the floorboards in the room above. A single thickness of plaster board would have provided half an hour's fire resistance – enough to have thwarted Fosdyke's plan.

He pushed the settee next to the dresser and balanced the dining table and chairs on top of them, building a bonfire which reached to within three feet of the exposed ceiling joists. He then soaked the bandage in paraffin and wrapped one end of it around the bottom of the candle, unravelling the rest, twisting it into a rope and sticking it beneath one of the settee cushions. He looked around the room. There was something he'd forgotten, there must be at least one about. Try the dresser drawers. Top, middle, bottom. Bingo! bottom drawer, three of them, candle holders. A bit exotic looking for his requirements, naughty even. One of them was a brass replica of a penis standing on three testicles. Sacrificing anatomical accuracy for the sake of balance.

He stood the candle in the phallic holder, on the floor, several feet away from the bonfire, slightly tilted so the hot wax would only run down one side, thereby not completely covering the paraffin soaked bandage leading from the candle to the settee – Fosdyke had done this before. The speed at which a candle burns down was one of the many useless bits of information stored in his odd mind. This candle would burn for about three hours before it reached the bandage. He then liberally doused the settee and wooden furniture with the paraffin and looked at his watch – 10.30. Sam would be back within an hour, probably asleep within minutes and hopefully dead to the world. For good.

The meticulous building inspector went into the kitchen and washed any paraffin off his gloved hands before carefully lighting the candle. He left the flat as quietly as he'd entered.

He was parked up the street when Sam's taxi dropped him off at 11.25. Fosdyke noticed his unsteady walk with some satisfaction. Things were going to plan. He smirked to himself. With him, things always did.

The phone was ringing as he opened the door. It was Kathy.

'Sam?'

'Correct.'

Where have you been? I've been trying to get hold of you all night.'

'Oh no you haven't. I'd have noticed, you naughty girl.'

'Sam, you're pissed.'

'Don't be so vulgar.'

'What are you wearing, big boy?' she asked, sexily.

'Navvy boots, vest and balaclava.'

'Leave them on. I'll be round at the usual time.'

The phone clicked off. Sam smiled at it, paid a very necessary visit to the toilet, then flopped into his chair to take off his shoes. Closing his eyes. As Fosdyke had hoped, he was dead to the world. In the flat below, the candle burnt steadily down towards the highly inflammable bandage.

Fosdyke sat on the wall outside Beverley's house and took out his mobile phone. Pay As You Go – completely untraceable. Especially with his fake Scottish accent, of which he was quite proud.

'Hello, Police? There's a man sitting on a wall outside Number Eight Nevison's Approach. He's acting very suspiciously.'

He clicked off the phone and smiled at his own ingenuity. This would be his fourth and last killing – and his most ingenious.

This was the only one he'd actually planned. At the moment he'd been directly, or indirectly, the cause of five deaths, and yet the police were only investigating one – a half-hearted investigation at that. Did this make him a serial killer? Hopefully not. Serial killers are just nutters who kill for the sake of it because they're no good at anything else. The three killings he'd carried out so far were all utilitarian, as was this next one. They served a useful purpose. The first one stopped Nicky blabbing her mouth off to all and sundry, the second stopped Mandy from blabbing to Carew, the third stopped Bev from running off with her boyfriend and depriving him of a home and the fourth would keep him out of jail. All justifiable killings.

His mother wouldn't approve, of course, although perhaps his dad would, wherever he was. Lousy bastard, leaving him, when he was what – two years old? In the care of a wimpy mother. God! She'd been embarrassing at times, with her doting, clinging ways. He'd been glad to leave home. Although moving from his mother to shack up with Beverley McAndrew had been a bit of a shock to the system.

It took a leisurely ten minutes before the police arrived. Perhaps they weren't in a mood to confront villains at a quarter to midnight. A police car pulled up in front of him. The officer in the passenger seat wound down his window.

'Good evening sir, do you mind if I ask you what you're doing here.'

'Minding my own business, what are *you* doing here, shit-face?'

The policeman was out of the car in an instant. 'I asked you a civil question, sir,' he said sternly. 'What are you doing here?'

'Who wants to know? Dickhead!'

'Okay sir, would you mind moving on?'

'Fuck off!'

The driver now got out of the car, more belligerent than his colleague. 'You've been told to move on. So DO IT!'

'Which part of fuck off didn't you understand?'

'You're treading very dangerous ground here, sir.'

The first policeman took Fosdyke by the arm and pulled him to his feet. Fosdyke lashed out, thumping the constable in the chest. A lame blow, but enough to earn him a night inside.

'That's it. I'm arresting you for assaulting a police officer, you do not have to say anything –'

'All right, all right, tosspots!' shouted Fosdyke. 'Could you finish it in the car please? It's freezing out here.'

Two hours later, Fosdyke, dozing in his cell, woke to the strident clanging of a passing fire engine. He smiled to himself. He had as good an alibi as he could come up with, given the time allowed.

The call came through at 1.50. It took Kathy a second or two to recognise the street name. House fire in Burroughs Walk.

'Did they say what number?'

'Barry took the call, I've no idea.'

She was in the cab, pulling on her jacket when Barry jumped in beside her.

'What number Burroughs Walk?'

'Forty-three. It's well alight apparently.'

Kathy's heart started pounding. Sam was in there, fast asleep. He'd been drinking as well. He slept like a log when he'd had a few. She'd grumbled about that in the recent past. Tears of fear appeared in her eyes. Fears for Sam's safety. Fear of losing him. Oh please God let him be okay. Let him have woken up. Let him be standing out in the street when they arrive, making some stupid joke.

She could see the glow in the sky as they raced down Station Lane. Bell ringing, not caring who they woke. Two tenders were approaching the blaze. They got there first. Kathy was out before it stopped, running forward, eyes darting round at the gawping onlookers. Looking for him. No sign.

'Is anyone still in there?' she shouted to the gathering crowd, obvious distress in her voice.

A woman stepped forward. 'A chap lives in t' first floor flat. I never saw him come out. Reckon he's still in there.'

239

Kathy looked at the house. The ground floor was an inferno. The first floor windows were breaking in the heat, releasing billowing clouds of acrid smoke.

'Kathy!' yelled Pete. 'We need a hand back here!'

Two fire fighters were connecting up to a hydrant, two more unravelling a hose. Others donning breathing apparatus. Kathy was oblivious to her duties. She only had one duty and that was to get Sam out of there.

'Kathy!' yelled her brother. 'What the he –?' He chased after her but was forcibly held back by a colleague. She was through the door, racing up the blazing stairs, two at a time. Halfing her chances of falling through. His flat door was locked, but not for long. One desperate kick sent it flying open. Smoke and flames hit her. For a second she saw through to the bedroom beyond, directly above the seat of the fire. An inferno. She steeled herself. He might be in the living room. Why? She'd no time to work out why, he just might be, that's all. There he was, slumped in the chair. She dashed in and, with a superhuman effort, grabbed him and dragged his unconscious body out on to the landing. He half woke up and erupted into a fit of coughing.

'Sam, she yelled. 'We need to get out!'

The coughing stopped and he became a dead weight again. She was beginning to lose consciousness herself now, the smoke was getting to her. A figure appeared on the stairs wearing breathing apparatus. With her last ounce of strength she pushed Sam towards him, causing them both to tumble back down the blazing stairs. Kathy passed out just as the landing collapsed beneath her, sending her crashing to her death in the furnace below.

27

Owen first heard about it when he arrived at work at eight o'clock the following morning; worse for wear after the previous night's session with Sam. He did a double take of Fosdyke at the custody desk, signing for his belongings before being released without charge, but with a mild rebuke from an inspector who didn't fancy arguing in court about the merits of arresting a perfectly sober man, sitting on his own garden wall, doing no harm to anyone apart from objecting to the police asking him to move on.

'What are you doing here, boyo?' enquired Owen.

'You tell me,' replied an aggrieved Fosdyke. 'Maybe your mates can explain it, I certainly can't.'

The custody sergeant released Fosdye and took Owen to one side.

'There was fire last night at Sam's flat.'

Fosdyke's ears pricked up.

'Oh, my good God!' gasped Owen. 'What happened? How's Sam? Is he all right.'

'He's in hospital,' said the sergeant. 'It doesn't look good.'

Fosdyke felt acute disappointment to hear that Sam was still alive. The sergeant looked up at him.

'You can go now.'

'Wait a minute!' said Owen. 'This fellow knows Sam.' He turned his attention to Fosdyke. 'Did you hear that? Sam's in hospital. A fire at his flat last night.'

'Oh no!' The distress on Fosdyke's face was genuine, but for reasons opposite to the distress felt by Owen. 'What time was this?' He felt a need to bring his alibi to bear at the earliest opportunity.

'About two o'clock this morning,' said the sergeant.

Fosdyke nodded. 'I heard the engine passing. It woke me up in my cell,' he said, with a hint of admonition in his voice. 'Where is he? Unsworth General?'

'That's where they usually take him,' said Owen, unaware of how odd this sounded.

'One of the firefighters was killed,' added the sergeant. 'A woman I think. She apparently saved Sam's life.'

'Oh no! Oh my good God!' Owen knew exactly who it would be. He looked at the sergeant. 'I'd like to see him. Is it alright?'

'Go on then. I'll square it with Sergeant Bassey.'

Owen was out of the door, leaving Fosdyke wondering what to do next. A perfectly good plan had gone slightly awry.

Tom and Jake were already there, sitting ashen-faced beside their mother, clutching each other's hands. Their darting, frightened eyes watching every movement of the adults around them. Looking for clues as to their father's welfare. Hoping these grown-ups weren't hiding anything. Sue stood up and walked quickly over to Owen as he turned the corner into the waiting area.

'We're not allowed to see him,' she said, in a low voice. 'He's suffering from burns and severe smoke inhalation. A lot worse than the last time he was in.'

'Did they – did they say what his chances are?'

Sue shook her head finding it difficult to talk. For an ex-wife she wasn't taking this too well. Over her shoulder he spotted Sally, approaching down the corridor. Her face asking questions. Owen shrugged at her.

'We don't know yet,' he said.

Sue turned and acknowledged Sally with a nod. There had never been any animosity between the two. Sally took her hand and asked, 'Are the boys okay?'

Sue shook her head. 'They're in shock. I don't know if I'll be able to cope with them if ...' The sentence remained unfinished, but understood.

There was a long silence. Owen looked at the two women, unsure how to say this. 'I understand a woman firefighter died in the fire.'

Sue looked at him, realising he didn't know for sure. 'It was Kathy,' she confirmed. 'She went straight in without any breathing apparatus and pulled him out of his room. She – she didn't make it herself.'

Sally sat down heavily in a chair. She didn't know about Kathy. 'Oh no! This is terrible.'

'He worshipped her,' said Sue.

Sally knew less about Sam's relationship with Kathy than Sue did, but she knew it was true. 'I don't suppose he knows yet?' she enquired of Sue.

'He hasn't regained consciousness. I don't think he should be told until he's strong enough to take it.' There was a measure of optimism in Sue's words, which the boys picked up on.

'So he's going to be okay then?' asked Jake. Four young eyes looked up at Sue for the right answer. She couldn't bear to disappoint them.

'Of course he is. You know your dad. This place is like a second home to him.'

Tom grinned and jabbed an encouraging elbow into his brother. 'Told you,' he said.

Sam awoke momentarily to a world that didn't make sense. He was panicking because he didn't know anything. He didn't know where he was, who he was, or what was happening to him. A man in white leaned over him. Why couldn't Sam talk to him? What was this thing over his mouth? The effort of staying awake exhausted him back into merciful sleep. The eyes of the waiting quartet were glued to the young doctor as he came out of Intensive Care.

'He woke up for a few seconds,' said the doctor. 'He, er – he seems to be holding his own.'

'Does this mean he's going to be all right?' asked Owen.

'Are you a relative?'

'Well, no. His only relatives are the two boys – his sons.'

'I'm his ex-wife,' volunteered Sue.

The doctor ushered Sue into a small room. He was young, with a nice voice and a kind, intelligent face. Under other circumstances she could quite fancy him.

'We're keeping him in Intensive Care for the time being until we're sure he's going to be all right. This is the second time in a few months he's damaged his lungs in this way, so we need to be doubly cautious.'

'So, he's going to be all right?'

The doctor screwed up his face. He hated being put on the spot like this. Everybody in this situation asked such questions, and of course it was understandable.

'You have cause to be optimistic,' was all he'd say. 'I'll have a better idea tomorrow.'

'Thanks doctor. Can I see him?'

'Just for a couple of minutes. Don't expect him to talk to you.'

'What about the boys?'

'That's up to you. He's on oxygen, and a drip to maintain his hydration. He looks very poorly.'

'They've seen him looking poorly before. He's a regular in this place.'

'So I understand,' smiled the doctor. 'Just you three and no one else – and only for a minute.'

The thing over his mouth was still there. An oxygen mask, of course. This certainly wasn't his first oxygen mask. His thoughts were jumbled, but the pieces were coming together. A woman, a nurse, leaned over him. Talking to him. If he could just get his act together he'd ask her something. God knows what though. He didn't know what to ask yet.

'Don't try and talk,' he heard her say.

Good. No talking was required, just thinking for the time being. He could manage a bit of that. He was a policeman. No, he was a builder. Which one was it? He'd just been to the pub, he knew that much. That was the last thing he remembered. Pieces of his memory dropped into place as his consciousness returned. He just needed someone to tell him why he was here. There was a vague memory of waking up in dense smoke and Kathy pulling at him. What the hell was that all about?

'Hello Sam.'

He forced his eyes open, his vision was very blurred. 'Who is it?' he asked. He recognised the voice, but couldn't place it.

'It's Sue.'

Sue, ex-wife Sue. Why was she here? He tried to ask, but no words came.

'He mustn't try to talk,' said the nurse's voice.

'Sam,' explained Sue. 'You're in hospital. Unsworth General. You were in a fire, but you're going to be okay. Tom and Jake are here to see you.'

Tom and Jake. Where are they? He moved his head and saw them at the other side of the bed. He hoped he was smiling at them but he couldn't be sure. They smiled at him.

'Hiya, dad,' said Tom with as much cheer as he could muster.

'Hiya, dad,' echoed Jake, whose eyes were fixed on the plastic identity band around his father's wrist. He didn't like seeing his dad like this. Helpless and weak. This was not how he wanted his dad to be.

Smiling was becoming to much of an effort for Sam. He hoped the boys didn't mind.

'We're going now,' said Sue, having taken a visual hint from the nurse. 'Owen and Sally are outside and send their love. They'll come and see you later, when you're a bit stronger.'

Kathy, thought Sam. What about Kathy? I hope they don't forget to tell Kathy. I'd like her to come.

Sue gave the boys some change to take to the drinks machine. She watched them walk away then turned to Owen and Sally.

'One of us three is going to have to tell him about Kathy.' She expelled a long breath, then added. 'I don't know which one.'

Owen figured it was down to him. The other two gave him no argument. He went to see her brother first. To offer condolences on his and Sam's behalf. Pete was back on duty, handling his loss in his own way. Judging from the state of him, he wouldn't be much use in an emergency. His face was drained of all its usual humour and his eyes were reddened. He took Owen's outstretched hand and enquired, sombrely, 'How did Sam take it?'

'He hasn't been told yet,' said Owen.

'It'll hit him hard. They were very close. I've never seen her so happy.'

'Sam was the same,' said Owen. 'She took his mind off all the other rubbish that's been going on in his life.' He looked hard at Pete. 'You know it was arson, don't you?'

'I heard. Have you got anyone?'

'No. Apparently someone piled all the furniture in the middle of the room and poured paraffin all over it. Why anyone should want to do that beats me. The heat was so intense, there's not much left to go on.'

'I'm surprised Sam didn't hear anything,' observed Pete, grimly. Whoever did it must have made quite a noise.'

Guilt overcame Owen. 'He'd been out with me. We'd been drinking, see. I suppose that had a lot to do with it.'

Pete could see his remorse. 'Don't go blaming yourself. If having a drink was a crime we'd all be locked up.'

'She was a brave woman.'

'That she was,' agreed Pete, with pride in his voice. Then he added, 'But what she did was daft.'

'Sam would have done the same for her,' said Owen. 'They were two of a kind, see. Daft about each other as well. God knows how he's going to take it. I've decided to tell him this evening. They reckon he's strong enough.'

'Best of luck – and thanks for coming,' said Pete.

Sam kept losing track of time. He'd been visited by Sally and Owen and Alec and Darren Feast. Even Mick and Curly had called in. He'd asked about Kathy and had been told she was in another part of the hospital and would come and see him as soon as she was well enough. She'd apparently been hurt in the same fire.

Owen came in on his own that evening. Sam was sitting up for the first time. Breathing without oxygen and eating proper food. For obvious reasons he'd not been allowed newspapers or television. Owen's face looked grave. A nurse hovered behind him.

'Hello, Owen.' Sam's voice was little more than a croak but it was a vast improvement on the last time Owen had seen him.

'Good to hear your voice again, boyo.'

'How's Kathy? Have you seen her?'

This was the hardest thing Owen had ever done in his life. He dropped his eyes at Sam's question.

'Owen?'

The Welshman raised his eyes again, looking straight into Sam's worried face.

'Something's wrong isn't it?'

Owen nodded and took a very deep breath, as did the nurse behind him. 'Kathy pulled you out of the fire, see. It was an unbelievably brave thing to do, but –'

'But – but what? Owen, what's happened?'

Owen shook his head and tried to summon up the right words. Sam closed his eyes and sank back on his pillow. His mouth trembled, uncontrollably. 'No,' he said. 'Oh, please, Owen, no.'

Owen took his friend's hand. 'I'm so sorry Sam. She died in the fire. They say it was very quick. We couldn't tell you before, boyo. You were too weak. I'm so, so sorry.'

'You mean she died saving my life? My sodding, useless bloody life?' Sam's face crumpled with grief. The nurse ushered Owen away and injected Sam with a sedative.

'How did he take it?' asked Sally, waiting outside. Sue was with her. Both had come to give moral support to Owen.

'He took it very badly,' said Owen. 'I only hope he won't have a relapse. He's sleeping now. They gave him a sedative.'

Sue took Sally's hand. 'Of all the people in the world, he's going to need you now.'

Sally took her hand away. 'I'm sorry Sue, but I'm not going to offer myself as a substitute Kathy. I'll visit him as a friend, the same as you two, but that's all.' She turned and walked away before they saw the tears in her eyes.

'She'll never be just a friend to him,' commented Sue, as Sally's footsteps faded in the distance. 'That woman's besotted with him. If Sam's to get over this, then Sally'll have a lot to do with it. Mark my words.'

'What about you?' enquired Owen, curiously as they walked away together. 'Were you ever besotted with him?'

Sue looked down at her shoes and smiled. 'In a way I still am,' she admitted. 'But don't you dare tell anyone, Owen Price!'

28

Owen and Sally took it in turns to visit. Sue took a step back and allowed one or the other of them to take the boys. Anything else wouldn't be fair on Jonathan, who had asked her to marry him. She didn't want anything to jeopardise that. The less she saw of Sam in his helpless state, the safer she was. As she'd often told him, as far as she was concerned he was unliveable withable.

Two days after he'd been told of Kathy's death, a detective called at the hospital to talk to him. He was an old colleague of Sam's, who managed to turn the visit into an interview. Sam could tell him little. The detective said it was routine in the event of arson. Sam understood and the man left him to grieve over Kathy. She was buried without Sam at her graveside. Still to poorly to attend.

Owen kept him up to date on progress. Sam had great difficulty concentrating on anything, but the Welshman pressed on. Somehow Sam must be made to take an interest in life once again.

'Whoever did it,' said Owen. 'Stripped some of the plaster boards off the ceiling before they lit the fire.'

Sam showed the first spark of interest here. Owen was hoping for this.

'That means they were after me,' deduced Sam. 'The plaster boards would give fire protection to the room above.'

'That's what the boys in CID think,' agreed Owen. 'I think Bowman might be wanting a word.'

'He can have two words, both to do with sex and travel.'

'Another weird thing happened that night as well,' said Owen. 'Your pal Fosdyke managed to get himself arrested.'

'Fosdyke? You're kidding!'

This was the most animated Owen had seen him for a week. 'He was arrested for assaulting a police officer. Turns out that it's a storm in a teacup, isn't it? He was given a reprimand and sent home the following day. But he spent eight hours in a cell. Picked him up at midnight outside his own house.'

Sam shook his head in confusion. Things were happening outside his own insular world. He knew he had to get on with his life. Get his act together, without Kathy. One thing for sure, there'd never be anyone else. He also needed to find out who had tried to kill him. Find him and he found Kathy's killer. It was to be his sole priority. He wasn't going to rely on Bowman for this one.

'I've already told your fellers everything I know,' said Sam. 'I appreciate you have to go through the motions, now that you have, goodbye.'

Bowman had come alone. He ignored Sam's outburst, it was milder than he'd expected. 'The arsonist attack was aimed at you,' he said, calmly. 'I need to know if you can think of any-one –'

'Look,' interrupted Sam, testily. 'What I don't know, is who did it. What I do know, is that it's somehow all tied up with your dead pal, Chisel Joo and all the other killings.'

'What makes you think that,' enquired Bowman.

'Call it gut instinct, call it common sense,' replied Sam. 'Will that be all?'

Bowman sat down beside his bed and shook his head. 'Not quite,' he said. He absently plucked a grape from a bowl on the bedside cupboard and popped it in his mouth. 'I don't know why I feel the need to tell you this, but as far as Chisel Joo was concerned I didn't accept any personal favours from him, finan-cially or otherwise.'

He paused, hoping for Sam's attention. Sam fixed his eyes on a wall chart, as though it was more interesting than anything Bowman had to say. The detective inspector decided to press on.

'Look, you've been around long enough to know that better men than me have tried to catch him. All I did was to utilise the resources available to me. Chisel Joo was an illegal businessman, who had the power to keep away undesirables from his patch, which also happens to be our patch. I turned a blind eye to certain activities of his in return for him pointing certain villains in my direction.'

He now had Sam's attention. Vague understanding for a fellow maverick. Understanding, but not admiration. Sam would never have done business with Chisel Joo. Bowman continued:

'Since he died, crime in Unsworth is increasing. I'm aware I might have lost my job if my methods had become public knowledge, but with his death, the episode is a closed book.'

He stood up and looked back down at Sam. 'I can't possibly see how this attack on you has anything to do with him or his organisation. The man's dead.'

'Okay,' conceded Sam. 'Let's just call it a gut instinct. I'm out in a couple of days. I'll find out who did it.'

'If you have any ideas at all, you should tell me.'

At that moment there was only one name running through Sam's head. He sincerely hoped he was wrong but his emotions were running so high and even the vaguest of suspects would be subjected to intense scrutiny. Losing Kathy was the worst thing that had ever happened to him and he needed desperately to strike out at someone. He had managed to cope with the loss of his dad because he knew that had been an accident. But his lovely Kathy had sacrificed her own life to save him being murdered. Someone had to pay for this.

'I don't have any ideas,' he said. 'I'd like you to go now.'

Bowman shook his head and left without another word. He lived in a different world from Sam.

One by one, the men on the site trooped over to the site hut to pay their respects. It was Sam's first day back at work and he felt uncomfortable. Of all the people who had visited him in hospital offering tears and hope, it was his old pal Darren who made the most practical offer. He offered Sam somewhere to stay until he found another place of his own. Sue had discussed the problem with him, but had quickly pointed out that Jonathan might not understand if she took her ex-husband in as a lodger. Moving in with Sally was out of the question. It was either digs or Darren. Jacob was the last to come into the hut. He was obviously nervous.

'Alec,' said Sam. 'Could you leave me and Jacob alone for a few minutes?'

Alec looked puzzled. 'Sure. I've plenty to do anyway. Take all the time you need.'

Jacob stood there, looking slightly apprehensive. Sam looked at him, steadily. His recent experiences had stripped him of any reticence he might otherwise have felt.

'Jacob,' he said. 'Whoever started the fire was trying to kill me, but they didn't, they killed Kathy.' At that moment Sam was scared what he might do if he found out it was Jacob.

'I know this, boss. Alec told us yesterday. Who the hell would want ter kill you?'

'Where were you on the night of the fire?'

'What?'

'You heard me, Jacob. Just tell me and I'll cross you off my list of suspects.'

'Surely you don't think I –'

'I don't want to *think* anything,' snapped Sam, his eyes were blazing. 'I want to *know*. Once you convince me you didn't do it, I'll give you a grovelling apology. If you don't convince me, I'll kill you.' There was an unbalanced sincerity in Sam's eyes that took Jacob aback.

'Jesus, Sam,' he protested. 'It happened in the middle of the damn night. Where the hell do you think I was? I was in bed with my wife.'

Sam didn't seem to be listening, he had his own agenda. He paced up and down the hut as he put his thoughts into words. 'You see, Jacob, I've been racking my brains to think of anyone who might have the slightest cause to kill me, and at first I couldn't think of anyone. Then I remembered that I'm the only person in the world who knows you killed Chisel Joo – the only person who could tell the police what really happened. On top of which, I know for certain that you're capable of killing

252

someone. It's also crossed my mind that you used to be a caretaker at Greerside Hall and that your sister used to be one of Chisel's prostitutes, which, in a way, connects you to the two dead girls. Added to which, I know for certain that the arsonist is in the building trade. Do you get my point?' He fixed Jacob with a piercing glare that Jacob returned, unflinchingly.

'I get your point, but it wasn't me, man. I didn't even know where you lived.'

'I need you to prove that to me beyond all doubt.'

Jacob sat down on a stool and rubbed his unshaven chin, thinking.

'Even if I knew where you lived,' he said. 'How would I know the flat below was empty? We've been talking about it. Whoever did that must have made a hell of a noise. Must have known you weren't in. How would I know that?'

'I don't know. You could have followed me.'

'Ring my wife.'

'How do I know you haven't told her? She might lie to protect you.'

'You don't know my wife, man.'

'No, I don't.'

Jacob shook his head. 'Look, my wife knows about Chisel Joo. She reckons I've got nothing to hide and that I should tell the police what happened. Live with a clear conscience. Me? I don't know what to do. I remember you telling me that if I owned up to the killing it wouldn't do anyone any good. It seems to me you were wrong and she's right.'

Sam thought for a long time, then picked up the phone and handed it to Jacob.

'You want me to give myself up?' enquired Jacob. 'Fair enough, it'll be a weight off my mind anyway. At least it'll stop you making these damn fool accusations.' He took the phone from Sam and asked, coldly, 'What's the number?'

'Just dial your own number. I want to speak to your wife.'

Jacob hesitated, then dialled the number and handed the receiver back to Sam.

'Mrs Marsden?' said Sam, managing a cordial tone. 'We haven't spoken before but my name's Sam Carew ... Thanks, I'm feeling much better. I've been talking to Jacob about the incident that happened at Chisel Joo's some months ago. I gather you know what happened and you've advised Jacob to take certain er, steps ... Really? ... Well, yes and no. It's sometimes not a good idea to have so much faith in British justice, Mrs Marsden ... Is he really?' Sam took the phone away from his ear as the noise level at the other end rose. 'Actually, I've always found him honest and reliable ... Does he? Well, I don't blame you. Anyway, at the end of the day it's up to you and Jacob. Personally I think you'd be wise to let sleeping dogs lie. Things like this have a habit of following you round for the rest of your life ... That's quite all right. I just thought I'd pass on my opinion first hand ... Not at all. Oh, there is one other thing. The police may well be asking my men where they were at the time of the fire at my flat ... He was? Yes, I assumed he'd be home with you. Just thought I'd mention it. Forewarned is forarmed and all that ... Yes, I'll be sure to tell him. Goodbye Mrs Marsden.'

He put the phone down and held out his hand for Jacob to shake. 'Okay, I believe you,' he said. 'I spent long enough in the force to know when a wife's giving her husband an alibi. No way in the world would a woman like that cover up for you if you'd burned my house down and killed someone.'

'I was actually thinking of telling the police just for a quiet life,' said Jacob, ruefully.

'You do have a point,' sympathised Sam. 'But on balance, I wouldn't, and I think you're wife now agrees with me, so maybe I've done you some good on that score. Anyway, she wants you straight home tonight and no calling in the pub. If I were you I'd do as I'm told.'

'I'll do that. By the way, what happened to the grovelling apology?'

'It'll be in your wage packet.'

'That's the sort of grovelling I like.'

Jacob left Sam with more on his mind. He had a point about the arsonist making a noise that he – or she – knew Sam wouldn't hear. Whoever did it must have made all the noise when he was still in the pub. Then they'd hung about until he came home and gave him time to go to sleep before starting the fire. But why wait so long? He'd been in bed two hours before the fire started. He allowed himself a rare smile. At least Fosdyke was in the clear. He was safely locked up at that time.

Fosdyke turned on to the site and saw Sam's Range Rover. He stopped his van at the entrance, considering whether to turn round and go away. Did Sam have any suspicions? He steeled himself. If he did, it would be as well to find out now.

'Morning Sam,' he greeted, as he entered the site hut.

'Ah,' said Sam, turning to face him. 'Morning James, how are you?'

'More to the point, how are you?' Concern showed on Fosdyke's face, which Sam thought was touching, considering the man was such a prat.

'I'm okay, thanks. Not a hundred percent, but alive and kicking.'

'Oh, and I was sorry to hear about ...' Fosdyke pretended to forget her name to illustrate his lack of detailed knowledge about the incident.

'Kathy,' said Sam. 'Yeah, well ...' He didn't want to talk about her, not to Fosdyke, anyway. 'How are things with you? I hear you had a run in with the law that night.'

'You might call it that. I can see why you packed the police in. Brain dead, some of them. I was sitting on my own garden wall, just thinking. I was still a bit brassed off about Bev leaving, and two idiots in a police car told me to move on. I shouldn't have lost my rag I suppose.'

'I was told you hit one of them,' said Sam, curiously.

'I pushed him away,' corrected Fosdyke. 'Silly sod arrested me. Something like that could have cost me my job. I'm still thinking of suing for wrongful arrest.'

'Join the queue,' said Sam, who considered Fosdyke's explanation plausible.

'What? You're suing them yourself?'

'Well, I was,' confirmed Sam. 'But it's too much hassle, so I dropped it.'

'Hassle? Yes, that's what I was told. Honestly, some people think they can get away with murder.'

'Not if I can help it,' muttered Sam, half to himself, but loud enough to re-kindle Fosdyke's worries.

At least Sam didn't suspect him. Which was something.

The men left Sam alone with his thoughts as he steadily worked away. It was a chill, dull day, one to suit his mood. Alec had asked him to bring up the brickwork on plot nine, which meant Sam would be standing on the ground. The scaffold was no place for a man whose mind wasn't right; although a cynic might argue that this category would include almost all bricklayers. Sam heard the phone ring in the site hut and ignored it, knowing Alec would get it. His partner slid down a ladder in the manner perfected by all young apprentices and dashed into the hut.

A few minutes later he walked over to Sam. 'That was Broughton from Manston Holdings. They had their planning application knocked back. It's going to put the Market Street job back a couple of months.'

Sam had little interest in any job, much less the Market Street one. 'Is that a problem?' he asked, absently.

'It's more of a puzzle than a problem. Apparently the chairman himself knocked it back without giving proper reasons. Broughton reckons he might be looking for a bung. He wants me to sound him out.'

'You what? You mean Manston are prepared to bung him?' Sam was interested now.

'If it oils the wheels, yes,' said Alec.

'This chairman, what's his name?'

'Laurence Dwyer. Now Sam, I don't want you to get involved in this. You could charge in there and blow it for everyone.'

256

'Put it this way, Alec. My fifty one per cent says we don't get involved in anything dodgy. If there's any sounding out to be done, I'll do it. The odds are that this bloke has an Achilles heel. All dodgy blokes have got one.'

'What's your Achilles heel, then?' asked Alec.

'Hey, I never do dodgy business,' retorted Sam, sharply.

'Well, I must admit, you certainly have a different set of principles as far as the firm's concerned,' observed Alec.

'I know,' accepted Sam. 'But you and me are only looking after it for my dad. These are his principles, not mine.'

29

Having an estate agent as chairperson of the Unsworth District Council Planning Committee was bound to result in a clash of interests. Especially if the estate agent in question is Laurence Dwyer, whose For Sale signs littered the streets around where Chisel Joo had had his properties.

Under normal circumstance Sam wouldn't have got involved, but the loss of Kathy had left such an anger inside that he wanted to hit out at any legitimate target. He waited a couple of days in order to regain the strength to tackle the situation, then he rang Dwyer from the site hut.

'Mr Dwyer? My name's Carew. We're the contractors for Manston Holdings on the Market Street job. We'll be doing the renovation work there when the planning's sorted out.'

'Are you now? And what's this got to do with me?'

'Well, with me being a builder I might have a better idea of how to satisfy your requirements. The people at Manston have never picked up a trowel in anger in their lives.'

'Working builder, eh? My sort of feller,' said Dwyer. 'Aye, it'll do no harm to have a drop o' dinner somewhere.'

'Shall I pop round and pick you up at twelve?'

'Aye lad. That'll give me a chance to get meself tarted up. 'Yer'll be taking me somewhere decent, no doubt.'

Sam had been thinking of the Pear Tree but changed his mind to the King's Arms. Somewhere decent – and expensive.

Dwyer's face looked familiar as he climbed into Sam's waiting Range Rover, but it took Sam a while to figure out where he'd seen the councillor before. He was a large, bald man in his sixties, with close-together eyes, blotchy skin and shrinking gums.

Sam made a good job of hiding his disgust at the man's principles. During their time in the pub, Dwyer's hands only ever ventured into his pockets once, and that was to make blatant adjustments to his privates. Sam was restricted to non-alcoholic lager, which he detested. Dwyer was on Glen Fiddich in large measures. He left it until the very end before he made his play. His voice, previously booming, became very quiet, very confidential.

'Right lad,' he said. 'We've talked about this and that and it's time for me and you ter stop beating about the bush. We're all on this earth for what we can get out of it and Manston Holdings are no different. They'll be making a very tidy profit out of yon building and they'll not be expecting ter keep it all themselves. That'll be why they've sent you ter see me.'

'You're right, Mr Dwyer,' said Sam. 'You don't beat about the bush.'

'No point, lad. No one got anywhere by procrastinating. Anyway, ten thousand pounds cash money represents a negligible percentage of Manston Holding's profits. I doubt they'll begrudge me it when you put it to them.'

'I'll be sure to do that, Mr Dwyer,' said Sam, amazed at how off hand these negotiations are carried out. 'One for the road?'

'No lad. Our business is concluded. I'd best be off.'

Sam was driving past The Clog and Shovel when he realised where he'd seen Dwyer before. This man had an Achilles heel if ever there was one. He allowed himself a thin smile. It had been a while since he'd done that.

'Do you ever go in there,' he asked, pointing to the pub.

'No, lad,' said Dwyer, a bit too hurriedly. 'Not since they did it out like a tart's boudoir.'

It had been done out like a tart's boudoir for three years to Sam's knowledge so he knew Dwyer was lying; maybe he'd figured a way to save Manston Holdings ten thousand pounds.

'I'll expect to hear from you shortly,' said Dwyer as he got out of Sam's car. 'You're more than likely to find me at home, this is me card. Me business more or less runs itself nowadays.'

'I'll be in touch within the next couple of days,' promised Sam.

He took Sally with him to the Clog and Shovel the following lunchtime. Sam felt he needed a chaperone.

Even with Sally on his arm he felt a bit self-conscious approaching the woman with the cat's head tattoo. Everyone in the place knew what she was. The management tolerated her because she was decorative and added a certain frisson to the atmosphere. She attracted spectators. Hence Sam's discomfort as he approached her.

'Buy you a drink?' he asked.

If the prostitute was surprised at a chaperoned man offering to buy her a drink she didn't show it.

'Sure, a large Courvoisier would be nice,' she smiled.

Sam ordered a pint, a large brandy and a white wine for Sally. 'Shall we go to a table?' he suggested.

She shrugged her agreement and smiled again, her teeth white and even. This lady was very expensive. Sally's teeth, also white and even, were firmly clenched.

'Sure, we don't want to be conspicuous now, do we?' The woman was reading Sam's mind very accurately.

'I'er – my name's Sam,' he said, placing the drinks on the table 'and this is Sally.'

The woman gave Sally a slight nod which was returned frostily. 'Sam Carew,' she smiled. 'I know about you, Sam Carew.'

'You do?'

'You're in the news quite a lot. Mad Carew, I believe they call you. Are you mad, Mr Carew?'

'Right now I am,' he said.

'I'm Gayle,' she said. 'Pleased to meet you, Sam – and Sally.' She raised her glass to him, took a polite sip and placed it back on the table, managing to make even this simple movement sensuous. 'Am I right in thinking you're not here on business?' She was surprisingly well spoken for a woman in her line of work.

'Er, yes. Well, not that sort of business anyway. I'm looking for information about one of your er–'

'Clients. I much prefer the words to punters.'

'Exactly.'

'I'm afraid I don't divulge such information. My work is confidential, as you might expect.'

'This information might be worth quite a lot on money,' said Sally, who knew how to cut out the crap.

'You now have my attention, carry on,' smiled Gayle, sparing Sally a brief glance before returning her attention to Sam.

'I came in here some months ago,' he said. 'Probably around February time, and I saw you leave with a man called Laurence Dwyer.'

Gayle laughed. 'You mean George Haddock – the fat man. They all give false names. Silly man thought I didn't know. He must think I don't read the papers. Anyway, what about him?'

'He'll shortly be under investigation for corruption by the police. I'd like to beat them to it.'

Gayle looked at Sally.

'You mentioned money? How much money.'

'A couple of thousand,' said Sam, suddenly doubling the price he'd intended offering. He wanted to be assured of her co-operation and by the look of her a thousand might not do it. Hopefully Manston Holdings would reimburse him.

'Two grand – hmm.'

The sum took her by surprise and merited an appreciative tilt of her head. Sam was glad he'd doubled the figure. She took a cigarette out a gold case, offered Sam one which he took, then she stuck hers in a gold holder and handed him a gold lighter for him to light both cigarettes. Sally, who didn't smoke, held up a hand and said, 'Not for me, thanks,' despite not being offered one. She just wanted to make a point.

'What do you want for your two grand?' Gayle enquired, cool-ly, blowing smoke over his head.

'I want to know just how corrupt he is. Am I right in saying he wasn't paying for your services himself?'

'Do I get my two grand now?'

'You get it the minute I nail him. Which means your information has to scare him.'

She studied him for a while, wondering if she could trust him to pay her. Then she shrugged and tapped the ash off her ciga-rette. 'What the hell,' she said. 'Chisel Joo was paying. Chisel rented out a lot of property. The word is he bought most of it through the fat man.'

'No doubt Dwyer sold it cheap at the vendor's expense,' guessed Sam. 'And made sure he got planning permission to convert them into whatever he wanted.'

'Chisel never paid full price where he could avoid it. I was an exception to this. I don't come cheap, not even for Chisel Joo.'

'Did you have many clients like Dwyer?' asked Sally, purely out of female curiosity.

'Hey! If you want more names you pay more money.'

Half an hour later, after gleaning further interesting information, Sam and Sally left the pub. Sam promised to return in two days with the money.

'Just one thing,' was Gayle's parting shot.

'What's that?' enquired Sam

'I won't repeat any of this in court.'

'She won't have much choice if push comes to shove,' said Sam, once they were in the street. 'Well, thanks for your moral support. Do you want me to drop you off at work?'

'I took the afternoon off,' said Sally. 'I want to see this thing through.'

Dwyer's wife came to the door in answer to Sam's ring.

'Is Mr Dwyer in? My name's Carew, I have a business matter to conclude with him.'

Dwyer appeared behind his wife. His face broke into a jowly grin. 'Don't stand on the doorstep, lad, come on in. We can discuss our business in my study, while the ladies take coffee in the lounge.'

'I don't need to come in, Mr Dwyer. I've come to ask you to resign your seat on the council so the planning committee can get on with their job properly without your corrupt influence.'

'I beg your pardon!' gasped Dwyer. 'Just who the devil do you think you're talking to?'

'I'm talking to a man who accepted bribes and sexual favours courtesy of a criminal called Chisel Joo in exchange for cheap houses and planning favours. I have the names of several prostitutes who will testify to that under oath. I also saw you in the company of one of them myself. Remember the lady with the black cat tattooed on her arm?'

'Sexual favours? What's he talking about, Laurence?' asked a shocked Mrs Dwyer.

'He used to take prostitutes to the Castle House Motel, Mrs Dwyer,' said Sally. 'Booked in under the name of Mr and Mrs Haddock. A bit fishy if you ask me.'

Sam frowned at her for this deplorable joke, then smiled at the shocked Dwyer. 'I expect to learn of your resignation tomorrow, Mr Dwyer. If not I'll take my information to the police.'

'Who are all these other prostitutes who are going to testify?' enquired Sally, on the way back.

'Gayle said there were others. I just can't remember their names off hand,' said Sam.

'She wouldn't give you their names. Honour among hookers and all that.'

'Anyway, did you see his face? It won't get to court.'

'I saw his wife's face,' grinned Sally. 'She wasn't best pleased.'

Sam laughed. His first since the fire. 'Thanks for coming along and giving me moral support,' he said.

'That's okay.' She placed her hand on his arm. 'I may be able to offer a bit of *immoral* support, should the need arise.'

She still loved him and Sam was aware of it. 'Don't take advantage of the flaws in my character, Sal,' he said. 'I'm just not worth it.'

'That's for me to decide.'

'Sal, I can't promise you anything. I'm still grieving over Kathy. You'd be much better off with someone you can rely on. You deserve better than me.'

'Jesus, Sam – I've always known that!'

He smiled. 'Incidentally,' he cautioned. 'If you ever come with me on a job like this again, don't make jokes. It's supposed to be serious.'

Sally shrugged, 'Well, it's nice to think there might be a next time.'

30

Gayle was pleasantly surprised that Sam kept his word. In her world this rarely happened. She stuffed the envelope full of cash into an expensive looking black handbag.

'It was two thousand well spent,' Sam informed her. He had already recovered the money from Manston Holdings who were in the process of rushing the contract through. 'Dwyer resigned his seat on the council yesterday.'

'Can I buy you a drink,' she asked. 'It seems I can afford it. I have many more names for you which are useless to me now that Chisel's gone. I could do you a job lot for a reasonable fee.'

Sam grinned at her cheek. Despite her profession he liked her. 'No harm in talking. You can buy me a pint.'

She brought the drinks to a table and sat down, elegantly, beside him. It crossed his mind to put her on to Maggie Jones. Perhaps not. The killer was still out there, he had other priorities.

'Something's just occurred to me about these names I was telling you about,' she said. 'I'er, I hope your friend won't get caught up in it all.'

Sam was puzzled. 'Friend – which friend? which friend?' He was hoping she didn't mean Owen.

'You know, you were in here with him a few months ago. I didn't recognise him at first, then I realised he'd grown a moustache.

Sam puzzled for a second, then he smiled, 'That'll have been Fosdyke.' His eyes narrowed, wondering what she knew about him. This could be very interesting. 'What's he got to do with anything? He's just a building inspector.'

'Fosdyke?' She turned the name over in her mind. 'Nicky never called him that. He had a funny name, but it was definitely him.' She snapped her fingers, 'Isaac! That was it. She called him Isaac.'

The initials JIF sprang to Sam's mind, as did something

altogether more disturbing. 'Isaac? – that's his middle name,' he remembered. 'James Isaac Fosdyke. What all this about Nicky? Nicky who?'

'Nicky *Fulbright!*' said Gayle. 'You know, the girl who was murdered.'

'You mean Fosdyke was her boyfriend?'

'Course he was. He was going out with her at the time she was killed – I thought you'd have known that.'

His mind was reeling. Fosdyke! Nicky Fulbright's boyfriend. What the hell did all this mean? Somewhere at the back of his mind he knew exactly what it meant, but he couldn't put it together. She'd given him the missing piece in a jig-saw, but where the hell did it fit?

'Hello?' she said, waving a hand in front of his eyes. 'Are you still with us?'

People on adjacent tables were grinning at her. He shook himself back into awareness.

'Look,' he said. 'Could you – could you tell me what you know about Fosdyke.'

She shrugged. 'Not much, only that Chisel had given Nicky to him on a long term basis, presumably for services rendered – and Nicky, the silly girl, had fallen for him. Much good it did her. I reckon Chisel had her done in.'

'Why didn't you tell the police any of this?'

The look in her eyes said, "Don't ask stupid questions". He accepted her unspoken answer with a nod. His mind was off again. Racing. Fosdyke knew the flat below him was empty, he knew Sam was in the pub. He'd left early, giving himself plenty of time to do the work. Getting arrested – that was so much out of character it had to be a ruse. Of course! He'd done it to give himself an alibi. Jesus, it was all so obvious now! It was Fosdyke who'd tried to kill him. Fosdyke who'd killed Kathy. Fosdyke who had killed Nicky and Mandy. An anger he'd never known before engulfed him. His fingers were shaking as he took out his mobile and dialled the site. It rang for a frustrating minute before Alec answered.

'It's Sam – is Fosdyke due today?'

'He's here, giving me all sorts of bloody grief.'

'Is he now? Well, keep the bastard there until I get there!'

'What –?'

'Just do it Alec!' Sam was screaming down the phone, oblivious to the attention he was attracting. 'Keep him there if you have to nail him to the floor. I mean it Alec. I'm coming over!'

Alec put the phone down, thought for a minute, then picked it up again.

Sam's Range Rover slid sideways onto the muddy site. He leapt out, leaving the engine running and the door swinging open. He looked around. Alec was at the hut door.

'Where is he?' he screamed.

'Sam – calm down,' soothed Alec. His eyes involuntarily flickered to the top of the scaffold where Fosdyke was criticising the positioning of a lintol over a bedroom window.

'The bearing's uneven,' he was saying. 'There's at least two inches more on this side than that. It'll have to be re-positioned.'

His attention was distracted by Sam's shouting from below. Arthur, to whom he was talking, looked over the scaffold at Sam, who was looking back at him. Why Sam was as mad as this, he'd no idea. He just hoped this anger wasn't directed at him, as did everyone on the site. This was a rare rage indeed.

Sam literally flung himself at the ladder and rushed up to the top scaffold, angrily kicking bricks and buckets and tools from his path as he stormed along the boards towards Fosdyke. Arthur, realising the object of Sam's anger was the building inspector, blocked Fosdyke's retreat.

'You bastard!' seethed Sam through clenched teeth. 'You murdering bastard!' He threw a venomous punch that broke Fosdyke's nose and sent him reeling down on to the boards. Men were gathering below to watch. Alec was climbing the ladder to stop it. Sam dragged Fosdyke to his feet and pushed him under the handrail. Fosdyke, his nose dripping blood, howled in terror.

'What is it?' he screamed. 'Leave me alone you bloody

madman!' Sam heaved him right over the edge until he was holding Fosdyke by his recently broken ankle. The terrified building inspector was dangling in mid-air, his head fifteen feet above a pile of loose engineering bricks. Hundreds of sharp edges awaiting his plunge.

'For God's sake, Sam! What the hell are you doing?' yelled Alec, halfway up the ladder. Uncertain where to position himself for Fosdyke's safety. 'He killed Kathy,' screamed Sam. 'This bastard killed my Kathy!'

'Okay Sam! Just calm down.'

Sam looked down towards where Owen had just arrived on site with Biggles, in response to Alec's phone call. Arthur was climbing down the scaffold, not wishing to be thought in any way responsible for what he thought was Fosdyke's fate.

'He killed Kathy, Owen,' shouted Sam. He looked back down at Fosdyke. 'He killed my Kathy. Didn't you, you bastard?'

Fosdyke had wet himself with terror. Peeing upside down; gravity making it soak through his shirt and out on to his face, mingling with the blood pouring from his nose.

'Don't let me go, please don't let me go,' he sobbed.

'You killed the girls and my dad, you murdering bastard!'

'I didn't. I didn't kill your dad.'

'But you killed Nicky Fulbright.' Sam was thinking clearer now. He was breathing deeply, trying to regain the control he needed to scare a full confession from this man.

'Yes,' sobbed Fosdyke. 'I didn't mean to kill her. I was just trying to shut her up. Oh my God! Please don't let me die. I didn't kill your father.'

'Who else did you kill?'

'I didn't mean to kill Kathy. Oh God! Somebody help me, please!'

'You started the fire didn't you? Didn't you, you piece of shit?'

'Yes, yes. Oh please God, Sam, don't drop me.'

'How did you do it? Tell us how you did it? I haven't got all bloody day!'

'I used a candle and a piece of bandage as a delayed fuse.'

'What else?'

'I don't know what else you want,' Fosdyke whined. 'I put the candle in a holder that looked like a penis.'

Owen ears pricked up. 'How many testicles?' he shouted.

'What?' Fosdyke couldn't tell where the voice was coming from.

'How many testicles on the candlestick?'

Normally, such a question might have provoked laughter amongst building workers, but so tense was the situation that they all looked at Fosdyke for his answer.

'Jesus Christ, what is this?' wailed Fosdyke.

'Answer the man!' roared Sam.

'All right, all right, three – three testicles.'

Owen gave a businesslike nod and wrote something in his notebook.

'Who else did you kill?' growled Sam.

'Oh for God's sake!'

Sam lowered his voice so only Fosdyke could hear. 'Who else? Tell me, you bastard, or I'm going to count to three and drop you!'

'Mandy – Mandy Jackson. She was going to tell you about me and Nicky!'

'Did you hear that, Owen? He killed Nicky Fulbright and Mandy Jackson.'

'We heard him, Sam,' shouted Owen. He burped, inadvertently, then thumped his chest with an apologetic fist. 'We've got all we need. Hang on to him, we're coming up!'

His job done, Sam allowed his hatred to return. He felt a desperate urge to avenge Kathy for the way she'd sacrificed her life to save his. Apart from the girls, this man had caused the deaths of his dad and Sean. He was hanging on to this vile murderer with every ounce of his strength, to save him dropping to certain death on the bricks below. Why? If ever a man deserved to die it was the man slowly sliding from his grip. Sam knew that in just a few more seconds help would be at hand and true vengeance denied him. If he had to sacrifice his own freedom in exchange for rough justice, then so be it; but first he needed Fosdyke to know what was in store for him. He called down, once again just loud enough for Fosdyke and no one else to hear. 'I'm going to count to three and realise I can't hold on to you, you evil bastard.'

'Oh God! Please – No!'

Fosdyke lost control of his bowels as Sam counted to three and let him drop.

Jacob had seen and heard enough to know what Sam ultimately intended. No way was Fosdyke going to climb down that scaffold. If ever a man was coming down head first, it was Fosdyke; and head first into the bricks would very likely be fatal. Jacob didn't want Sam to suffer the consequences of that, no matter how much Fosdyke deserved it. He climbed into the scaffold and stood on a putlog, his head level with the back of Fosdyke's head, which was upside down facing the site and occasionally looking in terror at the bricks below; only he and Fosdyke heard Sam counting. On three, Jacob made a grab for the hapless building inspector. For a split second he managed to hang on to Fosdyke's shoulders, just long enough to break the fall and for the rest of his body to somersault, heels over head, landing feet first on the bricks below. He was badly cut and bruised with another broken ankle, but alive. Jacob leaned forward and looked up into the disappointed face of Sam.

'I saw your hands slipping, so I made a grab for him,' he said.

Sam, who was in shock, said nothing. Tears were tumbling down his cheeks. Only now was his grief at losing Kathy finally pouring out. His thanks to Jacob would come later, when he was thinking straighter.

'For a minute there, I thought you'd dropped him on purpose, boyo,' said Owen, as Biggles went with Fosdyke in the ambulance. Owen had arrested him for murder but he didn't fancy a trip in an ambulance with a man who'd just shit himself. He let Biggles do that bit, besides, his stomach was playing him up. He had climbed up onto the scaffold to sit beside Sam, who was staring into space. 'Owen, I meant to kill him,' he was saying.

'You're in shock, look you.'

'I meant to kill him!'

'What was that?' said Owen, 'You say you couldn't hold on to him any longer?'

Sam shook his head; his face was the colour of putty and his cheeks glistening with tears.

'You couldn't hold on to him any longer,' repeated Owen, putting an arm around Sam's shoulders. 'You did your best, we all could see that, but he just slipped out of your hands. Good job Jacob managed to break his fall.'

'What?' said Sam.

'Just take your time, boyo,' Owen said. 'Me and you will stay up here until you remember exactly what happened. No point saying silly things and getting yourself into trouble because of a worthless type like Fosdyke.'

Sam sat there, gazing across the site which was returning to normality, thanks to Alec, calling out, 'Right, lads, show's over, back ter work.'

There was a man at the mixer, doing the job Sean would have been doing, had he lived. A load of bricks was arriving on site, with the driver, unaware of the recent drama, shouting across to Alec for instructions where to drop them. His voice was drowned by someone starting up a kango hammer and down below Arthur was calling up to Sam:

'Will yer be long up there? I need ter get that brickwork up ter wallplate by tonight.'

His request seemed to bring Sam back to his senses. He turned to Owen and said, 'He'll claim he confessed under duress.'

Owen gave a wide grin. 'Of course he will, boyo. But he'd no business knowing about that candlestick. That's enough to nail him on the arson charge, isn't it? And I reckon forensics will nail him on the other two murders, confession or no confession.'

'That's right!' realised Sam, nodding as he spoke. 'I – I'd no real need to shake a confession out of him, had I?'

'Oh, I wouldn't go as far as that, boyo. If anyone had a need, I reckon it was you. You know, if he'd landed on his head, you might well have been facing a murder charge – manslaughter at the very least. As it is, I should be arresting you for assault, unless of course you were trying to make a citizens arrest yourself and it got out of hand as these things sometimes do. Your method was a bit unorthodox, but that's you, isn't it? I imagine he tried to escape your clutches by climbing down the scaffold and of course you tried your best to hold on to him, but your strength failed you.'

'That's exactly what happened,' said Sam.

31

A faint smile flickered over Fosdyke's face as he stared up at the hospital ceiling; he was handcuffed to the bed despite his broken ankle. In the corner, a policeman was slumped in a chair, engrossed in the *Daily Mirror*. With DNA profiling to contend with, Fosdyke had no option but to confess to the murders of Nicola and Mandy, and they already had him bang to rights about Kathy – but there was nothing to be gained from telling them about Beverley. That was the perfect murder. He'd treasure that knowledge. Something to keep him going.

David Renishawe drove towards Unsworth, his wife beside him. It had taken months to get their marriage back on something of an even keel. Many months and many lies. All told in a good cause – in David's mind anyway.

This was the last step, the last phase in their marriage re-building programme. David was sure it would work.

He turned and smiled at his wife. 'I never loved her, you know. It's like they say, there's no fool like an old fool.'

Mrs Renishawe offered no reply.

'I realised that evening, as soon as I walked into her house,' her husband went on. 'She must have seen it on my face. I told her I could never leave you. It had all been a stupid mistake.'

'You never told me her name,' said his wife.

Renishawe looked at her, puzzled. 'You never asked. You didn't want to talk about her.'

'Well we're talking now, so what's her name?'

'Beverley – Beverley McAndrew.'

His wife said nothing for a while, then asked. 'Where is she now?'

'No idea. According to her ex-boyfriend she left the country that same night.'

'Ex-boyfriend? You never told me about an ex-boyfriend. When did you speak to him?'

Renishawe was uncomfortable, he was digging a hole for himself here. Oddly enough, during their brief meeting he'd been so preoccupied he had scarcely looked at Fosdyke's face. Since then, not once did he associate Beverley's ex-boyfriend with the picture of Fosdyke that had been plastered all over the papers. Beverley had vaguely referred to him as James, more often she had called him, The Plonker.

'Do you mind if we don't talk about it?' he asked.

'Suits me, you started it.'

'The main thing is we're still together. No more lies,' he assured her. 'I'm going to be totally honest with you from now on.'

He placed a hand on hers and squeezed it. 'Today is the first day of the rest of our lives.'

His wife felt the bile rising in her throat, but managed to suppress it. She'd taken him back for her own benefit. She was too old to start again. After this, she had him where she wanted him. But one more lie, one more deception and he was out on his ear for good. She'd made that very plain to him.

Owen drove on to the site. He was on his way home and had gauged it to coincide with afternoon tea break.

Sam and Alec were in the cabin, the paraffin heater on full, keeping out the winter cold. It was the day after Fosdyke's arrest, his identity hadn't been made public yet.

'Afternoon boys, do you have a spare cup for me?'

'Certainly constable,' said Alec. 'Any more news on the Fosdyke front?'

'Well, he confessed to everything.' He gave Sam a mock disapproving look. 'Without duress this time. As soon as we asked him to take a blood test I think he realised he'd no chance.'

'Well, it should speed things up for Sean's widow,' commented Sam.

'There is one other thing,' said Owen, looking at Sam. 'Did

274

you ever meet Fosdyke's girlfriend? The one he used to live with?'

Sam shrugged and shook his head. He found it difficult to talk rationally about Fosdyke.

'The one who left him, you mean?' enquired Alec.

'Beverley McAndrew,' nodded Owen. 'A few weeks ago, one of her relatives came down to the station and reported her missing. Apparently she went abroad, see, but no one's clapped eyes on her for months. Fosdyke's name's on the computer as her former co-habitee. He told our officers that she'd gone to live abroad with her new boyfriend. We didn't give it much thought until now.'

'What?' enquired Alec. 'Do you think he did her in?'

'Well, with his track record I'd say it was on the cards, wouldn't you?' observed the Welshman.

Sam nodded, slowly, and mused, 'I think if I was a relative of hers, I'd be a bit worried.'

'Hang on,' said Alec. 'She left him on his birthday, remember Sam? You took him to the pub that day.'

Sam forced himself to think back. 'That was the day Gayle saw us together.' He looked at Owen, who seemed puzzled. 'She was the one who told me about him and Nicky Fulbright,' he explained.

'How did he seem?' asked Owen.

'He seemed like a pillock,' scowled Sam. 'His normal self. Mind you, I did see him later that night, out in his van. Just passing this site as a matter of fact. I'd been to the pictures with my boys.'

'I tell you what,' said Alec. 'He was acting odd the following day, remember Sam?'

Sam tried to remember the day. 'Yes! he was. He reckoned he wasn't feeling well. I remember him saying something about how his girlfriend had left him and he'd been driving round half the night. I don't suppose you'd be feeling too clever just after you've bumped someone off.'

A removal van pulled onto the site, Alec went to the door. The driver looked at a piece of paper in his hand then up at Alec. 'Plot Five,' he called out, 'Mr Renishawe's house?'

Alec pointed up the site. 'Third on the right.' He acknowledged a thumbs-up from the driver then came back in the hut and swallowed the dregs of his tea. 'Plot five, eh?' he said. 'Funny that. I remember now – Fosdyke were checking the footings on that plot on the day we were talkin' about.'

'There was soft spot,' said Sam.

'That's right,' confirmed Alec. 'There was soft spot and the silly sod didn't want us to dig it out. He wanted us to leave it! I mean you can't do that – talk about going from the sublime to the ridiculous. I remember you giving Curly a bollocking about it. He swore blind it wasn't there when he dug the footing out.'

It took Owen to suggest the obvious: 'Maybe it *wasn't* there when he dug the footing out.'

There was a dramatic pause and a simultaneous 'Oh shit!' from Alec and Sam.

A car had driven on to the site and was pulling up behind the removal van. Alec, with Sam and Owen in his wake, approached the man emerging from the car. Wondering how to put it.

'Mr Renishawe,' said Alec. 'You'er – you might not want to move in today.'

Epilogue

'That's great, Norman. I've stuck an extra tenner in for a job well done.'

Norman the sign writer took the money from Sam and climbed into his van as Sally, dressed in torn jeans and a rugby shirt, came out of the shop where she'd been cleaning the floors. It was only a small lock-up, but it fitted Sam's needs. He put his arm around Sally's shoulder as he looked up at the sign above the window.

'Well, love, it cost a few quid but Norman's the best and you get what you pay for in this life.'

'Really,' commented Sally. 'You know, I'm still surprised you haven't been put off, after what you've been through in these past few months.'

'I don't know, maybe it's in my blood,' he replied. 'The very thought of spending the next twenty years laying one brick on top of another makes me cringe. Mind you, I'll only take the jobs that interest me and I'll always have building to fall back on. Can't lose when you come to think of it.'

He looked up at the sign again and read it out loud to Sally. 'Sam Carew Investigations Bureau – The Professionals.'

He turned to her and grinned. 'Short and to the point. What d'you think?'

Sally looked at the sign and frowned. 'Sam, I think – '

A white Porche growled to a halt at the side of them and a long haired beauty leaned out of the window. She wore dark glasses, but what Sam could see of the rest of her took his breath away.

'Are you Sam Carew by any chance?' she asked, her voice was husky and mid-Atlantic.

Sam had to clear his throat before replying. 'Er – yes, I am.' His voice was more hoarse than husky.

'I passed earlier,' she said. 'Just as the signwriter was finishing. I've heard about you and your unorthodox methods, and I think

I might have a job for you.' She lifted her sunglasses and thrust them into her silky blonde hair in that provocative way that only a few women can manage. 'What sort of work do you specialise in?' Her eyes, beneath her long lashes, were dark and alluring.

'Pretty much anything,' said Sam, quickly. Sally raised an eyebrow at this.

'I'm looking for the best,' said the woman. 'Someone who can think on his feet, with his finger right on the button – if you get my drift.'

'I can safely say very little gets past me,' Sam assured her. 'What sort of a job is it?'

'Forgery,' she said. 'Industrial forgery on a massive scale – mainly CDs and DVDs. The firm I represent needs a man with the instinct to spot the tiniest deviation from the norm – someone with a sharp eye for detail.'

Sam's sharp eyes were fighting the temptation to stare at the amount of cleavage on display. He gave a modest shrug and said, confidently, 'I'm your man.'

A boy walked by and stopped to admire the car. Then he looked up at the sign. 'I've been watching that feller paint yer sign, mister,' he said. 'I got into bother at school for doin' that. Will he get into bother?'

Four pairs of eyes studied the newly painted sign, glinting in the spring sunshine.

'What're you talking about, lad?' enquired Sam, annoyed at the boy for interrupting an important business discussion.

'There's only one "F" in professionals,' said the woman, just before driving off.

'I should stay clear of forgery,' said Sally.

END